There Goes Charlie

A Master of Foxhounds is murdered in mid-Hunt. Detective Chief Superintendent John Charter from Penfoldshire Area Headquarters takes on the case with the help of the highly intelligent local rural sergeant who is knowledgeable about Hunt customs, rivalries and politics. Together they question the victim's beautiful young Irish wife, his university lecturer brother, the Hunt members and servants —and the Hunt saboteurs.

The Chief Superintendent is unfamiliar with hunting and he experiences several moments of severe anxiety on horseback, not to mention a narrow escape from a nasty and deliberately planned death, as he pursues his inquiries from Hunt Kennels to farmhouse, from manor to market town and a run-down Irish estate, and of course to the chase itself.

Much fascinating country lore and a fair picture of the controversial subject of foxhunting are among the incidental pleasures of this first crime novel, in which the solution is cunningly delayed till the last page.

ANNE FLEMING

There Goes Charlie

A Rural Murder

COLLINS, 8 GRAFTON STREET, LONDON W1

William Collins Sons & Co. Ltd
London · Glasgow · Sydney · Auckland
Toronto · Johannesburg

Some of the incidents in this story are based on actual events in which I participated, but the Canfield and Old Ashley is an imaginary Hunt and all the characters are imaginary except the Huntsman, who will be recognized by many who used to hunt with him.

As for Penfoldshire, it could be found on the map south of Derbyshire if it were on any map.

First published 1990
© Anne Fleming 1990

British Library Cataloguing in Publication Data

Fleming, Anne
  There goes Charlie.—(Crime Club)
  I. Title
  823.914 [F]

ISBN 0 00 232303 6

Photoset in Linotron Baskerville by
Rowland Phototypesetting Ltd
Bury St Edmunds, Suffolk
Printed in Great Britain by
William Collins Sons & Co. Ltd, Glasgow

CHAPTER 1

'It was without exception the most entertaining murder that has ever fallen to my lot,' said Detective Chief Superintendent John Charter. 'But half way through it turned very nasty indeed. I nearly got killed in a particularly unpleasant way. I did get mildly beaten up. And I experienced several moments of sheer terror on horseback. I'll tell you about it.'

In the late afternoon the fox came hell for leather across the field of winter wheat, glanced back over his shoulder and stole into the hedgerow on the other side. A bright copper-coloured westering sun was branch-down behind the dark tracery of the row of alders fringing the field against the glowing sky. Their shadows reached across the grass towards a flock of sheep quietly grazing. The fox darted into the open and ran straight for the sheep whose panic-stricken ranks opened to let him through and, trembling, closed again as he emerged on the other side, melted into the ditch, sprang up the bright bank of golden-brown bracken and set off, straight as an arrow, across a sticky brown field of plough. From behind him, at least three fields away, came the music of hounds in full cry and the urgent, heart-stopping note of the horn.

In the first promising run of a poor scenting day hounds went in a body straight across the brave green fronds of winter wheat pricking up out of the heavy loam, and disappeared through the hedge into the meadow beyond, heads well down, speaking.

The mounted field came pelting round the headland.

The only way into the meadow was over one of the few Penfoldshire heave-gates remaining in the county. The farmer had nailed the top rail to the posts above the slots and it was over four feet high. Roger Pratt, the Hunt Secretary—tall and thin, a brave sight in his scarlet coat—

turned his dark bay thoroughbred towards the gate too
sharply, took off a fraction too soon, and hit the top bar
with a front hoof. Horse and rider somersaulted over the
rails and landed unhurt on the grass.

The Whipper-in, Peter Thorn, jumped off his horse,
handed the reins to a smart boy on a shaggy pony, and
vaulted over the gate.

'Haven't seen you on the floor before, sir,' he said, with
a grin, taking the reins of the bay as it struggled to its feet.
Roger Pratt jumped up, blinking and shaking his head. The
world was rocking about him gently but together he and
the Whipper-in set about removing the top rail. The terrier
man came with his tools and Peter Thorn began to lever
the board away from the posts.

Charles Hardcastle, Master of the Canfield and Old
Ashley Foxhounds, was fuming with impatience as he saw
his hounds disappearing into the distance. Six feet tall
and massively built, astride a three-quarter-bred Irish grey
which was wheeling and sidling and tossing its elegant head,
he was a formidable figure. His white hair curled over his
collar. Black eyebrows frowned in a heavy bar above frosty,
pale-blue, eyes. He forced the grey up to the gate and
brought his whip down hard on the rail in between Pratt
and Thorn, just missing their busy hands.

'Is there a man among you, or do I have to dismount and
get that rail down myself?'

Peter Thorn flushed darkly. The Hunt Secretary gave the
Master one look and dropped the rail at his feet. Stiff with
hauteur, he put on his dented and muddy top hat, tipped
it to the Master and said, 'There you are, Master, and I
think I'll go home now. Good night, Master.'

He turned away, caught up the reins, threw them over
his horse's head, climbed into the saddle a little stiffly and
trotted away round the headland in the opposite direction
to hounds as Peter Thorn vaulted back over the gate.

The Master gave an impatient glance after Roger Pratt,
gathered his reins up for the jump and stared, astonished,
as his first Whipper-in, who was still bright red from neck

to temple, mounted his horse, tipped his cap, said in a strangled voice, 'And so will I, Master,' and turned and trotted back the way they had come.

The Master turned purple in the face. The old Huntsman, Jim Caudle, froze in his saddle. The rest of the field stared after the departing Whipper-in in consternation. Then the Master jumped into the meadow, followed by the Huntsman, the amateur second Whipper-in, whose eyes were almost popping out of his head, and, one by one, by the rest of the field.

Hounds were feathering, fanning out over the meadow seeking the sheep-foiled line. Forced to swallow his bile, the Master followed the Huntsman closely as he picked up his hounds and cast round the field until they hit the line on the far side. Away they went and flew over the plough while the field cantered round the headland.

At about the same time two burly young countrymen and an elderly lady in a waxed jacket, tweed hat well pulled down, waited on a footpath some way ahead listening for the cry of hounds which had abruptly stopped.

'They've lost the line,' said one of the young men.

A flock of startled fieldfares flew up from beyond the hedge that rimmed the field of plough above the sloping meadow in front of them, and wheeled away, 'chack-chacking' nervously.

'And there goes Charlie!' cried the other young man. 'Look at him! He's been well worked, he has!'

The fox, wet and muddied to the shoulder, stole down the slope, crossed over the muddy path a few feet away from where they stood, turned to look them composedly in the face, then trotted off and vanished into the neighbouring field.

The young men were holloaing at the tops of their voices, hoisting their flat caps on their walking sticks and waving them in the air, almost jumping up and down in their excitement.

'I reckon they've started another fox,' said one man disconsolately. 'He'd surely have lifted 'em to the holloa.'

Then the horn sounded and hounds began to speak. By the time the mounted field came thundering down the slope the fox was minutes ahead of them.

Soon afterwards the Master instructed the Huntsman to blow 'Going home!' and they turned for home in the gathering dusk. The remnants of the field bade the Master good night and rode away in different directions.

'All on?' asked Jim Caudle.

'Two missing,' said the amateur Whipper-in.

'All but Jupiter and Juggler,' said Jim. As the distance was less than a mile they went home across country at a steady hound jog, touching the horn from time to time for Jupiter and Juggler, who found their own way home an hour or two later. As they came up the last hill to the Kennels the Huntsman sounded a long call on the horn to warn the girl grooms to look out for their charges and as they drew closer they saw the lights go on in the stables and the hound lodges.

The Kennels were Charles Hardcastle's obsession. He was head of the family which owned Finlay Hardcastle, the contracting firm, and his fortune was immense. When he became Master of the Canfield and Old Ashley he moved in on the Kennels with surveyors, builders, plumbers, carpenters and decorators. The Kennels acquired a well-equipped valeting room and a smart new dispensary. The flesh house was re-tiled, new plumbing and drainage was installed and the six great offal bins were replaced. The stables were already in good order but were repainted white so that all the buildings were matching—white-painted brickwork and pale-green-painted woodwork. The old fruit trees in the gardens were pruned and the garden hedges trimmed. Every other hedge on the place was cut and laid, ditches cleaned out, and the grassyards behind the Kennels were harrowed and cut and re-cut and re-harrowed until they looked like lawns. All wire fencing was removed and replaced with post and rail. The wooden fencing round the puppy show ring was newly painted white. Some distance from the complex on a slope further down the lane which led to the Kennels a new guest cottage was built. Every wheelbarrow, spade and bucket on the place was new and shining. Bay trees in pale-green-painted tubs stood at intervals round the yards. It was now one of the smartest Kennels in the country. In James Pierson's time it had been one of the happiest.

When hounds streamed into the stableyard followed by the Hunt servants, Nancy Thorn was working on the roan her husband had been riding. She was forcing him to keep his off hind hoof in a bucket of water and disinfectant by the simple expedient of lifting the off-fore from the ground. She was very pale and she looked up nervously as the Master dismounted, gave his horse to the groom and strode towards her.

'Where is he?' he asked abruptly.

'He's in the house,' she said. 'I'll get him for you.'

'No, you won't. I'll get him myself,' he barked and walked away angrily.

'Cheer up, Nancy,' said the Huntsman. 'The Master can't eat him.'

Then they busied themselves getting hounds into the lodges, looking them over for injuries, fetching and feeding to them great haunches of raw flesh from the flesh house. After such a feed they would eat nothing more for two days.

When the Master came out again he noticed Nancy looking anxious and called to her, 'Well, that's that. I'm sorry, Nancy, but he brought it on himself.'

Nancy let go the hoof she was holding, removed the pail and ran for the cottage without a word.

Charles Hardcastle got into his Mercedes, reversed it round to the hound lodges, opened the driving window to call out, 'Good night, Jim. Good night, Stanley,' and drove away without waiting for an answer.

When the men came out of the lodges Jim Caudle said, 'Best leave it to me,' and went to knock on the door of Peter Thorn's cottage. The Thorns opened it together, twined in each other's arms.

'He's sacked me,' said Peter. 'He's bloody sacked me, Jim.' He was shaking his head in disbelief.

'Can I come in?'

They took him into the neat sitting-room. It was newly papered. A brass canopy had been fitted over the old Raeburn. The curtains were fresh, sprigged, bright and new.

Jim sat down. 'Well, Peter,' he said, 'it was a right down foolish thing to do, wasn't it?'

Peter looked miserable. 'It was Mr Pratt going home,' he said. 'I shouldn't have done it but I thought to myself: If a gentleman like that won't let himself be made little of in front of all the field, why should I? We were getting that rail down just as fast as it could be done and Mr Pratt had just gone a real purler. "Isn't there a man amongst you?" he says and says he'll have to do it himself. He nearly got me on the knuckle with his whip too. It was more than I could stand, Jim, and it was the last run. I wouldn't have done it but for that. Mr Pratt'll speak for me. I know he will. We would have turned for home any minute. There, there, Nancy. It'll be all right.'

Nancy had covered her face with her hands. Peter patted her shoulder inadequately.

'I'll speak for you,' said Jim Caudle. 'I reckon he ought to change his mind. Cheer up, Nancy, be a good girl. I got to get home now, Peter. You'd better get on out there pretty soon. Mr Caldbeck can't be expected to stop any longer and there's hounds to be let out yet.'

Peter came to the door with him. 'She'll be all right,' he said. 'It's just that she loves this house and the new curtains and all. Made them herself. And Sally's top of her class at the school.'

Caudle clapped him on the shoulder. 'He'll let you off,' he said encouragingly but without conviction. 'But you'd better learn to bite your tongue. Send Nancy out to the stables in a bit. Take her mind off it. And there's four horses to be seen to. Good night, lad, I'm home to me dinner.'

'Good night, Jim. I just wish we still had Mr Pierson as Master. Kennels aren't the same. He treated you as if you were just as important as anyone else. This chap makes you feel like an insect. I can't be an insect, Jim. Not even for Nancy.'

'No, Peter. I don't suppose you can or ought to,' said Jim. He turned away and then turned back again. 'There's just one thing, Peter. He treats me like an insect too, *and* the terrier man. Mr Pratt's the only one I ever see argue with him. Only there's some sense in Mr Pratt doing it because Mr Hardcastle can't take away his house or his job nor yet his wife's new curtains. So think on that before you do such a stupid thing again.'

CHAPTER 2

It was twelve o'clock midday on Sunday morning at Hang-holt Manor and guests were expected for lunch. Siobhan Hardcastle was walking up and down her upstairs sitting-room, her lower lip jutting out and giving her exquisite little face a look of petulance.

It was a pretty, comfortable room with cream rugs on an apricot carpet. A box of chocolates was lying on the floor beside several glossy magazines in front of the neat white hearth with the blazing log fire. Two rows of bookshelves under the brightly-cushioned window-seat made a state-ment aimed at her husband. One said: 'These books on the Irish Troubles show that I'm an alien and you are the enemy.' Yet, in Ireland, Siobhan had never once picked up a book about the Troubles. The other shelf said: 'These pony books and dog-eared school stories show that it was my childhood days in Ireland that were the happy ones.'

On the window-seat an elegant orange and white pointer was sitting up, her front legs straight, her lovely delicate head with its gently challenging carriage touching the glass, her brown shining eyes fixed on something outside the window.

Siobhan was small and slight. Her pale gold curls were

neatly flicked up at the ends to frame the eyes blue as
hyacinths, the small straight Grecian nose and the full,
rose-pink mouth. She wore a lilac-grey-green tweed skirt
and a perfect grey shirt open on a delicate throat, thin pale
green lacy stockings and shining green calf shoes with
two-inch heels. Small gold earrings, a plain gold bracelet
and a delicate jade necklace proclaimed that she was both
wealthy and discreet. She was also very young.

This perfect appearance seemed lost on her elderly husband who put his head round the door impatiently.

'Will you please come down to the drawing-room. They'll
be arriving in exactly five minutes from now. You might
perhaps have checked with Maggie that everything's in
order.'

She turned to look at him with a consciously irritating
blend of indifference and dislike. 'Everything's always in
order in this house, Charles. It was always in order before
you brought me here and it will always be in order after
I'm gone. So I wouldn't worry myself about it if I were you.'
Her voice was soft, her Irish brogue slight.

'Well, perhaps you'll condescend to come down in time
to receive your guests!'

'Perhaps I will, Charles. Why don't you go on and do the
checking yourself and I'll follow you down?'

He frowned at her with profound resentment but, as
always, found himself in face of her indifference totally
unable to annihilate her as he could almost everyone else
who seriously annoyed him. He went away.

He was welcoming the Pratts in the pale green drawing-
room with its great bow windows, its Chinese carpets, its
Bonnard and its Stubbs, when Siobhan came into the room
followed by the pointer, Spindle, who ran among the guests
looking from side to side before returning to fawn on her
mistress.

If anything, Charles was slightly over-effusive as he
clapped Roger Pratt on the shoulder and kissed Mabel,
totally ignoring the unpleasant incident at yesterday's
hunt.

Mabel Pratt, elegant, well-groomed, ugly, but poised and charming, turned from Charles to Siobhan to give both hands to her unresponsive hostess.

'Siobhan!' she said. 'Haven't seen you in ages. Won't you come to lunch with me one day—just the two of us so we can talk?'

Siobhan kissed her cheek coldly and without a smile. 'Thank you, Mabel. It's very kind of you, but I've nothing at all to say.'

Mabel's eyebrows went up and Charles turned purple in the face. Before he could erupt, his son and daughter-in-law arrived with ten-year-old Abigail and eight-year-old Hugo, as well as an unexpected guest. The younger Hardcastles farmed a few miles west of Hangholt and after Charles had brought home his young bride they had often been summoned to lunch or dine to entertain Siobhan. As relations between Charles and his wife deteriorated, these invitations had become rarer.

Sara, plump and pretty, brought forward her house guest, Harriet Lincoln, a striking-looking young woman twenty-eight years of age.

'I'm sorry we announced Harriet so late,' said Sara. 'She's my long-lost cousin and she's stopping with us for a week. We didn't know she was coming but we're delighted and we're trying to persuade her to come out next Saturday on Atalanta. It'll be the first hunt of her life and since we've got the lawn meet here that day we thought it seemed a good idea. Don't you agree?'

Charles gave Harriet three fingers to shake. 'How do you do?' he said, then turned to Sara. 'I tell you what, Sara, you'll ruin that young mare if you keep sending her out with beginners on her back,' and he turned his back on them.

Sara flushed angrily. 'Bloody man!' she said, under her breath. 'I should have let Roddy introduce you. I can't stand his rudery. Rod's used to it.'

Harriet smiled at her, 'Look,' she said, 'next Saturday is likely to be my one and only time out with the Canfield and

Old Ashley. I'm going to enjoy myself and I don't care how rude your father-in-law is.'

'Well,' said Sara, 'he's a right sod, but I suppose you could say that of more than one Master of Foxhounds. Come and meet Mabel Pratt. She and Roger are the nicest couple in the country.'

Meanwhile Charles went beaming across the room to welcome Dr Cresswell who came hurrying in uttering apologies to which his hostess offered as blank a response as she had offered to the other guests.

'Sorry to be late,' he said to Charles. 'I'm expecting to be called out. Got my bag in the hall.'

'Glad to see you here at all,' said Charles. 'I hope you'll manage to get out with us next Saturday if you aren't too busy.'

Sara rolled her eyes at Harriet. 'What magic lies in Donald Cresswell's beautiful blue eyes?' she muttered. 'I suppose Charles is pleased with him for getting engaged to Siobhan's sister.'

Later Harriet found herself sitting with Donald Cresswell on a window-seat looking out over the lawns that swept down at the back of the house to a white gate leading into the Oak Wood. Dr Cresswell was six feet tall, heavily built but light on his feet. He had extraordinarily bright hazel eyes and a rueful smile which was rather charming. An unruly dark forelock kept falling into his eyes and he kept sweeping or shaking it back into place. Harriet looked at him with some interest, but he was gazing, frowning, at Siobhan, who was lolling gracefully on the tapestry-covered stool before the fireplace, stroking the pointer. Her eyes were on Spindle and only the jut of her lower lip showed her discontent.

Charles Hardcastle's hand came down on her shoulder not gently. 'Time we had something to eat,' he said in a loud jovial voice. Without a word, Siobhan rose and led the way through the double doors into the dining-room and stood there like a statue. After a pause Charles began to dispose his guests round the table.

Here, too, a bright log fire was burning. The air was so
unseasonably mild that the windows were open and when
the doors were opened the white and pink curtains flew up
and the pink linen napkins fluttered. The glow of the fire
shone rosily on the white panelling and was reflected in the
silver dishes and the silver vase full of tiny pink roses in the
centre of the table.

A tall young woman in a sloppy sweater, tweed skirt and
tan brogues was standing by the fire holding the hand of a
three-year-old boy in a striped pullover and jeans, with the
pale gold curls of his mother and the straight dark eyebrows
of his father. He looked at them all solemnly out of very
intelligent blue eyes. The girl's head was covered with the
same loose curls, black as ebony, curving round neck and
temple. Her eyes were dark blue and there were shadows
underneath them. The mouth was generous, the expression
unhappy, but when they came in she smiled a slow, shy
smile at them all.

Dr Cresswell walked over to Eithne, stood smiling down
at her for a moment, then bent to kiss her cheek. The girl
flushed and turned away awkwardly.

Twelve months earlier Eithne's young husband, Patrick
O' Dowd, the jockey, had been killed at the Curragh. Now
she was engaged to Donald Cresswell who had treated her
for influenza and depression but saw little of her outside his
consulting room. People talked of fixations and father figures
to explain Eithne's diamond engagement ring, but everyone
understood the affair from Donald's side, for Eithne was a
beauty and his very beautiful wife had left him two years
earlier.

Charles waved at the girl. 'You've all met Eithne, Siobhan's sister. Donald's fiancée. And this young rip is Daniel.
You all know him too.'

'Not Daniel, Dandy,' said Siobhan, and sat down opposite
her husband. She could hardly be described as presiding
over the party as she spoke hardly a word throughout the
meal and her husband never addressed a word either to her
or to the child. Eithne sat next to Dandy, whispering to him

and stroking his hair, but he too sat in silence, gazing from his silent mother to his expansive, smiling father.

Suddenly Dandy picked up his soup plate, lifted it high in the air and tipped the entire contents into his lap.

There was a moment of silent consternation. Then: 'What the devil was that about?' asked Charles Hardcastle, once more empurpled about the face. Siobhan looked at Dandy, knitting her brows as if not quite sure what he had done wrong.

'Poor little chap,' said Roger Pratt. 'Better mop him up.'

'I remember my little brother doing that when I was six,' said Mabel Pratt, who was adept at turning off difficult social situations. 'I always admired him for it. I would never have had the courage.'

Charles looked at her and smiled, pleased, as she had known he would be.

Donald Cresswell squinted sideways down at the child, took the napkin Eithne had tucked into the boy's jersey and dabbed ineffectually at the soaking jeans.

'Well, for God's sake, do something!' said Charles. 'Dry him. Take him up to Nanny and let's get on with it. There's a joint of meat shrivelling up in the kitchen.'

Siobhan turned a cool gaze on Charles and made no move. Eithne put down her napkin and stood up. 'Nanny's out today. I'll take him in to Maggie and give him lunch in there.'

Donald jumped up and drew out Dandy's chair. 'No, you won't,' he said. 'You'll stop where you are and enjoy your lunch. Maggie and I haven't had a good gossip in ages. Come on, young man.' The boy got down and Dr Cresswell took his hand and led him out of the room. Eithne, who had flushed scarlet, sat down again.

Roddy stepped into the breach, turning to Harriet.

'Well, love,' he said. 'Have you made up your mind? Are you going to hunt with us next Saturday?'

With an audible sigh of relief the rest of them joined in.

A plump, fair-haired, fortyish woman in a pink linen

smock appeared at the door with a trolley bearing huge dishes and Rodney went to help her. 'Look at that!' he said. 'You're brilliant, Maggie!' Charles carved with gusto, slicing into the glistening brown roast and piling the pink slices on the plates. Blood and juices ran down on to the roast-dish. Maggie handed gravy and crisp melting golden roast potatoes. Abby and Hugo took round fluffy swedes and snowy turnips, little onions in translucent white sauce, triangles of Yorkshire pudding light as a soufflé, a salad of lettuce and red peppers, speckled with garden herbs and redolent of garlic.

The conversation went on.

'I'm terrified of making a fool of myself,' said Harriet.

'So are we all,' they told her.

'And what's more we're just plain terrified too,' said Sara. 'Frightened rigid of all those enormous obstacles. And when you look at some of them next day you can't believe you jumped them. But that's what makes it all such enormous fun.'

'Sounds irresistible,' muttered Harriet. 'What happens if I fall off?'

'I pick you up,' promised Roddy with a mock leer.

'You'll be lucky,' said Sara. 'He'll be miles away on the horizon and even if you fell at his feet he's much too busy. The only people who'll ever bother to pick you up or to rescue your horse for you are the women.'

'I'll depend on you, then,' said Harriet, 'but you'll be busy with Abby and Hugo.'

'No, she won't. I'll be on the horizon too with Daddy,' said plump, fair Abby, leaning over to rub her head against his sleeve.

'Don't worry,' said Hugo, who was dark and skinny, 'I'll be glad to pick you up. You stay with me and I'll tell you what to do.'

'Hugo, you're a love,' said Harriet. 'I'll be glued to your side.'

Sara said, 'My common old Poppy can't keep up. But don't worry, Atalanta's a dream. After the first burst she'll be sure to settle down. I'd lend you Poppy but you're a much better rider than I am and she'd bore you stiff.'

'I must be mad,' said Harriet, setting down her glass with a snap.

'No, you're not,' said Roddy. 'You'll love it. It's all arranged.'

And by the time they gathered up the children and piled into the Land-Rover, so it was.

Roger and Mabel went back into the house with Charles.

'Have a brandy for the road,' Charles said, eager to make sure there was no resentment about the contretemps of the day before. 'Come on, Mabel. You too.'

'No brandy for me,' she said. 'I'll drive. Then Roger and you can drink a forgiving or at least a living-and-let-living drink together. I know you're spitting at each other.'

Charles looked surprised. 'No we're not,' he said. 'What bee have you got in your bonnet?'

'I don't know, Charles, but Roger came home swearing he would never hunt with you again. You behaved atrociously. Must have done. Or Roger would never had said such a thing.'

'Nonsense,' said Charles as they settled down in the leather armchairs round the library fire. 'Roger simply went off home and my Whipper-in had a brainstorm and fancied himself insulted and actually did the same—buggered off home (oh, sorry, Mabel) half an hour before we were ready to pack up. Extraordinary thing to do.'

'I agree that it was very bad,' said Roger. 'But don't *you* agree that sacking him is taking it a bit too far? It's the poor chap's job and his house too. They're very happy with the Can and Ash and I'm sure he regrets what he did and will apologize.'

'I don't want an apology. I want him out. It's tantamount to desertion. Deserters don't get a second chance. If I let such a shocking piece of insubordination pass they'd all get the wrong idea. If I'm going to run this Hunt successfully and kill foxes I must have a team I can rely on. Peter Thorn has shown that he's totally unreliable. It was unthinkable behaviour. I think he must be deranged.'

'Oh, come on, Charles,' said Mabel. 'If you sack Peter it'll unsettle all the others.'

'And if I keep him on they'll all think they can get away with murder.' The hectoring note had come back into his voice and the purple hue to his cheek. 'It's no use, Mabel. I've made a decision and I'm not budging from it. Out he goes.'

Roger Pratt was usually calm and level-headed but Mabel could see that his colour was rising.

'Roger,' she said quickly, 'I really think it would be best to drink up your brandy and come home.'

Roger put down his glass and stood up.

'Charles,' he said, his voice a little higher than usual, 'I don't think you understood me yesterday. When I said that I was going home I meant for good.'

'What on earth do you mean?'

'I meant, Master, that I shan't hunt with you again. Your behaviour to me and to Peter Thorn was objectionable in the extreme. You were violent and insulting. And quite unnecessarily so. We were doing the job as fast as it could well have been done. The Whipper-in quite rightly took exception to being addressed so rudely in front of the whole field. And so do I. He would have done better to have waited till he had taken hounds back to the Kennels before making his protest and I'm sorry if my behaviour induced him to make a fool of himself, but I've every sympathy with him and if you don't make allowances and take him back I'll not only consider you a damned poor Master of Foxhounds but I'll suspect that you have an ulterior motive.'

'What an extraordinary suggestion?' Charles looked at him in furious amazement. 'I suppose you're resigning as Secretary.'

'Of course not. I made a commitment to do that and I'm certainly not resigning until I can find a decent successor. And let me tell you, my successor will not be Hartley Godwin.'

'Typical!' cried Charles triumphantly. 'Typical fuddy-duddy!'

'Nothing of the kind,' said Roger, curling his lip contemptuously. 'I have the greatest respect for the man as a man, but you won't be able to foist him on the Can and Ash in any capacity whatsoever.'

Charles laughed rudely. 'Respect him my foot!' he said. 'You're falling over backwards to pretend to be so liberal but there's only one thing about Hartley Godwin that sticks in your gullet and we all know what that is.'

Mabel jumped up. 'That's quite enough,' she said. 'We'd much better go.'

'We'll go,' said Roger. 'And I hope you find a Whipper-in and a Hunt Secretary as loyal and efficient as Peter Thorn and me. Thank you for a pleasant luncheon. Now, Mabel, I'm quite ready,' and he walked to the door. There he turned round for a parting shot. 'I do seriously suspect that in sacking Peter you are influenced by your obsession with Godwin. My guess is that you want to make him your successor and I advise you to think again.' He went out.

Charles stood up and accompanied Mabel to the door, looking thoughtful. Mabel kissed him. 'What a pity,' she said. 'You must have behaved very badly, Charles. You know how long-suffering Roger is. You must try not to be so fierce. You've annoyed half the people in this Hunt. I'll admit that the two who've closed their land to us were always difficult. But if you can drive out Roger you'll end up by driving them all out. Do think about it, Charles.'

He kissed her in silence and she followed Roger. At the door she stopped and looked back at him, an unaccustomed hesitation in her manner. 'Oh, and Charles, I don't want to interfere—but you and Siobhan simply must try to hide your differences in front of Dandy. It isn't fair to such a small boy. You'll end up with a problem child on your hands. Now don't be cross. I know I ought not to interfere.'

He patted her arm clumsily. 'I'm not cross. You're quite right. But that's all much worse than you think. She's leaving me. I'm coming to talk to Roger about it next week.'

She took his hand in both hers.

'I'm sorry, Charles, but I can't pretend to be surprised.'

'You *will* be surprised when you know the reason.'

She looked at him questioningly.

'You'll hear in good time. These bloody Irish! I should have known. They're all alike. But I can tell you this, Mabel: nobody would believe it. Not for a minute!' He took her out to the car.

CHAPTER 3

The terrier man, young Tom Stringer, was out in the early hours on the morning of the lawn meet at Hangholt Manor, stopping earths in the Oak Wood (the morning draw). He moved softly and swiftly and calmly and purposefully like a wild animal. He knew this country as the fox and the badger knew it. He could tell where the old badger setts were and where the new. He recognized the badgers' scratching-posts and latrines, and he knew their paths through the bracken. He could tell at a glance, by the litter of food scraps, hair, bones, and fox billets round the entrances of old badger setts, when their original inhabitants had been succeeded by a lazier and a dirtier race. Because he moved like a breath on the wind he had seen things few others saw: a brood of wriggling 3-inch-long baby weasels, a stoat running a rabbit 50 yards along a woodland ride before going in for the kill, a roosting tawny owl mobbed by blackbirds, three hares leaping and tumbling and circling under the moonlight. He sometimes found the flattened beds where fallow deer had lain and the great muddied pools where they had wallowed in the dirt. The stillness of the night was for him alive with tiny sounds and breaths and whispers which others might fail to recognize. But once he started work he behaved like a wild animal, totally absorbed in what he was doing. He set to work stopping up the foxes' earths, pushing gorse and bracken and earth into the holes and sometimes using a bundle of blackthorn faggots tied up with baler twine.

What he was doing was hard on the fox but he did not think of it as cruel. He knew the fox for a killer, beautiful but vicious. But there was no real animosity in his attitude. 'There you are, Charlie!' he would say as he stopped the earth to prevent the fox from getting in after his night's hunting. 'That'll fix you for a while.'

Asked whether he did not find it cruel to hunt the fox, he would reply that there is an element of cruelty in everything. 'But,' he would add, 'if *we* didn't keep the numbers down he'd be gassed and shot and snared and trapped. He's far better off with us, is Charlie. We always hunt him fair. He always has a sporting chance with us.'

Not everyone agreed with him, but many of those who didn't, knew a great deal less about Charlie than Tom Stringer did.

At 9.30 on the morning of the lawn meet, Ramsay Hardcastle came out of his Victorian terrace house in Penchester and went down the steep steps to the pavement, which was shut off from the street by an enclave of grass and trees. Two of his most favoured students came out with him. All three joined the eight of the less favoured, some of whom Ramsay didn't even know by sight, who were gathered on the pavement beside the bright red, rented mini-van. They all wore shaggy pullovers, woolly caps and anoraks. They were larking about, teasing and punching each other, roaring with laughter.

Ramsay smiled at them indulgently. He was a very handsome man of fifty-five with a spare figure, a shock of white hair, and a healthy skin. Unlike his brother, Charles, he was bursting with charm and friendliness, longing to be liked. He smiled constantly but the wounded eyes never quite joined in the smiles. Nevertheless, he inspired most of his students with a burning desire to become members of the charmed circle; the few who were admitted to his house, allowed to answer his telephone, drink his Glenfiddich, and do those of his chores which were outside the province of his daily woman.

He was a lecturer in the University of Penchester with a useful capacity for racy and intelligible exposition. This, together with his undeniable charm, made him a popular speaker on Radio Penchester and almost indispensable on its phone-in discussion programmes. Fame indeed in Penchester, but he reckoned that his gifts should have brought him the infinitely greater rewards of Portland Place, and Wood Lane.

His colleague and Head of Department, Professor Lawrence Philbrick, was a rather mousy-looking little man, untidy of hair and of dress, devoid at first sight of charm, too busy to spend time with his students outside their regular seminars and tutorials, but concentrating on them a hundred per cent at those times. No asking them to sort out his bookcases or find a record he wanted to play for them during their scant and vital tutorial time. For Professor Philbrick the modern mysteries of structuralism and its developments represented a useful new armoury of intellectual probes for the stringent analysis of literary works. Stringent analysis was foreign to Ramsay Hardcastle, though he threw himself wholeheartedly into the exposition of the latest modes. Professor Philbrick was something of a philosopher; Ramsay Hardcastle a juggler with words and notions.

Twice in the Michaelmas term and twice in the Hilary term Ramsay Hardcastle would prevail upon his students to hire a van (paid for by sending round the hat—Ramsay always put in a ten-pound note) and accompany him on an expedition into the territory of the Canfield and Old Ashley Hunt with the purpose of sabotaging the foxhunting activities of the day. There were several country activities and other modern practices of which Ramsay disapproved quite as strongly as he disapproved of foxhunting but his energies were directed only against the evils perpetrated by the members of the Canfield and Old Ashley Hunt. Foxes could be hunted elsewhere or offered poisoned bait or dragged out of badger setts and hit on the head with spades. Badgers

could be dug out and sold to be baited by bull terriers.
Children could be starved and tortured. Ramsay Hardcastle
concentrated his protective forays solely for the benefit of
the Canfield and Old Ashley foxes. In this he differed from
his students, many of whom did what they could for as
many causes as they could well fit in to the intervals allowed
by a busy academic programme. As the years went by the
less militant melted away and a different sort of protester
joined in the fray.

Ramsay took no pleasure in violence or brawling of any
kind, whether vicious or well-meaning. His motive for organizing these sorties was personal. He hated his brother,
Charles Hardcastle, and deeply and corrosively envied him
his money, his position, his house, his heterosexuality, his
wife, his horses, his Mastership of Foxhounds and, most of
all, his sons. The excursions in the mini-van were for him
more or less punitive expeditions. His motive was not the
salvation of the fox but the chastisement of Charles
Hardcastle and all his works and pomps, his Hunt
servants, his mounted subscribers, his horses, and his
hounds. Though he would not have gone so far as to
injure the members of the Hunt he was quite prepared
for horses to be hit with sticks and hounds sprayed with
noxious substances. He wrote letters of encouragement to
local councils and other bodies who were considering
banning foxhunting over their land.

Ramsay was the only one of Charles's brothers and sisters
who hated him, though they all resented his having taken
to himself the lion's share of the profits of the family con-
struction firm. Small amounts of stock had been distributed
to the other members of the family but Charles had taken
over the firm and made it into the giant of industry that it
was now. He saw no good reason why the rest of the family
should profit from his monumental labours.

Ramsay's younger brother, Francis, took this philosophi-
cally. He was not at all fond of Charles but was not so
distressed or offended by his unpleasant behaviour as to
feel that he must be punished for it. He simply eschewed

Charles's company. Francis was an accountant and made a good enough income to keep himself and his wife and children in a pleasant Georgian house on the other side of the county.

His sisters, Gertrude and Dora, could not resist bringing their rather diffident husbands and their assorted hopeful children to stay with the Hardcastles at Hangholt as often as they could wangle an invitation, although Charles was invariably rude to his family. These occasions were fraught with tension and probably inflicted untold psychological damage on the young nephews and nieces of the Master as they were punctuated by furious rages and the exchange of noisy abuse. But both Gertrude and Dora felt that the cachet of occasional residence at the home of the Master of Foxhounds was, for worldly reasons, worth it. The children grew up to fear and hate Charles Hardcastle but the rest of the family stayed ostensibly on good, or at least on visiting, terms with Charles and Siobhan.

Ramsay might have done as his sisters did, and for roughly the same reasons, but it was now ten years since his elder brother had turned him out of the house and told him never to come back again. No one knew the reason for this banishment and neither Charles nor Ramsay ever referred to it again, but it turned Ramsay's sycophantic endurance of Charles's rudeness into a burning resentment and it created rumours of the wildest sort. Ramsay was variously reported to have seduced Charles Hardcastle's first wife, to have got one of the village girls pregnant, to have been caught stealing the silver, to have been found in a compromising situation with a local youth. It was a nine days' wonder in the Can and Ash country but only the vaguest of rumours got as far as the University. However, from the day he left Hangholt for the last time Ramsay never again received an invitation to dine with, drink with, shoot with, or accompany to the races, anyone living in the Can and Ash country. This was a considerable curtailment of his social life and the destruction at a blow of the prestige he had enjoyed at the University as one of the local bigwigs.

Ramsay blamed only Charles for this, although it was in fact the result of the cravenness and self-seeking of his former friends.

In some ways Ramsay was just as angry with Professor Philbrick (for denying him the position of most brilliant scholar in the English Department at Penchester and for being interviewed by Melvyn Bragg on the South Bank Show) as he was with his brother, but as he could not vent his ire on the Professor, this resentment, denied utterance for fear of repercussions on his academic career, simply added fuel to the fire of his obsessional hatred of his brother.

'Well,' he said, 'let's get this show on the road.'

Norman Little, his favourite post-graduate student, took the wheel of the mini-van. Ramsay got into the front passenger seat and the rest all piled into the back.

At eight o'clock on the same morning Rodney and Sara Hardcastle, Harriet and the children were out in the stables at Hangholt Farm, brushing and currycombing, plaiting manes, oiling hoofs, filling haynets looking over tack to see what last-minute burnishing and polishing was necessary. Then they all dashed for the kitchen where Jenny, the help, was dispensing bacon, eggs and sausages, coffee and milk and fruit juices, hot rolls and honey. The comforting warmth of the Aga cooker fought against the chill morning air pouring in through the half-open door.

'Wonderful hunting mornings,' said Sara. 'You have a perfect excuse for sheer greed at breakfast.'

'But not for lingering over it,' said Rodney. 'Come on, get a move on all of you. I expect you all ready for loading in fifteen minutes precisely. Anyone late gets left behind and that includes guests, Harriet.'

Atalanta was a thoroughbred bright bay mare. Kind and willing, and less nervous than she looked, she went straight up into the horse box followed by Sara's Poppy, Jenny's cob and Rodney's O'Halloran, a huge dark bay. Three-quarter thoroughbred, one-quarter Irish draught, short-backed, with plenty of bone, he was fit to carry a giant like Rodney.

Abigail's Welsh pony, Sage, and Hugo's remarkable-looking skewbald, known as Paintbox for his blue eyes and brown and white colouring, went in the trailer with Jenny. Sage was named for her sensible disposition. Paintbox was as sharp and bold as his rider.

Jenny was nervous about reversing the trailer so she always parked a long way from the meet to be sure of finding a suitable grass verge out of everybody's way. This was just as well, for it gave the children's ponies time to settle down as they trotted to the Meet. Sage took exception to some suddenly cackling geese in the field on the other side of a low hedge but Jenny got them mounted and sent them on ahead while she waited for the box to arrive with her cob.

Hugo went scuttling on ahead, heels well down, happy and confident. Abby, unnerved by the incident with the geese, was stiff with fright. She was a sensitive child, conscious that she was overweight, fearful of making a fool of herself and frankly nervous of jumping. She longed to emulate Rodney, who was her hero, but knew that she would have to go over some big jumps if she tried. She was deeply embarrassed at having announced that she would keep up with him. Whatever happened, she felt she faced ignominy. She held her head up and bit her lip, determined not to cry.

Several riders were titupping along the road before and behind her, when she saw, standing at the side of the road beside a wood not far ahead, her Uncle Ramsay. He was a great-uncle really, but when her mother had taken her to see him in Penchester she had been told to call him Uncle Ramsay. Would he notice her? Should she notice him? Would he remember her? Friendliness won the day and she waved a yellow-gloved hand.

Ramsay looked embarrassed, then he smiled across at her and waved back. 'Hello, Abby!' he called out. 'You look very smart, but you know what I think of what you're doing. Next time, you tell them you like foxes and won't come out to kill them,' and he went back into the wood.

She waved again and laughed at him, but inside she

thought: what if I did? I need never be nervous again.

It was a few minutes later that it happened. Six young men came out of the wood where Ramsay had been standing. They walked over to an old lady who was riding side-saddle just ahead of Abby. She wore a shabby old habit and slightly rusty bowler and sat very upright. The youths began to jeer at her. 'Hi, old girl!' they called out. 'Don't you think you're a bit long in the tooth for this sort of thing?'

Abby was horrified and felt she would never be able to look Mrs Granby in the face again after hearing such embarrassing things said to her. Mrs Granby was a very grand old person who owned a crumbling mansion in which she occupied two rooms. With the help of one elderly servant who lived in a cottage on her land she bred cattle, hunted, and in the summer judged at horse shows. She was immensely dignified. To Abby it was terrible to hear her treated with such disrespect.

Mrs Granby walked her horse straight on, looking forward between its ears and ignoring the youths completely.

'Not her,' said one of them. 'She might have a heart attack.' They turned away and saw a little fat, fair girl trotting along on a stylish pony. 'That's one of the Hardcastle children,' said the tallest youth. 'I saw her picture in the paper winning something with that white pony she's riding.'

'Right,' said another. 'She's the one,' and they walked over and surrounded the child. Abby opened her mouth to scream as they poured a pail of some sticky substance all over her and her pony. Her hands went up to her face, the pony began to dance and wheel, and Abby never realized that the second bucket they upturned over her was full of feathers.

'That'll teach you to kill foxes, you spoilt little brat,' said one as they turned away.

Abby grabbed at the reins in time to stop her pony from taking off. Mrs Granby had noticed nothing and went quietly on towards the meet. The people on the road behind gave a great shout and came cantering to Abby's rescue. The youths ran away and got over the stile. It was just as well that there was no way for a horse to get into the woods at that point or mayhem would have been done.

Abby sat looking down at her pony, white with shock, tears running down her cheeks. The first to reach her was Antonia Hyde, one of the finest horsewomen in the Hunt. Antonia dismounted, gave the reins to her sister, Vivian, who had driven up from Bath for the lawn meet, put her arms around Abby, and kissed her, sticky stuff and all. 'Don't you mind them,' she said. 'They're the biggest louts. Come to my box. I've got two huge bottles of Perrier water and we'll use one for you and one for Sage. Come on.' Antonia was leading the pony back to her box when the Hunt lorry came slowly past. Charles Hardcastle's astonished eyes saw his weeping granddaughter the centre of a sympathetic crowd, who were dabbing at the mess all over her and picking off the feathers and wiping off the paste. He leaned down, opening his door. 'What the devil has happened to Abigail?' he asked.

'It was those foul hunt saboteurs,' said Antonia. 'She was very brave. Anyone would have been justified in having hysterics. They poured paste and feathers all over her.'

'Look at poor Sage,' wept Abigail. 'Why did they do it to poor Sage? She hasn't done anything to them.'

Charles got down. 'Who was it, Abby?' he asked quite gently.

'I don't know,' said Abby, 'I never saw them before.'

'She'll be all right,' said Antonia. 'I'm taking her to my box and I'm going to clean her and Sage up, aren't I, my love?'

Abby smiled up at her through her tears.

'Go on,' said Antonia. 'You don't want to be late for the meet. We'll see you there.' She trotted off with her charges.

Charles got back into the lorry but just then he saw Ramsay Hardcastle and Norman Little come out of the wood over the stile and begin to walk along the road towards the meet.

A formidable figure in his scarlet coat, he got down again

and stormed across the road. Grabbing his brother by the shoulder, he swung him round so hard that Ramsay stumbled and fell forward on to his brother's chest. Charles pushed him away and raised his whip. 'Your revolting little blisters of students have attacked my granddaughter,' he said bitingly. 'Take them and your revolting self away and never show your face in this country again.' With each word he hit Ramsay hard with his hunting whip across the face and chest. Ramsay threw up his arms to protect his face, tripped and fell to the ground with a sound between a cry and a groan. Charles raised his arm again, then thought better of it, and stalked back to the Hunt box. Norman Little was still standing, stunned, with his mouth open. Charles climbed up to his seat and motioned the Whip to drive on.

A young police sergeant was standing by the gates of the Manor and Charles signalled Peter Thorn to stop the box. He beckoned to the policeman, who had the physique of a rugby forward and an open, guileless, fresh-faced appearance.

'Sergeant,' he said, 'my granddaughter has just been attacked by thugs. Can you arrest them?'

'Several people have already reported the incident, sir,' the sergeant answered. 'It seems to have been very nasty indeed. The nastiest I've heard yet.'

'Then you can arrest them?'

'I'm afraid not, sir. They haven't actually harmed the child or the pony physically. And they've scarpered. We're here solely to make sure there isn't any breach of the peace. Nobody has in fact started an affray. But perhaps you would like to take out a private prosecution?'

'Well, as you point out, Sergeant, they've bloody well scarpered. We haven't even got their names.'

'Trouble is, sir, they come from all over. They may not be local. But we'll keep an eye out for them.'

'You'd better watch out for my foot-followers too. There'll be trouble if they catch up with the swine. I hope you'll have the sense to turn a blind eye if any of them do,' and he waved Peter Thorn on.

On the terrace in front of Hangholt Manor Eithne and Maggie were walking round with trays, offering glasses of cherry brandy and plates of tiny hot savouries to the assembling members of the Hunt. The long low house of honey-coloured stone with grey stone quoins made a pretty backdrop with the gentle slope of the hill rising up behind the balustrade. A pale sun was fitfully shining in a champagne-coloured sky drifting with grey wisps of cloud. There was a damp feel in the air.

Several of the mounted followers were gathered together on the grass below the terrace sipping their drinks and talking hunting.

'They'll go like blazes today,' said Donald Cresswell, who always tried to come out for the Hangholt lawn meet although he was not often able to hunt on other days.

The Hunt lorry turned in at the gate and wheeled carefully to a stop below the terrace. Charles Hardcastle got down with a face of thunder followed by the Huntsman and the Whippers-in who looked almost equally angry. The horses seemed moved by their fury to a nervousness that manifested itself in sidlings and wheelings and sudden whinnyings. Newcomers who trotted up past the pack as it circled and jumped up round the Huntsman brought the explanation of Abigail's ordeal to the earlier arrivals.

It was beginning to rain gently and the raincoats and hoods were coming out among the group of foot-followers who were sipping cherry brandy on the terrace. A girl in a cloth cap, jeans and wellingtons, was holding three black labradors on a lead as she told every newcomer to the group the horror story of a small girl and her pony 'tarred and feathered' by six great louts. Voices were raised. Charles Hardcastle was not popular with the foot-followers, but Rodney, his son, was liked by everyone. He was friendly by nature and made no distinctions between people. Everyone who came to Hangholt Farm was welcome to coffee in the kitchen. When he entertained it was in the kitchen too. He was a working farmer and couldn't be bothered with dinner-parties. Gamekeeper or High Sheriff, if you wanted to eat with Rodney, you ate in the kitchen and took pot luck who you might find at his table.

Abby was known as a well-behaved and rather shy little girl. Even if she had been a little monster the anger against the saboteurs would have been considerable. As it was, the Can and Ash were beside themselves.

'I reckon they ought to ride 'em down in the woods,' said one young farm worker.

Frank Hardy, the chairman of the Hunt Supporters Club, a greengrocer from Stumpington, jumped on him at once.

'None of that,' he said sharply. 'That's what they want. *Us* in the papers doing *them* a mischief. Let it be. Mr Hardcastle will settle with them. You can be sure of that.'

All the same, he was tapping a heavy leather boot on the flagstones angrily as he munched a piece of fruit cake. It was he who started the cheering as Antonia trotted up the drive with a beaming, cleaned-up Abby at her side. Everybody clapped and cheered and Abby held her head high. All her fears vanished. Everyone smiled at her. The foot-followers came and patted her on the back. Her grandfather loomed over her on his huge hunter and said, 'Good girl. Full of pluck.'

Best of all, Rodney smiled at her and squeezed her hand and said: 'That's my brave girl!' She *would* keep up with him. She could do anything now.

And Hugo looked at her with awe.

'I'm terribly sorry, Abby,' he said. 'If I'd known I would have stayed with you. They'd better not try it again.'

The sexton from Hangholt Church, Mr Fenchurch, came up to them and gave Abby a holy picture. He was very religious and always gave them pictures when he was pleased with them. Abby thanked him and put it in her pocket carefully. An elderly lady came up to ask him where the morning's draw would be. 'Oak Wood this morning,' he told her. 'Taverners this afternoon.'

'Oh dear,' said the lady. 'Come on, Helen, we'd better get going. They've got that long gallop over the meadow. We'll lose them if we don't get on now.'

Grumbling, Helen went to put her glass back on a tray and they hurried away. The girl in the cloth cap smiled.

'They'll be hanging about for half an hour at covertside,' she said.

'Ah well,' said Mr Fenchurch. 'They can't move so fast any more. Just as well to get on with it.'

'Come on, my dears.' Rodney came trotting up to Abby and Hugo with Harriet in tow. 'Into position for the Charge of the Light Brigade. It's the Oak Wood so we've got the fifteen-acre meadow for starters. Abby, Hugo, you stay well behind me and keep well away from red ribbons and green ribbons and don't get in the way and don't forget to open gates if you're asked, and generally show you're an asset to the Hunt and not a bloody nuisance.'

'We're an asset anyway,' said Hugo, 'seeing we're farmers.'

'We'll discuss that remark tonight,' said Rodney ominously. 'You're too uppity by half, young man.'

The mounted followers were beginning to edge towards the open meadow. The Huntsman had collected his hounds and now the horn sounded, sweet and clear.

Huntsman, Whippers-in and Master, superb in their panoply of scarlet coats, black velvet caps, white breeches and shining black boots with glossy brown tops, set off at the trot, hounds streaming ahead of them on to the grass. The mounted field broke into a collected trot.

Maggie and Eithne stood by the table laden with empty glasses and watched. It was a magnificent sight. First went the Whipper-in followed by the Huntsman with the bitch pack at his horse's heels, sterns waving, heads up; some black and tan, some lemon and white, some badger pied, most of them smooth but one or two rougher and more hairy, showing their Welsh breeding. Then came the Master followed by the field, more than a hundred of them, in blue coats and black coats and scarlet coats, their mounts dancing and tossing their heads, waiting for the signal to canter.

The Master broke into a canter and now it was like a military charge; light thoroughbreds and heavy hunters, well-behaved cobs of unknown breeding but patent-safety character, well-bred ponies daisy-cutting and shaggy little commoners scuttling along.

'Lovely sight, isn't it?' said Maggie, turning to Eithne. Then: 'Oh my love, I'm sorry. I never thought.' Eithne's eyes were full of tears.

'Don't worry,' she said, putting out a hand to press Maggie's reassuringly. 'It's stupid of me. I really thought I'd be all right by now. It's all those great hooves thundering over the ground. I always see him lying there. He'd kill me for being like this. He said he'd make a jockey out of me. At this rate I'll never be able to get on a horse again. Never mind, Maggie. Let's start clearing up.'

'Come on then, love,' said Maggie, putting an arm round her. 'Come and help me. There's no need really but it'll keep your mind off it.'

CHAPTER 4

Harriet and Hugo were hurtling along together midway up towards the van of the troop of horses, Hugo's pony sometimes breaking into a gallop to keep up, and then being throttled back, Hugo hanging on to the reins with all his might.

They dashed along, the wind whipping round their ears, but in too short a time they were queueing up to pass through a narrow opening over a bank and a ditch into a field of faded last-year's grasses. They all trooped into a wide stretch of grassland at the edge of the Oak Wood into which the Huntsman was putting his hounds. 'Leu in! Leu in there!' he cried as hounds scattered along the ditch and made their way through into the scrub and thicket.

From a footpath at the far end of the field, Monica and Helen could be seen vaunting themselves on their position of vantage.

The mounted field spread out and for ten minutes they stopped there chatting. From time to time the Huntsman's voice could be heard from within the covert in a high screech, exhorting hounds to 'Push 'em up! Go at 'em! Yoi! Yoi in there!' After a while the Master dismounted and handed his bridle to the nearest rider, who happened to be Harriet. She sat there biting her lip and praying that Atalanta would behave. What horror if she lost the Master's mount! She could imagine the scene and the swearing and cursing. By the time Charles came out again and climbed on his horse with a careless 'Thanks,' her lip was bleeding.

Cries came from within the covert. 'Yip! Yip! Yip! Yoi on! Yoi on there! Rouse him! Push him up!' A hound spoke and the cry came 'Hoic to Juniper!' The riders began to gather up their reins. The Master swung round on the field with a huge bellow. 'Will you stop that coffee-housing and let me bloody well listen.'

Hounds were now speaking as the tension built up. A great 'Holloa!' came from the far end of the covert followed by the urgent doubling note of the horn and cries of 'Hoic Forrard! Hoic Forrard!'

'They're blowing him away!' cried Hugo. 'Come on!'

The Master was cantering along the edge of the covert, the field falling in behind him. As they rounded the end of the shaws the Huntsman and Whippers-in came into sight, galloping hell for leather across a broad meadow in pursuit of a moving white mass which was the bitch pack in full cry.

Before Harriet knew it, she and Hugo had taken a flying jump over a low hedge with several of the field and were heading for a set of rails. Harriet brought Atalanta up to the jump too close to the horse ahead. A clod of earth flew up into her face. Atalanta checked momentarily, losing momentum, and tried a cat jump which took her lopsided over the rails, depositing Harriet in a ditch. She hung on to the reins, was dragged on for a few paces at a run, then managed to lead Atalanta to one side, scramble up again and canter on without causing any commotion, covered with mud from head to foot.

Hugo came galloping up anxiously, having judged the rails too high for Paintbox and found a gate. Antonia and Vivian came flying past them and as Hugo and Harriet followed they passed by Rodney on one side of a fence exhorting Abby, on the other, to jump her pony out of an impenetrable spinney into which she had rashly jumped. Abby had lost her nerve and was weeping quietly.

'Come on,' said Hugo fiercely, 'pretend we haven't seen.'

'Hunting's very hard on nervous kids,' said Harriet, as they went on. Hugo shrugged. 'It's very character-building,' he corrected and grinned at her as they looked back and saw Abby wreathed in smiles trotting after them beside her father, who was smiling down at her and applauding.

The Hunt now seemed to have vanished across a field on the other side of an unjumpable hedge. They followed Antonia and Vivian along a narrow lane, keeping to the grass verge and pausing every so often to listen. Popping over a low gate into a field, they met with angry shouts of 'Hounds, please!' from the Whipper-in. They stopped dead. The Whip took off at a canter along the hedge to round up a straying hound and the guilty four trotted quietly away round the headland. Crossing a wooden bridge over a stream, they discovered the rest of the field beside a covert. Steam rose from the horses' wet flanks and nostrils. It was suddenly much colder and a mist had come down like a net, enveloping the countryside.

'Why has the Field Master gone off away from the field?' Harriet asked Hugo.

'I expect it's the railway,' said Hugo. 'Someone usually goes in that direction in case hounds show signs of getting on to the line.'

Then hounds were speaking, the horn doubling, and they were away again, thundering uphill and into a woodland ride, then on, winding through beech and oak trees with holly and hazel shrub layer and a carpet of decaying leaves and bracken.

Four young men in woolly hats and anoraks appeared on the path ahead of them waving sticks in the air and shouting obscenities. Harriet yanked at her reins but there was no possibility of stopping in time. Hugo cried out, 'Don't stop, Harriet! They're saboteurs!'

He rode straight at them and so, willy-nilly, did Harriet. At the last minute the young men jumped out of the way, hatred in their faces. Harriet heard them shouting, 'You might have killed us!' and managed to slow Atalanta down. She swung round and called out, 'I'm really sorry, but no one could have stopped!'

'Fucking shit!' they yelled, and one of them ran after her at speed and swiped the mare over the rump with a heavy stick he was carrying. Atalanta lashed out and he tumbled away out of reach of her hooves just in time.

'Stupid louts!' called Harriet, as she galloped on after Hugo.

Without realizing it, she passed by the turning he had taken, and by the time she retraced her steps there was nothing to show which of the many woodlands paths the Hunt had followed. She stopped to listen, but the thick carpet of humus deadened sounds and the mist seemed to shut her in. She had lost all sense of direction and began to feel a slight sense of panic alone in the misty wood. Then to her relief she glimpsed through the trees a grey standing still in the middle of the ride, and put Atalanta into a canter.

It was only as she got near enough to see which horse it was that she realized something was wrong. A shallow stream crossed the ride and in it Charles Hardcastle's grey was standing, riderless and looking oddly distressed. Then she saw the still figure lying half in the stream, the face pressed into the leaves on the bank, the velvet cap lying upside down in the water beside him.

My God! thought Harriet. It's the Master. He's been thrown and he's dead! He must be dead! I've never seen anything half as dead as this! She flung herself off Atalanta and ran to kneel beside the heavy, motionless bulk. She slipped an arm under the neck and struggled to lift the head high enough to see the staring eyes and awful flaccid face, then laid it gently down again. She had no doubt that he was beyond help but wondered if she ought to give the kiss of life. She tried to turn him over so that the dreadful face was clear of the bank but he was deadweight in her hands. And then she heard a flurry of lightly galloping hooves and Hugo came to a halt and jumped off his pony, splashing her and the scarlet coat of the Master with mud.

'No, Hugo!' she cried. 'Don't look!'

'Don't be silly, Harriet!' said Hugo, but with a gulp in his voice. 'He's dead, isn't he? We'll have to get someone.'

'I'll stay with him,' said Harriet. 'You go and fetch your father.'

'Are you sure you'll be all right?' he asked. 'You look all white and funny.'

'I'll be fine,' she said, 'but I can't move him. They can't be far away. Do hurry!'

'All right, I will,' he said. 'Those saboteurs have gone too far this time. But, Harriet, they might come back! I'd better stay!'

'Go on, Hugo!' Harriet almost screamed at him. 'They'd better not come! I can cope with them!'

'I'm going,' he said, jumping on to his pony again. 'If he's really dead you'd better calm the horse. I'll get Daddy.' He tore away, sublimely sensible and matter of fact.

Harriet remembered that you turn the heads of accident victims and clear the passages. She lifted the clammy, flaccid upper lip and put her fingers in the slack mouth, feeling for any foreign bodies at the back of the throat. She found nothing. The teeth scraped the back of her hand horribly. Then came the welcome sound of trotting hooves and Roddy and Dr Cresswell came and rolled him over and looked in the mouth. Then Donald Cresswell knelt over him and after trying a few great thumps on the chest with all his weight behind them so that the body jerked grotesquely, he began trying to breathe his own life and breath into the lifeless thing that had been the Master. He went on for what seemed a long time with passionate energy but Harriet knew it wouldn't work and at last he sat back saying, 'I'm afraid he's gone, Roddy.'

Rodney stood for a long time looking down at his father.

'Well,' he said at last, 'they've done it now. They've actually killed someone.'

'Someone had better fetch the police at once,' said Cresswell.

'It's either an accident or the saboteurs,' said Rodney.

'Any case of sudden death it's the same,' said Cresswell apologetically. 'Sudden death means police, statements from everyone, inquest. I'm very sorry but that's the way it is.'

'I'll go,' said Rodney. He turned to Hugo who was staring solemnly at his grandfather's body. 'You go and find Mummy and Jen and Abby, Hugo. You've been very sensible and very grown-up and now you must keep it up and get them all to go home. Can you do that?'

'Of course I can,' said Hugo and cantered off the way he had come.

Harriet got to her feet and took the reins of the big grey. She began to stroke and pat him, crooning to him in a voice that trembled.

Rodney had vanished into the mist. She began to feel both very cold and very wet. The gentle rain had long since soaked her black coat but she had had no time to notice it. Kneeling in the stream had drenched her breeches and water was squelching at the bottom of her boots.

'I hope they get a move on,' said Donald Cresswell. 'It's horrid cold.' He began to pace up and down. 'That's the way it goes,' he said. 'My one chance in a month to come out hunting. It's a hard life, a doctor's. If you're feeling fit enough we'd better walk these chaps up and down before they take a chill.'

Harriet looked at him in amazement at his egotism and walked over to Atalanta who was nervous and trembling.

'It's just the dead body,' said Dr Cresswell. 'Horses can't stand it. Very sensitive creatures.'

Harriet stroked the mare's ears. 'Does the grey kick?' she asked.

'Not that I know of.' said the doctor, 'And my old fellow is a hundred per cent steady. I'll lead these two and you lead yours. Lovely mare but nervous. Did she go well for you?'

Harriet gave no answer.

He led the two horses away along the ride but without touching or speaking to them. He behaved as if they weren't there. When he tried to turn them and lead them back they balked and the grey reared.

'Oh,' he said, 'of course! Never mind. I'll lead them on a bit. The mare all right? Follow me, then.'

Harriet had no intention of following him any further.

'I'm going back,' she called. 'We can't leave him alone.' She turned Atalanta who came sweetly round with her, followed quietly, nuzzling her arm, and showed no sign of distress when Harriet stopped near the still body and stood on guard.

The mist seemed to be lifting a little. Far away among the trees she saw something move and thought: Saboteurs! It was them, of course! Her heart began to beat very fast. What if they returned, as Hugo had feared? She scrambled back into the saddle, feeling safer at a more commanding height.

Someone was coming towards her through the trees. She leaned forward to peer through the mist and, just as suddenly, he was gone. She opened her mouth to cry out, but shut it again firmly, determined not to summon Donald Cresswell.

It was surprising how many rustling sounds disturbed the silence. Wild things were moving in the undergrowth. Or perhaps it was birds. And if they were humans, humans would not necessarily be ill-disposed. She dwelt on these thoughts to distract herself from the panic that threatened to have her screaming at the top of her voice.

Something flew past her head and landed with a thump in the undergrowth ahead of her. She jumped, as Atalanta, bucked, startled at the sudden movement. An arm came round her neck choking her and her hat was knocked to the ground. Atalanta reared and, as Harriet began to fall, her head seemed to split apart as a heavy blow struck her on the temple. The last thing she heard was the thunder of hooves all around her as she fell to the ground.

CHAPTER 5

The Assistant Chief Constable rang Detective Chief Superintendent John Charter of Police Headquarters at Penchester at 2 o'clock that afternoon and said, 'We've got a possible serious crime on our hands, John. I've been trying to get you for the last hour. Sudden death of a Master of Foxhounds.'

'Good God! Which one, sir?'

'The Can and Ash. He lives at a village called Hangholt near Stumpington. Chap called Charles Hardcastle. Big businessman and candidate for the European Parliament. Bit of a VIP.'

'I'd better go over and take a look. Do we know that it's murder?'

'We know absolutely nothing so far. On the face of it, it looks like heart failure on horseback but there's the possibility that the hunt saboteurs were responsible for bringing him down off his horse. That could be dynamite. And there's another sinister possibility. He was found by a young woman who was attacked and knocked unconscious a few minutes later. The inference is that someone wanted either to make sure he'd finished the chap off or to remove an incriminating piece of evidence. It's all a bit of a muddle. Just up your street, wouldn't you say?'

'Whatever you say, sir.'

'Well, wrap it up as fast as you can. Can't spare you for

long. Look on it as a spot of country leave but definitely a short break only.'

'I'll get out my Barbour and my green wellies, sir.'

'You do that.'

John Charter was welcomed with relief by Inspector Longfield at Stumpington Police Station. 'We're stretched about to the limit, sir, at the moment,' he explained. 'There's the robberies down Fawley way and we've got the royal visit to the local hospital. But we've been getting on with it. We're assigning you the sergeant who was at the scene. He's rural sergeant here and a very good lad. He accompanied the body to St Christopher's. Mr Harvey Knott has already performed the PM and the inspector who was present should be here any moment with Sergeant Cobbold and I reckon we'll have at least an interim report before long. They're in a right tizzy over this one. We've had the ACC on the blower practically non stop. They're setting up the Incident Room here and you tell us when you want the briefing. Then there's the Press. I'm afraid there's going to be a lot of interest. We've already got all the local papers and half the nationals.'

'I'd be grateful if your people could handle all that for the time being. I'll do my bit with them when the time comes but I've got to cover some ground first. You'll know what to tell them.'

'We'll cope for a day or two but you know how it is. Once they know we've got the Chief Super from Penchester they don't want to talk to anyone else.' At that moment Inspector Thompson and Sergeant Cobbold arrived and handed the PM report to Charter.

'Cardiac arrest,' said Charter.

'Yes, sir. He was on digitalis (or digoxin, I should say) according to his doctor who was on the scene—a hunting GP. He seemed to think it was only to be expected in a heavy man sixty years of age who had already had a mild heart attack and was on medication for high blood pressure too. Said he forbade him to hunt. If it weren't for the attack on the girl he'd have signed the certificate.'

Charter glanced at the window. 'It's getting on,' he said. 'Thank you, Inspector. I'd better get to the scene before it gets dark.'

The sergeant followed Charter to the police car, thanking his lucky stars for the robberies which were occupying the attention of his colleagues. The Chief Superintendent looked more like a university don than a policeman. His manner seemed slightly vague and apologetic and he kept running his hands through his shock of dark hair. But there was nothing vague in the way he set about things.

'Right,' he said, 'we'll go straight to the scene,' and then, once they were in the car, 'Now, let's be hearing.'

'Well, sir, I was in on it from the very beginning which was at about ten forty-five this morning when my colleague and I were in the police car at the lawn meet at Hangholt Manor, the home of the deceased. Several of the Hunt members asked us to arrest the hunt saboteurs who poured paste and feathers over a small girl on a pony who happened to be a granddaughter of the Master. I told them we were there solely to make sure there was no breach of the peace. The incident was a very unpleasant one and if we hadn't been there the six youths who did it would have been beaten up by the foot-followers. It's the foot-followers who see red.'

'What sort of people are they?'

The sergeant gave it some thought. 'I suppose, really, much the same as the people who hunt nowadays. All sorts. Butchers, bakers, builders, farmers, old colonels, young women with dogs and children, blacksmiths, stablegirls, vets. You name it. Lot of the nobs foot-follow when they get too old to hunt. Doddery old couples you'd expect would stop by the fire on a freezing winter's day. The foot-followers know more about hunting than some of the field and there's some of them I'll swear can tell all the local foxes apart. They collect money for the Hunt and buy some of the equipment and they get blind with rage when the "Antis" try to tell them what they can't do.

'Anyway, as it was, there was no affray as far as we know,

though we were told later that there had been violence done. The Master saw his brother going to the meet. That's Mr Ramsay Hardcastle. He blamed Ramsay Hardcastle for the attack on his granddaughter, got down from the Hunt lorry and lit into him with his hunting whip. Didn't do him much harm as far as we heard and no complaint was made to us.'

'So you stayed with it? Followed by car?'

'Yes, sir. We thought it best just in case the situation deteriorated. You could cut the tension in the air with a knife. Those chaps were wandering about in the woods for all we knew and might be ready for anything because of what the Master did to Ramsay Hardcastle.'

'Why did the Master beat up his brother?'

'Ramsay Hardcastle is well known around here for bringing his students over to disrupt his brother's hunting activities.'

'Good God!' said Charter. 'The £10 a day and a packed lunch lot?'

'I don't know about that, sir, but it's bizarre, isn't it?'

'So Charles Hardcastle blamed his brother for the attack on the little girl?'

'That's right, sir.'

'So what happened in the woods?'

'Nothing happened until, at twelve-thirty precisely, the Master's son, Mr Rodney Hardcastle, came out to us at the gallop to report a death in the woods. His father, the Master of Foxhounds.'

'Isn't that somewhat bizarre too, Sergeant? How often does a Master of Foxhounds get murdered in mid-Hunt? Surely he is usually in the thick of it?'

'Exactly, sir. We were sure it was an accident—something to do with the tension between the Hunt and the foot-followers against the hunt saboteurs. And that seems to me the most likely scenario.'

'So what did you find when you went in?'

'We found a shambles. The corpse lying next to a stream. (He'd already been moved away from it.) The doctor leaning over a young lady who'd been hit over the head in the last couple of minutes. Three horses reported loose in the woods. No one in charge. Of course the attack on the girl led us to suspect there might be something fishy about the death of the Master.'

'So what did you do?'

'Got in touch with the station. Called for an ambulance. Watched the doctor like a hawk as he looked after the girl in case he turned out to be the villain. Stayed there myself to protect the scene as best I could and start finding witnesses and taking statements. There were none bar the girl and the doctor, and according to his story no one actually saw the Master fall. Mr Rodney Hardcastle had come on the scene and he'd helped to get him out of the water and then come to us for help. Came back with a hurdle only to find we needed two. The girl came round but the doctor wouldn't let us talk to her. Then the police surgeon arrived, not at all pleased that the body had been moved, but we had to move the poor chap when the hounds found him. All over him they were. Then the Scene of Crime lads came and when they'd finished photographing him I went with the body to St Christopher's, where it was pronounced DOA and then to the hospital mortuary. Inspector Thompson was present at the PM. Which was done by St Christopher's consultant pathologist, Mr Harvey Knott. I took care to send one of our lads with the girl and told him to stay right with her in Casualty and to accompany her into the ward and make sure no one got to her before we did. The doctor seemed rather keen to go with her and I couldn't be sure it wasn't the doctor. He had all the opportunity. She must have seen something to make the murderer, or the "Antis" or whoever it was, try to kill her before getting away. Very dangerous thing to do with the woods teeming with possible witnesses.'

'He may have been trying to kill her, Sergeant, in which case he failed miserably or he may have just wanted to achieve what he actually did achieve—put her out for just long enough to finish the old boy off or to tamper with something or remove something from the scene.'

'I wonder what that might be, sir?'

'Did he have a flask on him?'

'No, sir.'

'Would a Master of Foxhounds go hunting without his flask?'

'I don't know, sir. We did have one who was teetotal.'

'Was this one teetotal?'

'No, sir, he wasn't.'

'Then we'd better start looking for the flask.'

'Right you are, sir. I'll get on to it.'

'And, Sergeant, you are known as the rural sergeant hereabouts?'

'That's right, sir.'

'Well, in my book of words you're streetwise. Much too fly for a rural sergeant.'

'Ah, sir, but we local cops are not your country bumpkins any more. Not in Penfoldshire we're not.'

'Well, I'll want you on the case with me. We'll need a rural sergeant, won't we, for a rural murder?'

Sergeant Cobbold drove as far as he could into the woods, then they left the car and walked. The rain had petered out and the mists were clearing. Pale sunlight streamed down through the trees, glistening on the wet boles of the beech trees and throwing dark shadows across the woodland floor.

As they approached the scene several uniformed men could be seen through the trees methodically walking up and down searching the undergrowth. Several square yards of woodland were cordoned off and a police constable stood on guard.

'It's a pity we couldn't leave everything as it was,' said Cobbold apologetically, 'but this place was like Piccadilly Circus even before the lab men got here. The Hunt people kept trotting up to see what was happening. No way we could stop them. We even had the whole pack of hounds at one stage and it was then they decided it was time to move the poor chap. It was the Assistant Chief Constable's decision. We tried to work out which were the prints of the victim's horse to see whether he was galloping. But the ground's too poached to tell one print from another.'

They stood by the stream and looked about them.

'I still think it was the saboteurs,' the rural sergeant added. 'We knew it was bound to happen one day. I thought it'd be a hunt saboteur killed by a foot-follower but it's the other way round.'

'So how did they do it?' asked Charter.

'Rope across the path?'

'Only if he was galloping.'

'He wasn't even cantering. He was a great heavy chap on a great stomping Irish hunter. If he'd been galloping or cantering the indentations'd have been through to Australia.'

'And was the horse brought down? He didn't just fall off?'

'We can't tell. The horse had slithered down a bank earlier, so the son told us, and it was covered with mud and cuts and scratches. So there would be nothing to show whether he fell again here.'

'A rope isn't the only way. What about someone jumping on him from out of a tree?'

'Robin Hood style? Could be.'

'Why would the saboteurs hit the girl over the head?'

'Same reason they attacked the Master. To disrupt the hunt. But I admit it's a problem because she wasn't hit till several minutes later. They'd be far away by then. When they saw the Master lie where he fell I reckon they scarpered at a rate of knots.'

'Then it's hardly likely they'd come back to hit the girl. You start looking for the flask, Sergeant. It's probably gone already but who knows?'

'They're quartering the area looking for anything that might be there,' said Cobbold. 'I'll just go and tell them what they're looking for.'

He came back and they walked to the car.

'One thing, sir,' said the sergeant diffidently. 'Poison in

the flask. They often swig from each other's flasks. He might have offered it to anyone.'

'Yes. We'll have to find out whether he did. It could be a nutter who wouldn't care. It could also be something in the flask to which he would be peculiarly susceptible. Something harmless to anyone else.'

'Who would know enough for that, sir?'

'His family might, or his doctor, or almost anyone who knew him well and could get at the flask. Anyone can buy a book on drugs.'

'There was a lot of talk about his relationship with his wife. She's Irish and a lot younger and beautiful. They say they hardly ever slept under the same roof. He'd sleep up at the Kennels most nights.'

'Then that's where we'll start. That's where the flask would be filled. Is it far from here?'

'Not far, sir. Three or four miles.'

They drove a couple of miles through winding country roads lined with leafless hedges and the winter skeletons of beech, oak, thorn, and ash, already misted over with young green shoots, with here and there a tall Scots pine. Away to the west a huge, rayless sun glowed, then, gathering all the pale light from the landscape into itself, slowly sank behind the low hills on the horizon, leaving the land grey and formless to the eye.

'What do you feel about foxhunting yourself?' asked Charter idly. 'Do you approve of it or have the saboteurs got a case?'

There was no doubt at all about the response of the rural sergeant. 'Well, I personally don't agree with it,' he said. 'Mind you, I can see the exhilaration of it. But all those people rejoicing in the death of a small animal! To tell you the truth I feel sorry for them.'

'You may be right to feel sorry for them but I'd have thought it's nothing but a cross-country course to most of them.'

'Maybe so, sir. Of course I don't allow my personal views to influence me in my work.'

'Of course not, Sergeant.'

'And I've known police officers who hunt in their off-duty time.'

'It's a funny thing, Sergeant, but police officers do as many daft things in their off-duty time as any of the rest of the population.'

'That's right, sir. You might like to know, sir, that the Old Rectory near Hangholt we're just about to pass by is where Mr and Mrs Pratt live. He's the Hunt Secretary and a solicitor. Very respectable old-fashioned firm in Stumpington. What they don't know about what goes on in the Canfield and Old Ashley Hunt isn't worth knowing! And they say Mr Pratt was going to leave the Hunt on account of Mr Hardcastle's behaviour.'

'We'll call in and see them, then.'

'Now, sir? Right you are.'

CHAPTER 6

It was a large Victorian house with a gravel sweep behind high brick walls. Stone balls topped the gateposts of the two entrances. Behind the house outbuildings of various heights and shapes could be seen and an archway in another brick wall led into gardens and orchards.

An elderly woman in a pinafore showed them into a room lined with bookcases filled with leather-bound books. Two portraits in oils hung in heavy gilt frames on either side of the fireplace, the meek lady with her hands folded submissively, the bewhiskered gentleman, hand on hip, conveying by both carriage and expression an almost aggressive self-assertion. The room was Roger Pratt's, as a glance at the books made evident. Half were concerned with the law. The rest were those of an historian, except for a large section filled with books on horses and hunting, including an entire set of Surtees.

Mabel Pratt came in carrying a bunch of daffodils.

'I'm sorry,' she said. 'Mrs Sims couldn't find me. I was feeding the guinea fowl. I'm a bit late tonight, having heard the terrible news about the Master's fall. Did you want to see my husband? I'm afraid he's away until Monday at a legal conference at York. I told him about it on the phone but he can't get away until lunch-time tomorrow.'

'May we have a word with you then, Mrs Pratt?'

'Of course. Do sit down.'

'In any case of sudden death the police have to question everybody connected in any way with the victim.' Charter began the soothing preamble he had so often used before.

Mabel had sunk rather wearily into an armchair but at this she sat up sharply.

'You're Penchester. You aren't local. Does that mean what I think it means?'

'I'm afraid,' said John Charter, 'that it means that I have to question several people as a matter of routine in connection with a death that may have been a suspicious one. This is the local rural sergeant who is helping me to deal with the case.'

Mabel nodded. 'I know Sergeant Cobbold well. Good evening, Sergeant. It's not the hunt saboteurs, then?'

'Much too early to say. It could be the saboteurs or it could be someone nearer to your Master. He could have been attacked because he is Master of the Canfield and Old Ashley but he may equally well have been attacked because he is this particular Master, Charles Hardcastle. Anything you have to say about that possibility could be a great help to us.'

Mabel sank back again in her chair as if exhausted. 'Good God!' she said. 'It's unbelievable! Murder! That stupid, stupid man! Why couldn't he behave like any sensible man would do? Why drive everybody over the edge? It's appalling, Mr Charter, if it's true. But it really isn't surprising.'

'That is a very interesting reaction, Mrs Pratt. On the face of it, most people would assume the saboteurs must be responsible for the attack on the Master. You must feel quite strongly that he gave people reason to want him dead.'

'No,' she said firmly. 'I can't say anybody would wish him dead. But many people wanted him out of the Canfield and Old Ashley.'

'Which might come to much the same thing?'

'Only if there is a murderer among us and I can't quite believe that.'

'What did he do to make himself so unpopular?'

'James Pierson and old Jim, the Huntsman, ran this Hunt like a dream for fifteen years. Charles took over and spoiled everything for everybody.'

'What exactly did he do that spoiled everything for everybody?'

'Well, for one thing he wasn't interested in the social side of hunting and could hardly bring himself to address a word to the subscribers. All he cared about was killing foxes.'

'Isn't killing foxes the whole purpose of hunting?'

'Well, yes, of course it is but there's a lot more to it than that. It's the whole life of the countryside in winter. A Master of Foxhounds has to be all things to all people. There are the landowners over whose land we want to hunt. The Master has to keep them happy, assure them that we'll take care of any damage, that sort of thing. And then the mounted followers provide the cash. You can't be consistently rude to them. And the foot-followers are frightfully important. They help us in countless ways, organizing the cars and raising money for the Hunt. Most Masters get along with them like anything and join in all the events they organize when they can. Charles couldn't be bothered with any of that.'

'Wasn't there a little difficulty with your husband?'

'They had a tiff at the end of a long day. That's all there was to it.'

'I'm told there was a little more to it than that, Mrs Pratt. They say your husband has been saying he wouldn't hunt again with the Canfield and Old Ashley while Charles Hardcastle remained Master.'

'Yes, he did say that, and he meant it. But that isn't the

end of the world. There's the Fillingham on one side and the Fawley Green on the other. He could take his choice. And everyone here wishes him well. They knew who was to blame. But in any case Roger would probably have relented in the end once he'd got Charles to take Peter Thorn back on the strength.'

'Why did he want Peter Thorn taken back?'

'It was Roger's fault. That's why he felt responsible. The Master ticked Roger and the boy off very rudely in front of the whole field when they were doing the job that had to be done, efficiently and quietly. You've no idea how horrid and belittling he could be. Roger had had enough and said he was going home. To his amazement the Whipper-in did the same. It was a very dramatic thing to do. It was the end of the day but the Whipper-in has the job of looking after hounds, rounding them up and taking them home. Charles regarded it in the same light as desertion in face of the enemy and would make no allowances. Roger tried to persuade Charles to have him back. It's not only his job, you see, but their home. His wife is a very clever woman. She's made it so nice and the little girl is doing well at the local school. They were so happy. Until Charles took over, the Kennels was the happiest of places.'

'Did the Hunt servants dislike the Master?'

'Well Jim, the Huntsman, got on with him. Had to or they couldn't have hunted hounds together. So Charles was all right with him. But I'm afraid the rest of them loathed him. Tom Stringer, the terrier man, certainly did.'

'Why?'

'I believe there was a dreadful row early one morning at the Kennels. Tom decided that Charles was there to spy on him, thinking he wasn't going out early enough or was skimping on his work. We all know what Tom is. There was no reason for Charles to turn up there in the pitch dark to check whether Tom had gone out. Tom swore at him and Charles wouldn't stand for that.'

'So it would be a heinous crime to skimp on his job?'

'It could lead to a thoroughly blank day. But Tom never

would. We all know that. Mind you, Tom may have been wrong. The Master often stays the night at the guest cottage at the Kennels. It's outside the complex down the hill. He may have just popped up to fetch something he'd forgotten at the Kennels. He built the cottage especially.'

'Why did he build it?'

'It's not what you think. Charles is a very moral man. There has never been the slightest scandal. He was a widower when he married the present Mrs Hardcastle.'

'Why build a cottage if the former Master got along without one?'

'Charles did up the whole Kennels. Wanted to make it a show-place. The cottage was for putting up visitors for hunting, or visiting vets and hound-fanciers or writers. Whatever.'

'And has it been used for any of these people?'

'Well, not that I know of. The Master often stopped there. But that was when he and Siobhan—' She stopped.

'Mrs Pratt,' he said, 'all these matters will have to be ventilated. We will have to go into the state of affairs at Hangholt Manor. If they are irrelevant they will go no further.'

'Well, they haven't been getting on too well and Charles practically lived at the Kennels. No one could understand it. She is a most beautiful girl. But she wouldn't hunt. That annoyed him. She's a perfectly competent rider.'

'I see. Can you think of anyone who might have had a motive for killing the Master?'

'No. Of course not. Not for *killing* him.'

'What about Ramsay Hardcastle?'

'Ramsay? I'd completely forgotten about him. You never see him about since the great row with Charles a few years ago. He's a lecturer at Penchester.'

'But I hear he was about today.'

'Yes, I believe he was. But I can't believe that it was his lot who attacked little Abby Hardcastle.'

'Did you see him?'

'Well, yes, I'm afraid I did.'

'Can you tell me about it, Mrs Pratt? I do understand your loyalty to the Hunt and to your friends. No one wants to stir up trouble or accuse anyone of murder, or even point a finger at anyone in a murder case but, you see, if it was murder, we've got to find out who did it. He might just decide to make a habit of it. Our experience is that anyone who kills and gets away with it can kill again.'

'Yes, of course. Well there was this very nasty incident. Ramsay often brings a handful of saboteurs in a van to disrupt the meet. I personally believe he only does it to annoy Charles. I don't think he cares a snap of his fingers for the fox. No one knows if it was his lot who behaved so horribly to little Abby Hardcastle. They poured paste and feathers over her and her pony as she hacked to the meet. When Charles came by in the Hunt box and saw what had happened he thought Ramsay was to blame, jumped down and beat him with his whip.'

'And did the saboteurs make themselves scarce after that?'

'They sloped off, or they'd have been murdered by the foot-followers and they knew it. But they were seen in the woods. They were about all right.'

'And Ramsay Hardcastle?'

'I don't know. I saw him with his face all bloody, looking absolutely beside himself, but I guess he would have gone home. It was humiliating for him. His own great-niece. Not a very heroic thing to be involved in. My guess is he'll go off as lecturer on some cruise. Leave the country, to let it all blow over.'

'Would he be capable of killing his brother? Did he hate him?'

'I doubt it. Much more likely to be the "Antis". Perhaps they hit him with those great sticks they sometimes hit the horses with. But I'm afraid Ramsay did hate Charles. He must have resented being turned out of the house and out of the social scene here. He used to point-to-point quite successfully. He was better than Charles and he qualified his own horses so he didn't care about the fox then. But he was reported for excessive use of the whip. He was much keener to win than Charles. Charles didn't care a damn. Just did it for the thrill.'

'And did Mr Hardcastle want to beat his brother.'

'No. Charles couldn't care less what Ramsay did. He's a completely self-sufficient man. He does what he wants to do and hang everyone else. He was simply obsessed with his hounds and his Kennels and with killing foxes to show what a good Master he was, but not to show anyone else. Only himself. He wanted to *be* a good Master but he didn't care whether people thought him one as long as *he* knew he was one. Do you understand?'

'Yes, I think I do. Did Mr Hardcastle carry a flask when he went hunting?'

'Yes. That's one of the things about Charles. Most Masters of Foxhounds wouldn't dream of carrying a flask. They're supposed to give a good example to the field. Mind you, that wouldn't stop them from taking a swig from someone else's flask. But Charles paid no attention at all to that sort of tradition. He did exactly what suited him and didn't care what anyone thought. And to him the field are just a damned nuisance. He had opened up his land from end to end with hunt jumps. It was all grass and woodland. Wouldn't hear of the plough. All the hedges cut and laid. He always said it was the best bit of hunting country outside of Leicestershire. But he didn't do it to let twenty subscribers jump a hedge simultaneously. He did it so that he and the Huntsman and Whippers-in could live with hounds and kill foxes. Anyone skylarking over a fence just for the fun of it got properly told off. There was no balance about it. In a Hunt you've got to have a balance between the need to kill foxes and the need to show the subscribers some sport. You can't ignore the wishes of the field when they provide the cash. And he couldn't spare the time to do the pretty with the bigger farmers and landowners as James Pierson always did. Two of them have closed their land to us this season and there are more to come. It could never have happened in James Pierson's day. He was on good terms with more or less the whole county.'

'It seems a pity you couldn't find a better successor for him. How did such a man ever get to be Master?'

'Money, of course. He was Finlay Hardcastles.'

'Oh, *those* Hardcastles! The ones in all the takeover bids?'

'That's right. He, single-handed, quadrupled the turn-over in no time and built it up to be the giant it is today. He was a godsend to us. If he hadn't taken it on we'd have been landed with four Joint Masters. It's fairly common nowadays but far from satisfactory. But you know, Mr Charter, you'd have to be absolutely mad to kill a Master of Foxhounds because you didn't like his methods or wanted his job.'

'There's no guaranteeing we aren't dealing with someone who *is* absolutely mad. Have you heard that Miss Harriet Lincoln was hit over the head at the scene of the murder to make sure she wouldn't see what he was up to? She was mounted at the time. The point is, he didn't very much care what damage he did to the girl. She could have fallen under the hooves of the horse. And it's impossible to judge the strength of a blow in those circumstances. I want to find this murderer pretty smartly, Mrs Pratt, before he goes on the rampage.'

She looked at him in consternation as he rose to take his leave.

'So if you can think of anything further that might help in any way you will get in touch with me at once, won't you? Here's my number. The local police station. That'll reach me.'

She looked down at the piece of paper. 'Yes,' she said tonelessly. 'Yes, of course I will.'

'Please telephone me as soon as your husband comes home. I must talk to him as soon as possible.'

She looked at him challengingly.

'Mr Charter,' she said, 'there is simply no possibility that my husband killed the Master.'

'No,' said Charter, 'but you must see, Mrs Pratt, that I can't possibly take that on your assurance alone.'

'He is the gentlest, kindest, most level-headed man you

ever met,' she said, her voice a little higher than normal.

'In that case, Mrs Pratt,' replied John Charter, 'you have nothing at all to worry about.'

CHAPTER 7

'She *is* worried though,' he said to Sergeant Cobbold as they walked to the car. 'She was going to tell us something, but she thought better of it. Perhaps we'll get it from the husband. We'll have to see him about the will as soon as he gets back. Now for the Kennels.'

On the way up the lane that led to the Kennels they passed by a square, white-painted, Georgian-style brick house standing in three-quarters of an acre of lawn fenced with new post and rail.

'That's the new guest cottage put up by Mr Hardcastle when he became Master.'

They pulled up outside Jim Caudle's house. The Huntsman, an elderly man in a brown overall, answered the door to them with a worried look.

'Good evening, Jim,' said Cobbold. 'I'm sorry about what's happened. Must have been a nasty shock.'

'Yes, it was,' Caudle said. 'I hope Mr Pratt'll come and see to things. I can't get along without the Master. Did you want to come in?'

'Yes, please. This is Detective Chief Superintendent Charter from Penchester and he has to ask some questions about the Master's death.'

The Huntsman led the way into a neat sitting-room, cleared some knitting off an armchair and motioned them to sit down.

'It's gone too far,' said Jim. 'It's time the police did something about the "Antis."'

'It may not have been the "Antis",' said Charter. 'We have to ask a lot of questions now that may seem to you rather pointless, but when someone dies as suddenly as your

Master I'm afraid we have to go into all sorts of details about them and the people who know them and work with them.'

'That's all right, sir. Don't you disturb yourself.'

'Well, Mr Caudle, you're a very important man in the Hunt. Have you any idea of what was going on in the woods today?'

'No, sir. When I'm hunting, sir, I've no eyes and ears other than for me hounds and me Master, and me Whippers-in and me fox. That's the lot. I don't pay no attention to what's going on other than that.'

'They tell me you're a very good Huntsman and know how to show them good sport.'

'I should be, shouldn't I, sir? I been doin' it more nor forty year.'

'Tell me, Mr Caudle—'

'You'd best call me Jim, sir. Nobody calls me anything other than Jim.'

'Very well, Jim, can you tell me what happens in Kennels on the morning of a meet?'

'At seven o'clock I draw me hounds I want for that day. The rest of 'em stop behind and get fed. I'd draw eighteen and a half, maybe nineteen and a half couple out of the thirty-five. Bitch pack or dog pack or sometimes I'd mix 'em. That's what the draw yard's for. While I'm drawing me hounds, the Whippers-in and the terrier man, if he's back in time, they wash the lodges down. Wash 'em with hot water, we do. We don't put nothing in the daily wash. The disinfectant gets up their noses. Some do, but we don't other than the once a week when we wash the lot with disinfectant and soda crystals. Three times a week we take the beds down and wash the benches and put down new straw bedding. When I've drawn me hounds we walk the rest out for a half an hour. Then if the terrier man's there he looks after the bitches in the whelping pens. When we come back we all have breakfast. Then we load hounds and horses and off to the meet for ten fifty-five sharp, and then they tell us where the draw is.'

'And when you bring them home?'

'Well, first you gotta feed 'em. It don't take too long to feed 'em. But if you got some lame ones you've got to look at 'em to see what's the matter. It might be a cut or it might be a thorn in there.'

'Would you call a vet if a hound was injured?'

'I could do a lot myself but as often as not I couldn't get the stuff I'd need. Sometimes you'll get a nail or something down in the quick, all swollen and ready to rot away. I've been to the chemist to ask for what I'd want to put on it and they've asked what I wanted it for—was I going to make a bomb? So then I'd have to call the vet. He don't know much more than me for the simple things.'

'I think we'd better have a look at your medicine cupboard. Where do you keep your medicines?'

'I used to keep 'em in a cupboard in the feed room but Mr Hardcastle he made a dispensary so we keep 'em there now.'

'Locked up?'

'Oh no, sir. Everybody needs to go in there.'

'And are the cupboards locked?'

'Well, no, sir. What'd be the use of that?'

Charter sighed. 'I'll come over there and have a look. You must get very fond of individual hounds looking after them as you do.'

'Well, I do 'ate to see 'em get old and can't get out to hunt. They fret so, the old ones. I always try to clear off out of it the day the vet comes to put one down. I used to do it myself. We'd take 'em right down the grassyards so as not to frighten the rest. Those Webleys they got now, you can hold them against their heads. The old Greeners had a bell on 'em. You had to hold up the gun and tap it. But the last couple o' year I got fed up of shooting 'em so in the end I got the vet. They go to sleep and by the time I get back on the place they're gone. He'd put a double dose in the vein and put 'em to sleep that way.'

'And I suppose the Master was fond of them too?'

'Knew every one of 'em like they were his children.'

'And would the Master come up here on the day of a meet?'

'Come here? He nigh on lives here. Sleeps down in the guest house when he's not in London. Yes, he's here all right most mornings. He goes to the meet in the lorry with us. Keeps his horses here now too.'

'Did the Master carry a flask?'

'Yes, sir, he usually did. Mr Pierson never did but Mr Hardcastle liked to carry his own.'

'And would he fill up his flask here?'

'Well, he could, sir, if he wanted to. There's always liquor in the cupboard in the feed room. That *is* locked up. But he'd likely have plenty at the guest cottage.'

'So he wouldn't bring it from Hangholt Manor already filled?'

'Well, yes, sir, I expect he would if he stopped the night before the meet at home.'

'And did he do so last night?'

'I can't tell you that, sir. The guest cottage being down the hill we don't see whether there's lights on there.'

'Right. Now when the Master comes up here the morning of the meet what does he do? Would he take his coat off?'

'He wouldn't even have it on, sir. He'd come up in his waxed jacket and an old pullover to help me draw me hounds. He leaves his scarlet coat and his cap and his boots in the valeting room as there's hooks there to hang things. He'd come up in rubber boots so as to keep everything clean.'

'I see. And his flask would be in the pocket of his scarlet coat?'

'You're thinking, sir, that someone might have put something in that flask?'

'I have to find out whether anyone could have done that, Jim.'

'There's no one here would have done such a thing, sir.'

'No, I'm sure you're right. You must get to know them all pretty well. You're the boss at the Kennels.'

'Under the Master I suppose I am.'

'And do you plan the routine and send them out on their jobs?'

'There's not much call for me to interfere, sir. They all know their jobs. There's not much I can tell 'em.'

'And were you sorry that the Master sacked Peter Thorn?'

'Well, young Peter, he did a very foolish thing. The Master pretty well had to sack him. Going off like that before the end! I never heard any Whipper-in ever did such a thing before!'

'But everybody put in a good word for Peter, did they?'

'They did, sir, and so would I have done. But first we left it to Mr Pratt. It weren't no use. But he might have give in in the end.'

'And if he hadn't?'

'Then young Peter would have lost his job *and* his house.'

'Was he very upset?'

'Well, it was Nancy, you see, and her new curtains. He's been no use to me at all the last few days. But Peter wouldn't do a thing like that, sir.'

'I suppose the Whipper-in has an important part to play? What would Peter have been doing? Presumably he would be working out his notice till the end of the season, so he was out today?'

'Oh yes, sir, we couldn't have managed without him.'

'So where would he be?'

'Well, sir, I can tell you where he wouldn't be and that is knocking Mr Hardcastle off his horse somewhere out in the middle of the woods with never a hound in sight. Either he'd be stood at the end of a covert on the most likely line we know the fox would take from that particular place, to holler when the fox goes away and to tell hounds to hark forrard. Or he might be in covert with me rather than the amateur Whip pushing hounds on.'

'So it's the Whips who tell the field and the Master where the fox is?'

'That's right, sir. Mind you, as often as not you'd hear the old jay start up or even a blackbird'll do it. Then you pretty well know a fox is moving. The old jay, he'd spot him all right.'

'So the wild life help you to locate your fox. That's interesting.'

'Oh yes, sir. They'll fly at him, magpies too. Mobbing the fox, they call it. Many's the time when hounds are checked I've seen the birds mobbing the fox and lifted my hounds and hit the line again and all thanks to that old jay bird.'

'But even so you'd need Peter?'

'I would.'

'And if the Master went off alone into the woods would Peter be likely to go too?'

'Only if it was after hounds into a covert.'

'And he wouldn't go off to have a quiet swig at his flask?'

'There's some as would because they don't want to offer it around like, but Master'd take a swig whenever he wanted and never think to offer it. No time for that when you're hunting hounds.'

'There's one other thing you can help me with, Jim. What about these hunt saboteurs, the "Antis", as you call them? Do they make you angry?'

'When I'm hunting hounds I've no time to spare to be angry. I just carry on as best I can.'

'And do any of the hunt followers get angry?'

'I'll swear they just about do, sir. Throw a brick through the window of the van they would as soon as look at it. It's the foot-followers want to fight them. Well, those people, they're town people: they don't understand how it is in the country.'

'Do you think they have a point, Jim? Is it cruel to hunt a fox?'

'Well, sir, what would happen to the old fox if we didn't hunt him? The gamekeepers'd set wires for him, the local authority'd gas him, the farmer'd shoot him. There'd be a lot of cruelty going on. I've found plenty of foxes with the wire eaten into 'em—right to the backbone I've seen it. And

I've seen a cat drag a trap right across an eight-acre field with the bones showing.'

'Wouldn't shooting be kinder?'

'No, it wouldn't, and for why? If you shoot a fox you must be sure to kill it dead. A fox won't carry lead. I've known a keeper just touch 'im with a couple of pellets knowing he'd get the gangrene. We've found plenty with the gangrene. They won't carry lead.'

'Then the gamekeepers are cruel?'

'No, sir, I wouldn't say that. A lot of the keepers are pretty good on the whole. If they set a trap or a snare they'll go round every day. If you set a snare you ought to go round twice a day to look at it. But them fellows on the estates, they do the job pretty well.'

'Does the Hunt have any trouble with the keepers?'

'None at all, sir. Mr Pierson, and now Mr Hardcastle, he'd talk to the landowners and they'd work out the meets so as not to interfere with the shoots. Sometimes a keeper will say to me, "We've got a fox in this covert or that," and he'll keep it for me.'

'And then some people would say he'll be torn to pieces by hounds. Not a pretty death.'

'Better nor gangrene, sir, if it were true, but it isn't true. When hounds kill a fox he's dead in the instant.'

'And doesn't he suffer from fear during the chase?'

'Not 'im, sir, not till the last few minutes. He's crafty, is the old fox. We don't kill more than one in six we push up. We won't often kill a fit fox. It's the weak ones we kill and what have they got to look for? They'll get too weak to hunt and then they die slow of starvation.'

'Jim, what do you think about Mr Hardcastle's fall? Could anyone think a fall like that would kill a man? Could a murderer be sure it would?'

'No, sir, he couldn't. The worst fall I ever had I thought I was dead that time. I fell flat on my back in a ditch with my horse on top. His hooves were up in the air and he was going up and down on top of me with the saddle denting me middle. Down Fawley way it was and the Master he'd gone on ahead. Nobody knew I was there. Hounds had found the fox and they'd all have been miles away in a minute, but thank the Lord they checked and the tail hounds come back to me and then the rest, like they always do, though I couldn't even get at my horn to blow it. Look, sir —' and he pointed to one of a set of silver and copper horns on a shelf. 'That's the one, sir, dented in the middle. That's what it did to the horn and that's what that old horse was doing to me. Major Hooper give it to me. It's a very good horn that one. Hounds saved my life that time coming back to me. The Master followed hounds and found me. They sat on my horse's head so he couldn't move and they pulled me out. Funny thing. Me feet came right out of me boots. That was a killing fall by rights. But the Master was on an open ride, and no rocks about to fall on. Unless the horse fell on him, and why would he do that? He's carried him five season and never a fall. And on an open ride like that he'd never be swept off by a branch.'

'Well, thank you, Jim. You've been a great help. Nice pictures you've got there.'

'Me five best hounds ever, sir. The Master before this one give me those. It's a lady over at the Green. She come over and done them when I was off sick. And that's the Duke of Beaufort, His Grace the Duke of Beaufort (*we* call him the Master) congratulating me on winning at Peterborough. Best hound, we got that year.'

'Congratulations! And now may we have a look at your dispensary?'

Jim got his cap and put it on as they went through the hall. He led them out through the dusk to the hound lodges. Bats fluttered to and fro with an intermittent sound as of faint far-away breathy squeaking like telephone wires singing in a high wind.

Jim took them into the dispensary which was all shining glass and chrome and tiles with neat cupboards lining the walls—drawers below, glass-fronted cabinets above.

'You keep all medicines in the dispensary?'

'Yes, sir. That's to say—all the medicines for hounds.'

'What others have you on the premises?'

'Why, the horse medicines, sir.'

'And where are they kept?'

'In the tack room, sir.'

'In a cupboard?'

'No, sir. On the shelf.'

'Good God! Well, let's be seeing what you've got here.'

Jim opened the shining glass doors to the cupboards. There was hydrogen peroxide, anti-histamine cream, bicarbonate of soda, soda crystals, pads of lint, gauze, olive oil, bandages, plastic syringes, antiseptic creams, boric acid crystals.

'Nothing very alarming here,' said Charter. 'Will you show me the tack room now?'

There on an open shelf he found brandy, whisky, liniments, embrocations, gamgee tissue, kaolin, Dettol, Friar's balsam, acriflavine, carbonate of ammonia, carbolic acid, linseed oil, turpentine, iodine and Epsom salts, and a large box of tablets labelled digitalis. At the back of the shelf was an old discoloured bottle labelled chloral hydrate.

Charter pointed to the bottle. 'This is restricted and dangerous,' he said. 'And the rest should be under lock and key. Who is in charge of the horse medicines?'

'Nancy Thorn. They live just across the yard.'

'She'd better put them all away. We'll go and talk to her.'

They walked across and Nancy answered their knock. She looked guilty when he said, 'Now go over there at once, Mrs Thorn, and get the horse medicines stored away under lock and key in the dispensary. Do it now, girl. The stuff is standing about on a shelf.'

'I'll go right over,' she said, slipped a jacket on and ran across the yard.

'Now,' said Charter, 'who else have we got here?'

'There's Peter Thorn, the Whipper-in,' said Cobbold. 'Nancy's husband.'

'The one who quarrelled with the Master?'

'That's right. And there's Tom Stringer, the terrier man. He lives over at the back near the flesh house. He's boiler man, too. Skins and joints and boils the carcases for feeding hounds. But he's not there tonight. He come back from the meet and, Master or no Master, he had to clean up and get over to Fawley for his young sister's twenty-first. But Peter's about.'

'Right,' said Charter. 'We'll try Peter Thorn.'

'If you've finished, sir,' said Jim, 'I'd as soon be getting back home. Mrs Caudle, she'll be waiting on me.'

'Right, Jim. Thank you. You've been a great help.'

The old man walked away slowly, limping a little.

Charter put his finger on the bell again and Peter came to the door and stood there unsmiling.

'Good evening, Mr Thorn,' said Charter. 'I'm Detective Chief Superintendent Charter from Penchester and I have to ask some questions of everyone connected with the Canfield and Old Ashley Hunt. Purely routine. It helps to give us an over-all picture.'

'From Penchester!' said Peter, taken aback. 'Do you want to come in? If you could get it over before Nancy comes back . . . I don't want her upset again.'

'We've very little time ourselves,' said Charter. 'And we won't come in, thank you. Have you anything to tell us about the death of Mr Charles Hardcastle?'

Peter looked at him, surprised. 'Well, sir,' he said more politely, 'I wasn't anywhere near him in the woods there. I didn't hear about it till the fox brought us round in that direction and hounds went to the Master and we found all those policemen and photographers there. I was pretty well flabbergasted and it took Jim and me and Mr Caldbeck all our time to keep hounds away from him lying there on the ground. Pretty shocked we all were, I can tell you.'

'You didn't have any reason to murder the Master?'

Peter stiffened. 'I didn't know he *was* murdered.'

'That doesn't answer my question.'

'Well, some people might say I had very good reason to murder him seeing I'd been sacked by him from my job and likely to lose my house too. But as I never was anywhere

near him there in the woods I couldn't very well have done
it.'

'Could you have put something in his flask?'

'In his flask!' Peter looked dismayed. 'Yes, I suppose if it
was in the pocket of his hunting coat. Anyone in Kennels
could have got at it. Is that what killed him? Something in
the flask?'

'We don't know yet. He may have died quite naturally.
I don't suppose you actually did murder him, did you?'

'No, sir, I didn't and I never would no matter how often
he sacked me. And neither would Nancy. So leave her
alone.'

'Thank you, Mr Thorn. You won't be leaving the Kennels
for the time being, will you?'

'No, sir. I may not have to leave at all now Mr Hardcastle's gone.' And, uttering this last remark with some
bravado, he nodded to Sergeant Cobbold. ''Night, Derek.
Good night, sir.' He went inside and shut the door.

'Not him,' said Cobbold as they walked back to the car.

'Oh yes, very possibly him,' said Charter. 'He's a cocky
young man and you often get that sort of cockiness in
murderers who think they've got away with it. There's a
deep resentment there. Of us or the Master or of life. You
always get that in a murderer and they can very rarely hide
it successfully.'

'But he wasn't trying to hide it at all, sir.'

'True.'

'The only one here who might possibly do such a thing,
sir, is Tom Stringer. He can be a right sod and I wouldn't
put it past him to do something silly and violent if he took
it into his head. He's big-headed and he loathed the Master,
as Mrs Pratt said. Where now, sir?'

'Penchester. Ramsay Hardcastle may be able to help us
with the saboteurs.'

CHAPTER 8

Ramsay Hardcastle answered the door of his house and took the Superintendent and the sergeant into a room which was lined from floor to ceiling with bookshelves. Every piece of furniture, including the Blüthner grand piano, was piled high with books, papers and records.

They sat down.

Ramsay Hardcastle was very pale. His face was covered with strips of sticking plaster and he wore a bandage round the knuckles of one hand.

'I suppose,' he said, 'you're here about my brother's fall.'

'About your brother's death. Yes, sir. How did you know about it?'

'We heard it on the news,' he said. 'It was a shock. I don't feel at all well.'

He got up and poured himself a glass of whisky from a cut-glass decanter. 'Would you and the sergeant like a whisky?' he asked and they shook their heads.

'No, thank you, sir. We're on duty.'

He sat down again, drank largely and put the glass down.

'Have you been in touch with any members of your family, sir?'

'Francis, my younger brother, telephoned from Lamford-ham when he heard the news. I telephoned my nephew Rodney to find out what had happened and I rang Francis back.'

'You weren't at the scene when the Master fell?'

'Of course not. If I had been there I wouldn't have had to go through the shock of hearing it on the news.'

'I believe you disapproved of your brother's foxhunting activities?'

'Well, I don't exactly love "*le son du cor le soir au fond des bois*".'

He waited to be asked for an explanation and looked

rather cross when Charter replied. 'Nor yet *"le son du boa au fond du cor"*?'

'Isn't Saki rather undergraduate humour for a Chief-Superintendent?' he said crossly.

'And isn't it rather worse than undergraduate behaviour to bully a small girl on her way to the meet?'

'I had nothing to do with that.'

'And what about your young friends?'

'Not my young friends. Only Tony and Jill and Norman. I didn't know any of the others.'

'I should make quite sure that you do know who the others are in future, sir. You might be held responsible for anything they get up to.'

'I can't possibly be held responsible. They're all adults.'

'There's such a thing, sir, as conspiracy to cause an affray.'

'God!' He held his head in his hands. 'This is all too much.'

'When did you leave for home, sir?'

'Directly after my brother attacked me. I was bleeding from the head. Ruined this pullover. I could have had a heart attack.'

'So you were extremely angry.'

'I was drained.'

'Did you wait for your young friends?'

'No. Norman called a taxi and we came back here. Tony kept the van so he could drive the rest of them home.'

'Did you murder your brother?'

'Murder? Who said he was murdered? He had a fall out hunting. Happens all the time. Just bad luck that he hurt himself. Or perhaps he had a stroke or a heart attack.'

'So you didn't hold a rope across the ride with one of your students to make him fall off and then hit the girl over the head so you could finish him off?'

'What girl? Of course I didn't. That's a monstrous and ridiculous suggestion.'

'Possibly. Are there any witnesses to the time of your arrival back at Penchester?'

'Norman was with me. And we said good afternoon to Mrs Robinson from the house next door. She sits by the window all day and calls out to anyone who goes in or out.'

'Right, sir. We'll check that. We may need to question you again so please don't leave Penchester. And you may be called to give evidence at the inquest.'

'I'm not well enough.'

'You would have to be very seriously ill to fail to appear if the coroner wants you there. Now, I'll need to talk to your companions in the van today. Can you give me a list of their names and addresses?'

'I'm afraid not. Except for Tony and Jill and Norman. I didn't know any of the others. Tony and Jill are upstairs.'

'May I see them in here?'

'If you must.'

'If you'll be so good as to leave us for a few minutes.'

'If I must.' He went to the door and called, 'Tony! Jill! Can you come down for a minute!'

A tall, curly-haired young man with wind-burned red cheeks and very bright eyes popped his head round the door.

'Hello! Do you want me? Jill's gone over to the takeaway.'

He was health personified, slim and wiry with bony features and a wide smile.

'Tony Redfern, Chief Superintendent Charter. He wants to ask you a few questions.'

He went out of the room, shutting the door behind him.

Tony turned to Charter. 'We've been awfully worried,' he said. 'We were afraid you might think it was one of us. I hope you don't.'

'Just a minute,' said Charter. He walked quietly to the door and flung it open. Ramsay Hardcastle was standing in the passage.

'I'm just going,' he said. 'You're paranoid, Superintendent. I wasn't listening. This is my house, after all.'

Charter stood in silence holding the door open until Ramsay had disappeared up the stairs. He shut the door and came back into the room.

'Right,' he said. 'Now we can get on. Sit down.'

'He's not a bad old stick,' said Tony, flinging himself into a chair and stretching out his long legs. 'He gets very fond of us all and he wants us all to love him. He misses all that lark at Hangholt Manor; the hunt and the races and all that nonsense. Pretends he hated it but it isn't true. Hard to believe it, but he was once a great point-to-pointer.'

'Why didn't he go on with it?'

'Well, he's much too old now but he hadn't got a bean. Couldn't afford to keep his own horses, so when his brother chucked him out it broke up his life. Well, half of it, anyway.'

'Why did the brother throw him out?'

'I don't know, but we all suspect it may have been the revelation of his homosexuality.'

'Surely the chap can't have been unaware of it all those years? His own brother!'

'You'd be surprised. In any case it might be that Ramsay was discreet and had suddenly ceased to be discreet enough and circumstances threatened a public disclosure. You know how hidebound that generation were.'

'It seems a pity. Now, you say you feared you might be suspected of murdering the Master?'

'Murdering him? Good heavens, no! You might have thought we'd brought him down off his horse. I couldn't answer for half our people. I know I didn't and Jill didn't and Norman didn't. But the others—I don't know them. But it wouldn't have been murder. Nobody could have intended to kill the bloke. It was an accident. Well, all right, a very culpable accident. A bloody dangerous thing to do. But why would they murder him? That would do the Anti-Blood-Sports thing no good at all. We're always being told we'd rather see humans killed than animals.'

'And would you?'

'No. Well, I personally wouldn't.'

'How did the ones you don't know come to be there?'

'We have a notice permanently up in the JCR inviting people to apply for seats in the van.'

'Don't you take their names?'

'We used to but we got sort of lax about it. They bring their own sandwiches and we provide the transport. They have to produce the money a week before the day.'

'And it hasn't occurred to you that you might be liable for anything the more violent members of your party got up to?'

'We did warn Ramsay but we were only too glad to get enough volunteers to fill the van. Otherwise it would have cost us. Ramsay puts in a tenner, so if it's full it's only a quid or two each. On the whole we keep to ourselves and they go off and do what they like.'

'Was it Ramsay Hardcastle who made you a champion of beleaguered animals?'

'No, of course it wasn't. I liked old Ramsay because he seemed sincere about things like that. Any sane person must disapprove of killing innocent animals for sport.'

'So you have always held these views?'

'Since I began thinking about things. Since I was sixteen. I became a vegetarian just about then. And I don't wear leather.'

'Is Ramsay Hardcastle a vegetarian?'

'Not he! Look, sir, you have to take old Ramsay with a pinch of salt. He's very mixed up. I sussed him out very soon. He isn't really in the least sincere but he's quite convinced that he *is* sincere, and that comes to almost the same thing. He has all sorts of dark motivations about everything, but he's one of the walking wounded. You have to make allowances. I don't think he'd hurt a fly. He's against all real violence. And so am I. I wouldn't even go so far as to wish the old MFH a fall. Would bringing him down off his horse without intending to kill him count as murder?'

'Is that what you did?'

'No. But it could be that some of the wild fringe might have done. I don't know. I can't be sure how far the real activists would go. And I don't know if there were any of them with us today.'

Charter got up. 'Then you'd better find out, hadn't you?
And . . .'

A plumpish girl with marvellous red hair tied back in a
ponytail, wearing black leggings and sweat shirt burst into
the room carrying foil-wrapped packets of food clasped to
her chest.

'Oh, I'm sorry!' she said. 'I didn't know you had visitors.'

'It's the police,' said Tony. 'This is Jill Cattermole. We're
engaged. She was with me today so she can't tell you
anything more than I can.'

'Good evening, Miss Cattermole,' said Charter. 'We'll
want your account of today's events. You can report to the
Incident Room.'

She dropped the parcels on a chair and turned to face
him, putting her hands on her hips.

'You're after the Animal Rights people, I suppose,' she
said challengingly.

'No, Miss Cattermole,' he said wearily.

'How do you know it was one of us?'

'I don't know anything of the kind, Miss Cattermole, but
we have to question everybody who was in those woods
today.'

Tony came over, looking embarrassed, and took her arm.

'Don't be silly, Jill,' he said.

'Just for the record, Miss Cattermole,' Charter asked, 'do
you subscribe to the view that the rights of animals are more
important than those of human beings?'

'Humans can protect their own rights,' she said. 'Animals
can't.'

'And if you could save a child or an animal, but not both,
from a nasty death, which would you save?'

'I can't answer that question.'

'I see,' he said. 'Thank you, Mr Redfern. We'll be
in touch with both of you and if you do remember the
names of any others who were there today you'll let us
know.'

'Yes,' said Tony.

'No,' said Jill.

Charter sighed and followed Sergeant Cobbold out of the door and down the steps.

'We'll leave that young woman to your lads at Stumpington,' he said. 'It's all far too predictable for this time of night. Nice boy. Sensible.'

'He wanted to shut her up,' said Cobbold. 'Poor chap. She'll drive him to drink.'

'Not necessarily,' said Charter. 'She may have all sorts of qualities of which we know nothing. She probably gives him sheer delight in bed.'

'Good luck to him,' muttered the rural sergeant. 'Where to, sir?'

'Nothing more tonight, Sergeant. Back to Stumpington. They've booked me in to the White Hart. Where are you for?'

'I live in Stumpington, sir.'

'Married?'

'No, sir. I'm living at home just now. My mother can't get about much. I've got someone looking after her but it's easier to keep an eye if I sleep there.'

'Join me for breakfast at eight, then.'

'Thank you, sir. It's a great chance for me, working with you.'

'Don't let your rapture run away with you, Sergeant. People who work with me sometimes end up beside me in the doghouse.'

From the White Hart he telephoned the ACC and reported progress.

'So far the Incident Room hasn't come up with anything on the anti-hunt people who were in the woods today. They've got to be traced. I'm told they come in different brands and from different localities. The Yard collater may be able to help with that. It doesn't look as if the university lecturer who brought a lot of them in a van is going to be able to help us, but he, and the three of them he does know, will have to identify the others when we lay our hands on them. We'll have to get some chaps over to the university asking questions, but they may have come from anywhere.

Then there are the foot-followers, any number of them, milling about in the woods. They may have seen something. And the mounted followers too. I've set up the briefing for tomorrow and then I'll get on with talking to a few more of the principals. I imagine they'll be hunting again soon. That may be the way to suss out a few more of the "Antis" if we have no luck before then. I reckon I'd better borrow a horse and see what I can see.'

The Assistant Chief Constable laughed placidly at the joke, blissfully unaware that Detective Chief Superintendent Charter was absolutely serious and intended to hunt with the Canfield and Old Ashley next time they went out, come hell or high water.

CHAPTER 9

After the briefing at Stumpington police station on Sunday morning they walked from the White Hart across the Market Square to St Christopher's. The sergeant headed for the wards but Charter stopped him.

'Not there,' he said. 'We'll leave the girl to recover. She'll be available at the farm tomorrow. I've already been busy this morning, Sergeant, and I've found out who we want to talk to. She's a young pathologist called Dr Prideaux. What we want is a little hypothetical reasoning ahead of our evidence. We're more likely to get it from a relatively unimportant young woman. You'll find these senior medical chaps will never commit themselves to anything unless it's cut and dried in the PM report.'

'You have a theory, sir,' said the rural sergeant.

'Hush,' replied Charter, with a smile.

Dr Prideaux summoned by bleep, led them into a tiny room. She was dark and thin and looked rather solemn in her large round spectacles but she proved to have a charming smile.

'I got your message,' she said. 'But I think you must be

making a mistake. The consultant pathologist is Mr Harvey Knott. He did the PM yesterday and the inspector took the report.'

'We won't keep you long,' said Charter. 'But it's you we want, Dr Prideaux. May we all sit down?'

They did. Dr Prideaux folded her hands and looked at him calmly.

'The thing is,' said Charter, 'we've got a very peculiar case here and I need a little reasoning ahead of our facts. I know what the PM says—but I've got to get on with it and I'd like to test one or two ideas I've got. I knew you'd help. You see my difficulty? Couldn't expect a peep out of Mr Harvey Knott before the PM and these senior medical chaps are always as cagey as all get out even after it. None of this is on the record, so Sergeant Cobbold is going to wait downstairs.'

Cobbold smiled and left and Dr Prideaux waved him goodbye. He could see that Charter had landed his fish. She was both amused and intrigued.

'Now here's the position,' said Charter. 'Solid, sixty-year-old Master of Foxhounds. Drinks a fair amount of spirits, leads an energetic sort of life. Business in London. Hunting in the country. High blood pressure. Already suffered one mild heart attack.

'Now. Out hunting he suffers a fall from his horse and is found dead. Three possibilities:

'1. Natural death as result of fall.

'2. Murder or manslaughter because the fall was engineered. Physical signs would be the same as for 1.

'3. Poison in hunting flask.

'I tend, for reasons I won't go into, to favour solution 3. I need some theoretical guidance, which will never be quoted as coming from you, Doctor. I guarantee you that.'

She smiled at him. 'Superintendent!' she said, 'you're babbling. All this is my meat. I can't wait to hear. Just get on with it.'

He laughed back at her. 'Right you are. Now what he

might have been fed in the brandy must probably satisfy these conditions:

'1. It must be harmless to most other people. A murderer couldn't guarantee the Master wouldn't offer the flask around, thereby causing mayhem among the Canfield and Old Ashley hunt people.

2. It ought to be something that would not show up in the PM except under the appearance of natural causes— say, heart attack or heart failure. This because the flask was removed at the cost of knocking a girl unconscious. If he knew whatever was in the flask would show up in the PM there would be no point whatever in risking the attack on the girl to remove the flask. If we found something toxic in the flask we'd only be learning something the PM would tell us anyway. Have you any suggestions about what might have been put in the flask to nudge him along a bit without betraying its presence?'

'I think it's got to be digitalis,' she said. 'He'd be taking it anyway if he'd already had a heart attack. The trouble is it might be rather nasty for anyone else who took a swig at it. Might make them very sick.'

'I don't think our murderer would mind very much about that.'

'Another condition for your poisonous substance would be that it must be soluble in alcohol. Digitalis is and it has no taste and no smell. So he wouldn't realize what he was taking. I imagine the lethal dose would be about half a teaspoonful. But it's all very doubtful. He might not drink the whole flask. The murderer couldn't be sure.'

'I suspect we've got a fairly hit or miss sort of murderer,' he told her, 'a pretty irresponsible chap whom I want under lock and key. Would an extra large dose show up in the PM?'

'It would be very hard to judge. If you want to give cardiac glucosides like digitalis in large enough doses to increase the strength of the heart contractions you've got to go canny. You need a concentration not far from the level at which you'd expect to get toxic reactions.'

'Like cardiac arrest?'

'You could well get cardiac arrest.'

'And would there be physical signs?'

'There was marked venous engorgement of the intestines with hæmorrhage and œdema of the intestinal wall. And of course the waterlogged lungs, the typical sign of cardiac arrest. All possible results of digitalis intoxication. You say the victim had been suffering from high blood pressure. Then he'd probably be on one of the thiazide diuretics. Prolonged use of diuretics tends to cause the loss of potassium. It's excreted in the urine. Potassium depletion makes the myocardium more sensitive to digitalis and you're more likely to get digitalis intoxication.'

'And sudden death?''

'There have been fatalities. But we avoid the danger by prescribing potassium salts in entericoated tablets in slow-release form.'

'Ah! Now you're talking!'

'I get your drift, Superintendent, but you're off target. If anyone substituted diuretic tablets without potassium for the combined tablets he may have been taking they wouldn't need to pop anything into the flask. He'd just quietly die one day and no one would ever know. To give him an extra dose would be absurd.'

'Yes, it would, wouldn't it? So he would need a very pressing reason for speeding up the plan.'

She smiled at him. 'Well, if you find someone with such a reason and some knowledge of drugs all this might hang together, but it's the wildest speculation.'

'My dear young lady pathologist, nobody is more aware of this than I. And you need have no fears. No one will ever know that this interview took place. I'm deeply grateful.'

Sergeant Cobbold was waiting for him downstairs. Charter clapped him on the shoulder in great high spirits.

'Now,' he said, 'it's high time we called on Mrs Hardcastle senior. We'll see the doctor later. Our young lady pathologist has given me furiously to think about the amiable

doctor.' On the way he told Cobbold what he had learned
from Dr Prideaux.

As they drove up to the Manor through Hangholt village
the church bells were pealing and a row of cars and Land-
Rovers were parked outside the little Norman church on
the hill.

Siobhan received them in her sitting-room. They found
her crouched on the window-seat with Spindle curled up
beside her. Maggie brought them up and had to be almost
forcibly turned out. Siobhan watched them dealing with
Maggie's fierce protective ardour without a flicker of a
change in the sombre gaze. Then: 'It's all right, Maggie,'
she said. 'I can cope.'

'Very well, love, I'll go,' said Maggie. 'But I'm coming
up in twenty minutes with a hot drink for you and then
you're going to lie down. You can't go on sitting here all
day and all night without a thing to eat.'

She flounced out and Siobhan waved them to sit down.

'I'm very sorry to trouble you, Mrs Hardcastle, at this
time.'

'They told me you'd want to talk to me. Better have it
over and done with. What is it you want to know? It was a
perfectly horrible accident and I can't think how it happened. He never fell. He'd better not. Such a big man as he
was is bound to fall hard and hurt himself. He wasn't all
that young either.'

'Mrs Hardcastle, has it occurred to you that your husband's death might not have been an accident?'

The colour drained out of her face, leaving it pinched and
strained and childish.

'Not an accident?'

'I'm sorry to distress you. But there is the possibility that
it might have been murder.'

'How could it be murder? No one could make him fall off
his horse. Unless it was the "Antis"?'

'Accidents on horseback can be engineered in a number
of different ways. There could have been a rope across the
path. Do you know of any enemies of your husband?'

'There's very little I do know about my husband, Mr Charter. I've no doubt you've already been told that we hardly ever slept under the same roof. He'd stay at the Kennels except when I'd go to Ireland to my parents or when we had guests here.'

'You were on bad terms?'

'We were hardly on speaking terms.'

'I'm sorry I have to ask these questions but do you think your husband may have been unfaithful to you?'

'No I don't. It's my bad luck that he never was. There was never any scandal about him. I don't suppose you could say it of any other Master of Foxhounds in the whole length and breadth of the land.'

'Was he a moral man, then?'

'I couldn't say. He was a busy man. I think it was that company of his he was really wedded to. And the Hunt next after that. And he wasn't young. He may have had enough of all that. I don't know how he behaved when he was young.'

'Were you unfaithful to him?'

'No, I was not. What good would that have done me?'

'But if you had divorced?'

'After the life I led with Charles would I let another man into my life to bully me and upset me and make me do things I don't want to do?'

'Why did you marry him?'

'My mother thought I'd be rich and have an easier life than she's had. But my father knew it wouldn't do. He warned me Charles would be mean like a miser once we were married. And so he was. Would you believe it, he closed my account at Harrods one day without a word to me because he said I was spending too much of his money. He'd only have had to tell me. But that's the sort of man he was. To him money wasn't just bits of paper. It was shining gold. After that I never wanted to spend a penny of his, but I've none of my own so I had to. That's when I decided to go back to Ireland.'

'You told him you were going to leave him?'

'Of course I did, but he knew already. We couldn't go on as we were and he knew it.'

'But, forgive me, wouldn't that have meant a great financial sacrifice for you?'

'How could it be a sacrifice? It was his money, not mine, and he made that clear to everyone. And I wouldn't have hurt Dandy. Charles set up an enormous trust for him when he was born. I can't touch it and the trustees will look after it for him. Eton, Oxford, all that's taken care of.'

'But what of yourself, Mrs Hardcastle? You are used, if I may say so, to enormous luxury.'

'And much good it's done me. I was happier in Wexlow where we had buckets in every room to catch the drops from the leaking roofs.'

'So would your husband have made provision for you?'

'I don't know whether he would or not. I never discussed it with him.'

'That sounds a little unlikely if you seriously planned to leave him.'

'Does it?'

'If he was faithful to you so you would have had little ground for demanding a large settlement.'

'I didn't want a large settlement.'

'That seems quixotic.'

She made no reply.

'Your husband's death has done you a favour as you will now inherit a very large sum of money.'

'You've seen Roger Pratt. Yes. The house goes to Rodney. The rest of the money is of no concern to me. Dandy has his trust.'

'You're a very unusual young woman if that's true.'

'Where I'm going I'll have no use for it.'

'Where are you going?'

'Has no one told you that? I'm going into a convent.'

'You're what?'

A flicker of a smile acknowledged his astonishment.

'I'm going to become a nun.'

'But your little boy—'

'I don't care for children all that much. Of course I'm very fond of him. I'll see him every week of my life, if not every day. My sister is going back to Ireland. She's marrying again. Dr Cresswell is going to marry her. They'll live in Wexlow near St Mary's. They'll take Dandy and I'll see him every day.'

'So you had it all arranged between you. But what would your husband have said to that? Wouldn't he have wanted Dandy?'

'I shouldn't think so. He pays him no attention at all. Of course when he gets bigger, then Charles might possibly have wanted to see more of him. He could have gone between Hangholt and Wexlow. Anyway, by the time Dandy gets to that age who's to say Charles wouldn't have been dead and gone? We knew from the first we weren't going to grow old together.'

'And you wouldn't have minded giving up this house and your expensive clothes?'

'That's nothing.'

'Have you always been religious?'

'I go to Mass. Charles didn't like that. He's not religious but in the country in England you're supposed to be Church of England even if you just put up a show of it. I wouldn't put up a show.'

'And now you are about to inherit a quite staggering amount of money.'

'So you're thinking I killed Charles to get hold of his money. Did I lie in wait for him in the woods, I wonder?'

'No, Mrs Hardcastle. I don't see how you could have done that. But, just as a matter of routine, where were you yesterday?'

'I was here. With Maggie and Eithne. The whole of the time. All day.'

'Neither you nor your sister was out hunting? Don't you hunt?'

'We did when we were small but we don't any more. Sister Imelda at the Convent taught us that it's cruel to hunt animals. Once you've got that thought in your head you can't do it. My father was furious with Sister Imelda but it was nothing to Reverend Mother. She'd have slaughtered her, she was so angry. All the nuns bet on the horses and go to the meet when it's near enough. But my mother understood and made them all let us be. We never let on to my father's hunting friends why it was we wouldn't hunt. You can't argue about it. Of course we did ride. Eithne used to help exercise for the racing stables when Patrick was alive. I was never so brave but I used to hack about the country at home.'

'And would you trust your sister and her new husband to look after Dandy and be good trustees for him?'

'They won't be the trustees. That'll be Roger Pratt, the lawyer, and Rodney, Charles's son by his first marriage. And you'll see that they'll make quite sure Eithne does what Charles wanted for Dandy. It'll be me will have to see they do what *I* want for him. Charles always gets his own way even from the grave. That's one thing you can be quite sure of.'

'I see. Can you tell me whether your husband slept here on Friday night?'

'I doubt it but I couldn't be sure.'

'So he wouldn't have filled his flask here?'

'I don't know. If he was here he could have done.'

'Can you perhaps tell me anything about a feud or quarrel between your husband and Mr Roger Pratt?'

'That was all about Hartley Godwin.'

'Hartley Godwin?'

'He was one of Charles's crazes. He used to go in for these mad crazes. They lasted about two or three years. I was the last craze before Hartley.'

'Who is Hartley Godwin?'

'I suppose he's a businessman. Charles met him at the Institute of Directors in Belgrave Square and they got on very well together. Hartley is very political and he persuaded Charles to stand for the European Parliament. Charles was very flattered and Hartley knows all sorts of famous people he used to introduce to Charles. Charles took it into his

head to make Hartley the next Master and Roger Pratt
thought he had fired the Whipper-in because he wanted to
make Hartley Whipper-in so that he would get experience.
That wasn't it at all but it made Roger very cross with
Charles. They used to get on much better before Charles
met Hartley.'

'Did Hartley Godwin stay here when he came down to
hunt?'

'Oh no, he was much too tactful. He knew I didn't like
him. He stays at the White Hart in Stumpington and
Charles used to dine with him there. But he does keep his
horses here, so he is often about the place in the stableyard
and the paddock.'

'Surely it would have been more convenient to have let
him stay at the Kennels and keep his horses there?'

'Not for Charles. He likes to have the place to himself.'

Maggie knocked at the door and walked in belligerently,
carrying a tray covered with a napkin.

Siobhan looked up at Charter with great eyes surrounded
by dark shadows in a weary, pinched white face.

'I really am a little tired,' she said, and they got up.

'Thank you, Mrs Hardcastle,' said Charter. 'You've been
most helpful. I'm afraid there will be an inquest, I'll inform
you as soon as a date is set for it and then we'll be able to
let you go ahead with the arrangements.'

'Leave all that,' said Maggie. 'You can arrange it all with
Rodney. Come on, my dear. Can you show yourselves
out?'

'I'm afraid not,' said the Superintendent. 'I want a word
with you, Mrs . . . Miss . . .?'

'Mrs Philpot.' She gave them a fierce look but followed
them downstairs and took them into the drawing-room.

She smiled then, warmly. 'I'm sorry,' she said, 'I can't
help getting angry when I see people being victimized. I
know you're only doing your job but that's what I'm like
and I can't help it.'

'Well, Mrs Philpot, can you tell me whether Mr Hardcastle spent Friday night here?'

'No, I'm quite sure he didn't.'

'He couldn't have come in late at night without your knowledge?'

'Yes, I suppose he could have done that, but I knew he didn't spend the night here because the bed was still made up on Saturday morning.'

'You looked in specially?'

'It's my job to see that the house is kept in order.'

'I see. And you don't think he could have spent the night in Mrs Hardcastle's room?'

'Certainly not.'

'So they were on bad terms?'

'He behaved abominably to her.'

'So she was going to leave him?'

'Yes, she was, but she was going to the convent. She had no reason to do him any harm and she wouldn't have wanted to. She just wanted to escape from his bullying.'

'Now, to me, Mrs Philpot, Mrs Hardcastle doesn't seem a young woman it would be at all easy to bully. She seems quite composed even in these difficult circumstances and well able to hold her own.'

'I suppose she is, now. He made her like that. I watched her change. She was quite different when he first brought her here. Bright and happy and laughing. And so young!'

'Do you know anything about the medicines Mr Hardcastle was taking? Did he keep them here?'

'I suppose, if they were here, they'd be in the cupboard in his bathroom, but he probably took them to the Kennels with his hairbrushes and everything else. Why are you asking these questions? I thought he fell, out hunting.'

'Yes. He did. Was Mrs Hardcastle here with you all day yesterday?'

'Of course she was. She doesn't hunt.'

'May we see Mr Hardcastle's bathroom?'

She took them up to a room on the same floor as Siobhan's sitting-room, a starkly masculine room with a mahogany bed, bare and cold and forbidding, with the curtains half drawn and the windows shut. In the adjoining bathroom they found a stock of aspirins and mouthwash but no diuretic pills and no digitalis.

Charter turned to Maggie.

'Weren't you surprised when Mrs Hardcastle told you she planned to become a nun?'

'Yes, of course I was, until I thought about it. She needs to be looked after and the nuns would do that. And that way she could take Dandy.'

'Surely he would never have let Dandy go?'

'Why not? The man couldn't be bothered with the child. He's only concerned with the Hunt and his own ambitions —the European Parliament. Though who he thinks would ever vote for *him* I can't imagine. Finlay Hardcastles! Who are they?'

'But surely the nuns wouldn't have agreed to her seeing Dandy and having him so near her?'

'They wouldn't have been asked. He'd just be living there with Eithne and when Siobhan went to see Eithne Dandy would be there.'

'And would Mr Hardcastle have agreed to that?'

'In the end I think he would. She would have kept on at him and finally he would have given in. She'd learned how to handle him.'

As she took them downstairs Charter asked, 'And what about this contretemps with the Whipper-in? Were you on Peter Thorn's side?'

'Everyone was. Not that I think much of that young man. He's too conceited by half. He's got ideas above his station. He keeps a thoroughbred horse at the Kennels for his wife. Where does he get all the money from, I'd like to know?'

As they got into the car the sergeant asked, 'What about *her*, sir? Couldn't she have switched the tablets?'

'Yes, she could. If he kept them here, which seems un-likely. But it's a bit far-fetched. All she'd achieve would be to lose a very cushy job. She clearly enjoys doing the earth mother thing with the two girls.'

*

'That young woman frightens me,' said Charter, as they drove towards Stumpington.

'She's extremely pretty, isn't she?' said the sergeant.

'Yes. Very pretty. Just like the cover of a chocolate box. Not in the least what I expected.'

'Sir?'

'I expected—oh, I don't know—Deirdre of the Sorrows. Ireland personified. Raven locks. Long limbs. Diana rather than Venus, and a pocket Venus at that.'

'That's the younger sister, sir. I've seen her picture. It was in all the papers when her husband, that young jockey, was killed at the Curragh. I expect the old boy thought this one was a dolly. That's the way she might like it.'

'I wonder whether Charles Hardcastle could have had designs on the sister.'

'Hardly, sir. She's getting married again. I must say it seems a shame. Dr Cresswell is far too old for her.'

'He's roughly about my age, Sergeant. But I do see your point. Siobhan, however, married a man who might have been her grandfather.'

'Can't understand it.' The sergeant shook his head sadly. 'Well, at least, sir, we've learned something about Mr Pratt's relations with the Master. Mr Hartley Godwin seems to have been the problem. I suppose that's what Mrs Pratt was keeping back.'

'At this stage, Sergeant, I'm not swallowing a single word from this young woman. For my money she's by far the most likely suspect. Time will tell. But all that chocolate-box prettiness hidden away under a veil! It's unthinkable! And all she'll need for the convent is a small dowry in cash. She'd be throwing away a staggering amount of money. I think we have to look for a lover. Her story of becoming a nun is a nonsense. No convent would accept a young wife who would be abandoning a husband and a small child. As for letting the child live with the sister near the convent and visit the mother regularly, I don't believe it for a minute. It would cause misery for everyone.'

'Why should she make up a tale like that?'

'As an alibi. To prove to us that she had no use for Charles Hardcastle's money. That little story puts her right at the top of the list.'

'Couldn't we check with the convent, sir? Just in case it's a true bill?'

'Yes, Sergeant, we'll certainly check with the convent.'

'So she'll inherit all that money and doesn't need it.'

'Looks like it, but I can't swallow it. We reserve judgement. And we don't forget that the son too has quite a motive if the father gave him nothing but huge expectations. Now, Sergeant, we'll tie up the Kennels by talking to the terrier man.'

CHAPTER 10

Tom Stringer lived in another white-painted brick cottage in the Kennels complex. They walked up the path between rough lawns and gnarled old apple trees. At the side of the house were the terrier pens. Cobbold knocked on the pale-green-painted door with the brass angel knocker. No reply. They walked round the house and came upon an open door leading into a small outhouse. Something small and white flew through the air and fell at their feet. A wiry young man in blue denim overalls came running out after it and dived to the ground to grasp the object, which turned out to be a small, very clean, white animal with longish fur, luckily somewhat stunned by its fall. The hands which grasped it were covered with blood.

John Charter stared, fascinated. 'What is it? What's happened to you?' he asked.

The young man laughed up at them.

'I'm sorry, sir,' he said. 'Give you a nasty shock, I expect. I've just been paunching a rabbit for the pot and without thinking I gave the liver to one of my ferrets before I'd washed the blood off my hands. He grabbed my finger and

I flung him off so hard he flew out the door. I'll soon have him back in his pen.'

He got up and they all went in to the clean, whitewashed outhouse which smelled revoltingly of polecat. He placed the ferret gently into a large cage with a fresh bed of clean straw and a drinking trough.

Tom Stringer was well over six feet tall and so thin as to be almost emaciated. His longish dark hair was almost black and the long sideburns gave him a gipsyish look. His eyes were so dark as to be impenetrable. This gave his companions an uneasy feeling that there was something behind them that could not be seen or reached. He was very neat and clean.

Charter looked into the cages.

'Do you use them for rabbiting?' he asked.

'That, or ratting. Can't use poison where there's livestock about. The ferrets and the terriers together make short work of the rats.'

'Do you use bleepers?'

'Don't need them. Mine are so well trained they'll send the rabbit up all right and then you'll see the old ferret's snout coming out after him.'

'They look very clean and well fed.'

'Come into the house, sir, and I'll wash my hands. Yes, they're well looked after. We'd have the Ferret Welfare Society after us if we didn't take care of 'em.'

'Ferret Welfare Society! I've heard everything now! Next you'll be telling me there's a Rat Lovers Association.'

'Wouldn't be surprised.'

They went into the house through the back door which led into a neat kitchen. A cast-iron stock pot stood on the stove and on the chopping-block beside it was a pile of onions, carrots, and leeks, and a sharp kitchen knife. Tom Stringer put the rabbit down on the wooden draining-board and scrubbed his hands and nails long and fastidiously in the sink. Then he led them into the sitting-room, which was quite unlike those of Peter Thorn and Jim Caudle. The floor was bare pine boards. The walls were painted white. The

only furniture was a plain deal table, four pine chairs, and
a fine Bentwood rocking-chair by the wood-burning stove
which was blazing away in a corner. Bookshelves lined one
wall from floor to ceiling, full of books on wildlife and
hunting. On another wall was a gun rack with an array of
guns.

'Do you shoot the rabbits?' Charter asked.

Tom Stringer laughed. 'No, I don't,' he said. 'I catch 'em
in purse nets pegged over the openings in the warrens. No
point in shooting 'em. It's messy. All you have to do is hold
'em up by the legs and get a hold of the neck and just give
it a good yank. I used to set snares for them but never since
I killed my own cat. The wire got her round the middle and
she jumped over a low branch trying to escape and hung
there and suffocated slowly. Will you sit down, sir?'

'You know what we're here for?'

'Well, I know Derek Cobbold, so I reckoned he'd brought
the officer from Penchester to ask me a few questions. I
didn't expect you quite so early of a Sunday morning but I
knew you'd come. I heard you talked to old Jim Caudle and
to Peter last night.'

'Good.'

They all sat round the table in the comforting warmth
from blazing logs and the yeasty smell which came from
four tins of bread dough standing beside the stove.

'I hear you had a row with Mr Hardcastle.'

'I don't think there's anyone in Penfoldshire hasn't had
a row with him at some time or another. He had a very
rough side to his tongue.'

'Did he make the Kennels an unhappy place?'

'You've hit the nail on the head. Old Jim, he's been here
forty years and more. He's an old countryman and he'd put
up with it. But Peter Thorn and me, we're young. I'm not
married so it don't matter so much to me. I can go as soon
as stay. But you can't go so easily if you've a wife and
children.'

'Do you think Mr Hardcastle was a cruel man?'

'Well, not exactly that, sir. I think he did some cruel

things, but *he* don't think he's a cruel man so he thinks the things he does can't be cruel. It's like he was saying, "I know you aren't going to like this but I'm doing it just the same and you mustn't be angry because it's only Charles Hardcastle doing it to you." I don't think he understood people's feelings at all.'

'That's good psychology. You've missed your vocation. That's tremendously helpful to me. So what was the bit of trouble you had with the Master?'

'I swore at him, sir. He said he'd sack me but he hasn't yet. Nobody saw it so perhaps he would have passed it over. He knew he'd never find a terrier man to beat me.'

'Why did you swear at him?'

'Well, sir, I thought he was questioning my doing the job right and I won't take that from any man.'

'But surely an employer is entitled to criticize an employee?'

'Not when he's got the best man for the job. Ask anyone. He came up here early one morning on a hunt morning when I was loading my Land-Rover and he said what was I doing there at that time and I ought to be miles away. I'd gone out at ten the night before and I was out until three. I never stint on my work. He knows that. There was plenty of time or I'd have been long gone. I swore at him and he said he'd fire me, but he hasn't and he would have passed it over. No one heard it.'

'What exactly do you do, Mr Stringer, besides the terriers?'

'I help with hounds and I'm the boiler. I skin and joint the carcases and boil the meat for hounds. Peter does that too. And I drive the pick-up to collect the carcases from the farmers. I know all the small farmers. On good terms with all of them. They all know me, don't they, Derek?'

'Yes, they do,' agreed Cobbold. 'And if we have an animal killed by the roadside I get on to Tom and he'll come and pick it up.'

'That's right,' said Tom. 'The knacker won't come out for small animals. It's a service we do for the farmers. We don't charge for it either like the knacker does. Dead calves or lambs or dogs or horses. It's all one to hounds. We hang 'em up and skin 'em and stick 'em in the deep freeze.'

'You must have a thumping great deep freeze.'

'We do. You could lose a few horses in there.'

'Why did Mr Hardcastle insist on firing Peter Thorn?'

'Because he wanted his job for someone else.'

'And who was that?'

'Mr Hartley Godwin.'

'And would Mr Godwin have made a good Master of Foxhounds later on?'

'I reckon he'd never get the job though he's often acted as Whip and he knows what he's doing. He's a very rich man too.'

'Then why wouldn't he get the job?'

'Because he's a darkie.'

'A what?'

'A black man.'

'Good God! But I don't see why that should make a difference if he's good at the job.'

'You'll see, sir. The nobs won't wear it.'

'Would you?'

'It's not my place to yea or nay it but I don't want rich foreigners taking jobs from us Penfoldshire men. What Peter Thorn did was foolish but he's a good Whipper-in and he shouldn't have lost his job for it. We all knew the reason old Hardcastle fired him was to make room for Mr Godwin.'

'So that's the reason for all the fuss about Hartley Godwin.'

'Yes. But he's a very good horseman and a credit to the Hunt. He knows what he's doing better than most and he's a very nicely spoken gentleman. We all get on with him a treat.'

'Well, now Mr Hardcastle is dead you won't lose your job and neither will Peter Thorn and Mr Godwin is unlikely ever to become MFH. Have you thought about that?'

'I've been thinking about it ever since the Master was

killed and they said it might be murder, though I can hardly credit it. It gives me a good motive, I suppose, for killing him but I don't reckon you think I'd do such a thing for a reason like that. I'd get a job in better hunts than this if I wanted and I'm fancy free. I can go where I like. You don't kill a man because you're going to lose your job.'

'Some might. What about Peter Thorn? He *had* lost his job. And he stood to lose his house. I heard that his wife was hysterical.'

'Not she. She was upset, was Nancy, but she's a good girl. She's pulled herself together and faced up to it and they were trying to work out where they'd apply to go. Peter might have sloshed old Hardcastle one in a fury but he'd never plot and plan to bump him off by poison. I don't reckon there's any of us here at the Kennels could do a thing like that, much as we'd have liked to have Mr Pierson back.'

'Who do you reckon will be the new Master?'

'That I can't say, sir. Mr Pratt, the Hunt Secretary, perhaps. He ought to have got it last time and none of us can tell why he didn't unless it was that he's a bit short of money for it. The Master needs a pile of money. This Master smartened up the Kennels a treat.'

'And you don't think Hartley Godwin could do it?'

'He could do it better than most but he wouldn't be given the chance.'

'Why not?'

'Well, sir, I can't see him going round to keep the land-owners and the big farmers sweet. They might not like it. Though as far as I can see he's more of a gentleman than most of 'em. Except Mr Pratt.'

'Would you object to his being MFH?'

'Oh, it don't bother me, sir. I can get along with anyone as long as they do the job right. I just can't see the nobs standing for it.'

'Can you tell me about the flask the Master usually carried with him? He did carry a flask?'

'Yes, he did. A glass one with a silver case with a pattern

of vine leaves. It was a very nice piece of work. It had a silver stopper. Small and neat.'

'Where did he carry it?'

'In the inside pocket of his coat, sir.'

'And did you see the flask on the morning of the meet at Hangholt Manor? Did he fill it at the Kennels?'

'Couldn't say. He often slept in the guest cottage at the Kennels but whether he was there or not on any particular night I wouldn't know. You can't see from here if the lights are on not unless you walk over that way. I was off in the other direction that night.'

'So the Master came up to the Kennels at nine or ten?'

'Half nine, sir.'

'And was he wearing his scarlet coat?'

'No, sir. He never put that on until we were ready to load up the horses. He'd come up in his breeches and rubber boots and a pullover and Barbour and he'd leave the leather boots and whip and gloves and cap and coat in the valeting room. No one goes in there much and there's hooks for hanging things up and a good big chair he could sit on to drag his boots on.'

'So the coat would have been hanging there from nine-thirty until about ten-thirty?'

'Reckon so, sir. Ten-fifteen more like. If the flask was in it anyone could have just about got to it. But I can't tell you I saw it because I didn't.'

'And what was your job yesterday? Were you about in the woods?'

'I'm always about during a hunt. I take the terriers along so we're ready to bolt the fox if he goes to ground.'

'And did he go to ground yesterday?'

'The first one did, but it was over on Mr Harvey's land and he always wants them killed so we killed him with the humane killer and gave him to hounds. Then the second fox took us back into the woods and we found the policemen there.'

'What do you think the Master was doing alone in the woods?'

'I know what he was doing. He was cutting through to make sure Mr Kingsley was keeping hounds away from the railway line. We lost hounds in the woods when the first fox went to ground. At least five couple were away off towards the line. The Master couldn't trust anyone to do their job without him. In fact, Mr Kingsley'd already brought hounds back another way and we met him as the second fox broke.'

'Did you see the "Antis" in the woods?'

'I saw some of those chaps in the woolly hats buggering about in there.'

'Would you recognize them if you saw them again?'

'No, sir, I never looked at them. Silly buggers. They ran off when they saw me coming.'

'And did you see the Master fall?'

'No, sir.'

He looked Charter very straight in the eye but his eyes were black and secretive. Charter felt instinctively that he was lying.

'You're sure?'

'Absolutely sure.'

'Thank you, Mr Stringer,' said Charter, standing up. 'You've been a great help.'

He came to the door with them and stood watching them drive away.

'Twelve o'clock,' said Charter. 'We'll look in at the station and then a pint and a sandwich in a pub. But first this cottage where the Master spent most of his nights.'

'I'm sorry, sir,' said the rural sergeant as he drove down the hill. 'I should have told you Mr Godwin was a black man. Somehow it never struck me that you wouldn't know. It seemed a bit of a stunner for you.'

Charter smiled. 'It was the best thing I've yet heard about Charles Hardcastle,' he said. 'I think he was having a bit of fun with the Can and Ash, trying to land them with a black MFH.'

'If he was, sir, I don't think he did it for fun. Malice more like it. But I don't think they'd turn a hair, most of 'em, so where's the joke? As long as he was good at his job. It's a very down-to-earth set-up and unless you're born to it you've got to earn your place in the Hunt. I've got to hand it to them—as long as you pull your weight and don't make a nuisance of yourself I don't think they care what colour you are or where you come from.'

As they came to the guest cottage, Charter signed to the sergeant to stop. 'We'll have a quick look at the bathroom cupboard in here,' he said.

The cottage was by no means perfunctorily furnished for the temporary accommodation of short-term and not particularly welcome guests. Charter walked round it in growing astonishment. Either a decorator had been at work or Charles Hardcastle had given more time and skill to it than was remotely possible. Everything was perfectly simple and therefore perfect. The china, the pictures, the great baskets of dried flowers in subtly blended colours, the flag-stones, the pale wood of the wall cabinets, corner cupboards, kitchen chairs and table, the crewel work rugs and bed covers and cushions.

Cobbold and Charter turned to each other with a single surmise.

'The other woman,' said Charter, and started opening wardrobes and looking into drawers. He found nothing to show that a woman had been living there until he went into the bathroom and there he found two toothbrushes and mugs and a box of pale pink tissues. He opened the bath-room cabinet carefully, using a tissue on the handle. 'Here it is,' he said. 'Potassium and what I suppose must be a diuretic. Get those hieroglyphics down and then this is a job for the lab. He won't have left prints but they may be able to put him in here by one means or another.'

It was the sergeant who found the broken window in the pantry.

Charter looked at him with a great light dawning in his eyes. 'Do you know, Sergeant,' he said, 'it all seemed too far-fetched by half. But I'm beginning to think there may have been something in it after all. This is where he got in after the murder to change the tablets round. He broke the small pane so he could reach in to open the window. He closed it again carefully, no doubt wearing gloves, and hoped we'd think it was a casual attempt at a break-in or even an accidental breakage. No one would see it unless they were living in the house or searching it, tucked away behind the shrubs at the back. Sergeant, I do believe we're really getting somewhere. Now for the doctor.'

CHAPTER 11

Dr Cresswell lived and had his surgery in a pleasant red brick house in Stumpington High Street. He opened the door himself in shirtsleeves and led them into a characterless drawing-room furnished with ugly chintzes which clashed with each other and the carpet.

'I've been expecting you,' he said. 'Any answers from St Christopher's?'

'Cardiac arrest,' said Charter.

'Yes. He should never have been hunting with high blood pressure and heart trouble. He was a very difficult patient. I lunched at Hangholt last Sunday and I told him then he ought not to hunt.'

'So you'd expect cardiac arrest, the waterlogged lungs and all that?'

The doctor looked at him calmly. 'No. I wouldn't expect anything in particular. But I wouldn't be surprised at his suffering cardiac arrest while under the stress you get out hunting. And in this case it's very likely that he came on some of the hunt saboteurs. God knows what they did or said, but whatever it was, he would have been furious. Might have ridden at them. In any case he'd have been under the sort of stress a sixty-year-old man with his problems ought not to subject himself to.'

'Was he taking digitalis?'

'Digoxin. Yes. I prescribed it after the heart attack—a very mild one—he had a few weeks ago.'

'Would that make it more likely that he'd suffer cardiac arrest?'

Donald Cresswell got up and began to walk around the room.

'Well,' he said, 'you've got to be very careful. He was already on a thiazide diuretic for high blood pressure. That causes loss of potassium, which causes susceptibility to the side effects of digitalis. I prescribed oral potassium to guard against digitalis intoxication. And as the dosage of digitalis has to be very carefully measured I thought it best to refer him to a heart specialist for a second opinion to make sure the dosage was within the safe limits. Fortunately for my *amour propre* he set a dosage almost identical with mine, but he preferred to prescribe the potassium combined with the diuretic. It's a pity it went wrong, but with a pig-headed chap who insists on hunting it's a problem. A sudden powerful shock such as an attack by the saboteurs followed by a heavy fall could of course do terrible damage. If he'd taken my advice and stopped at home he'd still be alive. We did our best for him. Mr Cheney is a first-class man.'

'An unfortunate end to your day's sport.'

'An unfortunate end to more than that, poor chap.'

'Do you often hunt?'

'Not often enough. Far too busy.'

'I hear you are to live in Ireland. I imagine a country doctor might have a quieter life over there.'

'I sincerely hope so. I've just sold my practice so I'm committed to it.'

'And you won't miss the Canfield and Old Ashley and the rest of this neighbourhood?'

'Oh, no. They're much too toffee-nosed for me.'

Charter looked at him in surprise.

'Yet you lunch at Hangholt Manor.'

'Only since I got engaged to Eithne. They still think calling the doctor is getting in the quack. Like getting in the plumber.'

'Or the police superintendent.'

*

'Seems a pleasant enough chap,' said Charter, but he's got a chip on his shoulder and I didn't much like the look he gave us when he brought up the second opinion—as if that was his trump card. We'll bear him very much in mind.'

'I thought he was protesting too much over the digitalis too,' said Cobbold.

'Absolutely right,' said Charter.

'But he did get the second opinion,' said the sergeant, 'so he can't have done anything wrong. He wouldn't have mentioned the potassium if he had.'

'My dear young Rural Sergeant,' said Charter. 'Think again, and think harder. His records are open to scrutiny. It would look very fishy if he hadn't mentioned it. He simply knew that no one could prove the chap was getting too much digitalis with malice aforethought. As our lady pathologist explained to us, it's a grey area.

'Supposing he decides to murder the chap. He prescribes digoxin or digitalis. Because the MFH is already on diuretics, he has to prescribe potassium tablets as well. Now, he starts him off on the potassium. Then he suddenly tells him he's taking him off them for a time. Spins a tale explaining why. Tells him he'll be back on them again soon to make sure he keeps them in the cupboard to be found after his death. Even that isn't important as people lose their tablets, even throw them away. This is all done by word of mouth, so he keeps a record of prescribing the potassium but none of taking him off it. But now the specialist prescribes the diuretic combined with the potassium. That makes it a bit more difficult but not impossible, especially if he has an accomplice in the household (e.g. the young wife). He prescribes the diuretic with potassium but substitutes for it some diuretic tablets without potassium. The complication is that after the murder he has to swap the tablets prescribed by the specialist for the ones he had substituted.'

'Then he wouldn't have had any reason to attack Miss Lincoln.'

'He must have put an extra dose in the hunting flask to make sure.'

'But why would he do that? If he just let the chap go on long enough he'd quietly die, apparently quite naturally.'

'The only possible reason would be if he suddenly found he had to speed things up. Some urgency had arisen. We know the MFH had made an appointment with the solicitor, Roger Pratt.'

'Would that affect Dr Cresswell? Unless they were all in it together—Mrs Hardcastle, her sister and the doctor, and when she inherited the money, Mrs Hardcastle was going to split the proceeds? Otherwise he stood to gain nothing from the will.'

'If we're right about the method (and we can't be sure of anything), the doctor isn't the only suspect. Anyone who is getting on in years and might be taking diuretics himself might have switched tablets with him. Anyone can buy a book on drugs.'

'They'd need a pretty good motive.'

'Well, what about Roger Pratt? His wife didn't mention his quarrel with Charles Hardcastle over Godwin, which shows that she thought it was important. But supposing Pratt had another motive? Perhaps he helped himself to some of the money from the trusts set up for the two sons. He is obviously not loaded and part of his resentment against Hartley Godwin may be owing to the fact that *he* very obviously is. Suppose Hardcastle had discovered a discrepancy or was likely to discover it. He had made an appointment for one day this week. Now he isn't going to keep that appointment.'

'But his death would bring it all to light.'

'Pratt might have won himself a day or two to sort it out. If so he'll be very busy now. We'll go and see him first thing tomorrow.'

'I can't believe it, sir.'

'And you needn't. It's pure speculation. So far. And on the face of it we've a much likelier suspect at the Hunt Kennels.'

'Peter Thorn?'

'Or his wife Nancy. Cast your mind back to the horse medicines we found on the shelf in the tack-room.'

'The digitalis?'

'The digitalis. In vast quantities. Presumably for administering to a horse. Nancy Thorn is in charge there. We're going back to see her for a serious talk about horses with heart trouble. You know, it's not a bad idea if you want to use a drug for nefarious purposes to leave it on a shelf so that anyone could have got hold of it.'

Nancy Thorn was in the stable block when they put their heads round the door. She was standing quietly leaning over the door of one of the stalls to fondle the ears of a tall grey. She turned in surprise and her face was sad and strained.

'Mrs Thorn,' said Charter, 'I'm extremely sorry to trouble you again but I must talk to you about your horse medicines.'

'Come into the dispensary,' she said, 'it's no trouble.' Her voice was very quiet and gentle and defeated. She led the way.

Charter pointed to the large box of digitalis tablets and she unlocked the cupboard and brought it out.

'Presumably these tablets were prescribed by a vet?'

'Of course. They're for my grey mare, Star.'

'What's wrong with her?'

Her large grey eyes filled with tears. 'She's got heart trouble. Quite suddenly. She's a great jumper. We bred her ourselves. I was going to compete on her. Then she suddenly went off her feed and began to look all tucked up and the vet found she was fibrillating.'

'Well, cheer up! If he prescribed all this he must think she's got a chance.'

She smiled. 'He says we've caught it just about as early as possible.'

'It seems an enormous quantity of digitalis.'

'You *need* an enormous quantity for a horse. It's a large

animal. You have to give it for ten days to prepare her for defibrillation.'

'And you give it yourselves?'

'Yes. We can't do the defibrillation. The vet comes for eight days to do that. He gives her quinidine through a tube. Then we give her digitalis for another ten days.'

'So he prescribed the whole twenty-day course right at the beginning?

'No. Just the first ten days. And he didn't give me a prescription. Just the tablets. That's what vets usually do in the country.'

'So what's the dosage?'

She picked up a piece of paper and read aloud. 'On the first day you give 40 tablets twice a day, on the second, thirty, on the third, twenty, and for the remaining seven days twenty.

'How far have you got?'

'This is the sixth day.'

'So you've used two hundred and forty tablets and there should be eighty left over. Let's count them.'

Nancy stood looking from one to the other of them as the rural sergeant counted the remaining tablets into an enamel bowl.

'There are only sixty-five here,' he said. 'Could you have given more than the prescribed dose by mistake?'

'No, I couldn't possibly have done that,' said Nancy, looking distressed. 'He must have counted wrong.'

'It looks as if fifteen tablets have gone missing.'

Her eyes widened at the implication. 'You think some-one might have stolen them and given some to the Master?'

'We don't think anything of the sort at this stage. We're simply collecting information.'

'Ring Andrew Frick, the vet. He'll know how many he gave me.'

'Yes. We'll have to check. Now how do you administer the tablets?'

'In the feed or a bran mash.'

'I suppose almost anyone could have walked into the tack-room and helped himself to a few tablets?'

'I'm afraid so,' she said. 'They were lying about on the shelf until you came. I feel very guilty. But who'd think anyone could do such a thing?'

'It's just because no one ever thinks it will happen that you have to guard against it by always keeping medicines locked away.'

She looked at him miserably and he patted her on the shoulder.

'Don't fret,' he said. 'We've all done careless things. I hope the vet manages to cure your mare. Is the prognosis good?'

'It could be,' she said with a lift in her voice. 'She could be as good as new. We'll just have to wait.'

'Now have you any idea who was in the tack-room while the tablets were on the shelf?'

'They were there for three days up to Saturday. We've had troops of people on the place. All the Hunt staff. A party of schoolchildren with their teachers. The blacksmith. And Eithne and Mrs Hardcastle and Maggie came to look at my mare. When I was foot-following with Eithne last week I told her about Star. She knows a lot about horse complaints.'

'Thank you for your help, Mrs Thorn. Now all I need is the address of your vet.'

As she handed it to them she said urgently, 'You can't think it was Peter. He wouldn't ever.'

'I don't think anything yet,' he said. 'Don't worry. If you *know* it wasn't Peter we'll find out that it was someone else, won't we?'

As they drove away the Sergeant said, 'I'll get on to Andrew Frick right away.'

'You'll find he counted them all right. Vets don't make that sort of mistake. It puts the stuff in reach of all sorts of people, including Nancy and Peter Thorn, who have the best motive for wanting the Master dead.'

'She seems a gentle, kind girl.'

'So have many murderesses. But the husband seems more likely. He's very protective towards her but that could be because she's in it with him and he knows she wouldn't stand up as well as he would to interrogation.'

'Would they have known enough to be dosing the Master with the wrong blood pressure pills, sir?'

'I doubt it, Sergeant, but we've no proof that anyone was doing that. The Thorns may simply have administered the *coup de grâce*. They'd guess he was on digitalis already for the heart attack and hope the extra dose wouldn't show up on the post-mortem.'

'It's not the doctor, then, sir, is it? He'd have no call to steal digitalis from the Kennels. And for another thing, he wouldn't even know the tablets were there.'

'No. But Siobhan could have taken them. Or she could have got the housekeeper to do it for her.'

'And used them to kill her husband?'

'Perhaps, but more likely to throw suspicion on the Hunt staff. Or at least to show that several people besides Cresswell had access to digitalis. The point is that whoever took them took far too many. Presumably to make it obvious that some were missing. Not too bright. It could have been ignorance or it could have been design. The dose for a horse is enormous. That might mislead the Thorns who know the dosage the vet prescribed. Now, Sergeant, that will do for today. Eight-thirty tomorrow at the White Hart.'

CHAPTER 12

Early on Monday morning a polite secretary told them that Roger Pratt would be in court all morning. Charter announced firmly that he would call on him at 2.0 p.m. and headed with the sergeant for Hangholt Farm.

Harriet had been kept in hospital for observation on Saturday night. Sara had collected her on Sunday and was given instructions to keep her in bed.

Harriet woke up at ten on Monday morning and raised her head gingerly from the pillow. It appeared to be rather more firmly attached to her neck than it had seemed in the morning and the pain in the centre of her forehead had dulled to an ache in place of the intolerable pain she had experienced the night before. The sickness had gone and she felt slightly hungry.

The door of the pretty bedroom opened and Sara's head popped round it.

'Feeling better, love?'

'Yes, thank you. I'm sort of hungry, I think. Thank you for these,' pointing to a vase of roses by the bed.

'Right, I'll get you some thin bread and butter with honey and some weak tea with lemon, and lots of sugar. OK?'

'Lovely. Thanks. I'm sorry to be such a bore.'

'Don't be an idiot. There's someone to see you. Do you mind? He wants to ask you some questions.'

'The police?'

'He doesn't exactly look like a copper but he says he's Detective Chief Superintendent John Charter from Penchester.'

Sara beckoned to the man in a tweed suit on the landing.

He stood apologetically at the foot of the bed.

'Good morning, Miss Lincoln. May I come in? I'll make it as brief as possible and we'll take a statement when you're feeling more the thing. I'm sorry you got banged on the head. Must have been a nasty experience. Never happened to me, so I can't tell. I suppose it must make you feel a little confused?'

He was tall with thick dark hair, untidy because he kept running his fingers through it with looks of desperation, although Harriet could see that he was entirely self-confident and level-headed and the desperation was nothing but an affectation. He had a long face and slightly drooping eyelids which gave him a faint resemblance to a bloodhound, but a rather nice-looking bloodhound with a kindly expression and very intelligent blue eyes. Harriet found his manner irritatingly apologetic.

'Well, yes, I do feel a little confused,' she said, unsmiling. He drew up a chair and sat down.

'Did you see anything? Have you any idea who did it?'

'No. No idea. They came up behind me and I heard nothing except the sound of hooves all round me.'

'And it was you who came upon the Master. You must have been very surprised to see him lying on the ground.'

'Surprise doesn't in any way describe it.'

'Horrified? Shocked? Afraid?'

'Yes. That's it. I was terrified all alone there with him. I *thought* he was dead. But how could I tell? I've never done the kiss of life. I might have worked out how to but I couldn't move him. You can't give the kiss of life to a mouth facing into the earth.'

'No, of course not. You weren't at all afraid for yourself?'

'Well, no. I could see it must have been an accident. But then when Dr Cresswell was out of sight—I can't think why he had to go so far—it was all misty and damp and a wind had come up and was whipping through the trees and things were rustling and crackling all around. I felt petrified. There was this sudden feeling of utter panic. I knew something awful was going to happen and then—bang! I was falling on the floor.'

'And you can't remember hearing or seeing anything?'

'No, I can only remember the hooves thudding all around me, it seemed, though it can't have been. She must have run away.' She suddenly sat up urgently. 'She *is* all right, isn't she?'

'Yes. I believe from the local rural sergeant that all the stray horses were safely rounded up. Only one of them got on to the road and a farmer caught that one and put it in a loose-box to be collected. Would you be surprised, Miss Lincoln, to hear that the Master was murdered?'

She looked at him quite crossly as she lay back on the pillows. 'Well, I don't want to be rude to you, Chief Superintendent, but what a stupid question. Of course I'd be surprised. He fell off his horse, didn't he?'

'Yes. But we have reason to believe that he may have

been dead before he fell. I can't say any more than that but I would like to know what you think about it. Can you imagine that anybody would have wanted to murder him?'

She looked at him without friendliness. 'Well, considering that I only met him for the first time on Sunday I'm not the best person to answer that, but from what I saw of him I should have thought every single member of the Hunt might have wanted to murder him. But I don't want to think about it and I saw him there, his face not human— and I do wish you'd bloody well go away.' She burst into tears.

He stood up, looking really desperate this time and running his hands through his hair wildly. 'I'm so sorry . . .' he began when Sara came into the room, took one look and said, 'For goodness' sake, Mr Charter—' Sara usually got that sort of thing right—'can't you see that she's not well enough for this? She got jumped off her first time hunting and found the body, and then this.'

'Did she indeed? Stayed out after a cracking fall? My compliments.' He saluted Harriet with a smile. 'I'm sorry I upset you. I'll go. We can do this later. I hope you'll be feeling better by tomorrow.'

'I shan't,' she said crossly. 'And I certainly shan't feel well enough to make a statement. And anyway it wasn't a cracking fall. I wasn't hurt at all.'

He withdrew and Sara looked after him with interest.

'My poor dear, eat up your honey bread and then try to sleep again. I'm sorry I let him come in but he seemed so gentle and self-deprecating. You never can tell with people, can you? What a bully! But dishy in a funny way.'

'He is most hideously ugly,' said Harriet unmollified.

'It's the eyes,' said Sara firmly. 'An un-Superintendent-like look of sheer naughtiness. Now go to sleep, honey: Donald Cresswell says there's nothing to worry about. You'll feel much better in the morning.'

*

Charter was waiting for Sara when she came downstairs. He was dwelling on thoughts of Harriet, whom he found quite charming in spite of her bad temper.

'I'm sorry, Mrs Hardcastle,' he said apologetically. 'I had no intention of upsetting Miss Lincoln.'

'No lasting harm,' said Sara.

'May I have a word with your husband?'

'Oh!' She looked surprised. 'Well, yes, I expect so. He'll either be up in the thirty-acre field or with the shepherd.'

She sent them out across the stableyard and through a gap between two loose-boxes to the farmyard, where Rodney was talking to his shepherd in the big covered yard. Some of the ewes had been brought under cover to have their lambs. Walls made of stacked bales of straw protected them from the winds and, within the compound thus prepared, small separate enclosures had been made to give each of the ewes which had already lambed a separate space. The rest occupied the open area in the middle. A thick bed of straw covered the whole floor.

'Comfortable lodgings there, sir,' said the rural sergeant approvingly as he introduced the Superintendent.

'This is the maternity ward,' Rodney said, smiling broadly at them both in welcome. 'The fitter ones are dropping them all over the shop out there. Off you go, Jack. The boy'll manage now. Go and get an hour or two while you can.'

'Lambing going well then, is it?' asked Sergeant Cobbold as they waved to the departing Jack and strolled into the yard.

'Splendidly,' replied Rodney. 'They're all dropping twins and triplets. We got some Kent half-breeds up from Devon —marvellous ewes—tough as old boots and prolific! We've only one pair of motherless twins. The children have got them on the bottle in the kitchen. I think they'll do all right. Poor Abby came out to fetch them just as Jack was showing me the lamb he found this morning with its head bitten off. It's either the fox or wild mink. We're going to get some cage traps from the Ministry. Now what can I do for you? Come into my office.'

He led the way across the stableyard, through a stable door into a comfortable room with a huge open fire, a couple of deep armchairs, a huge shabby sofa, a desk, several filing cabinets, a bookcase, and a large deal table covered with piles of papers, and copies of *Farmers Weekly*, *The Field*, *Horse and Hound*, and *Country Landowner*.

They sat opposite each other in the easy chairs with the sergeant at the desk with his notebook. Jenny tapped at the door and came in with three steaming mugs of coffee sent by Sara and a plate of Maggie's gingerbread which was regularly distributed among family and friends and kept in tins on pantry shelves for unexpected visitors. The rural sergeant leaped to his feet to help with the sugar and milk and exchanged flirtatious smiles and nods with Jenny as she crept out again and shut the door with exaggerated caution.

'Well,' said Rodney, 'have you traced the saboteurs?'

'No, sir. Not yet.'

'Aren't you rather taking your time over it? There they were, bullying my child, milling about in the woods. Who else is likely to have brought my father down and attacked young Harriet Lincoln?'

'It's not quite as straightforward as that, sir.'

Rodney looked at him very hard, frowning. Then he relaxed. 'I see,' he said. 'Then I'll have to rearrange my ideas. It seemed so obvious. What's the problem?'

'The problem is that your father died of heart failure, which may have been caused by a fall engineered by the "Antis", as you call them. But it may have been caused by something in the hunting-flask.'

'An accident?'

'Possibly.'

'Or something put there intentionally?'

'That's a possibility too.'

'Then anybody could have done it.'

'I'm afraid so, sir.

'Good God! It's unbelievable!' He got up and began to walk up and down, his hands in his pockets. 'Murdered! My father! I don't believe it!' He swung round on Charter.

'Surely you ought to check on the "Antis" before you run away with that idea. They don't care what they do. Surely if they attacked him he might have had a heart attack.'

'Yes, sir. He might. But the fact that Miss Lincoln was hit on the head several minutes later does seem to indicate that someone wanted a clear field to remove evidence. It could have been a rope used by the "Antis" to bring your father down, but that seems unlikely in view of the fact that he wasn't galloping or cantering. It's at least equally likely that someone was after his flask.'

'You mean to say that someone laced my father's brandy with something poisonous?'

'It's a possibility we have to consider.'

'Far-fetched in the extreme. How could the chap expect to be on the spot to remove the flask? Have you any idea how much ground an MFH might cover during a hunt? And all of it totally unpredictable. No one could be sure of being there when he fell.'

'One person could be pretty sure of being first on the scene once he was found.'

'Oh, the doctor! Well, I suppose he could, but why on earth would Donald Cresswell want to kill my father?'

'This is all speculation as yet. The most likely motive in this case must obviously be the money. It is a very large amount of money, I believe?'

'Yes, it is. But Donald Cresswell couldn't get his hands on a penny belonging to my father. There's Siobhan and us and Dandy. Who else could expect to benefit from it? Oh, I see. *We're* the suspects.'

'You, or anyone else mentioned in the will, or anyone who might expect to marry Mrs Hardcastle, the widow.'

'Well, I was out hunting that day. I was busy looking after Abigail, but I suppose I could have done it. Or got hold of the flask somehow, if I'd known where he was the night before. But as for Siobhan, I'll swear she hasn't got a lover. And Cresswell is engaged to Eithne, not Siobhan. He wouldn't get a penny.

'Siobhan was going to leave my father and she was doing it with her eyes open. She wanted to go back to Ireland to become a nun, and she didn't care about the money. There's a trust for Dandy, so he's all right. I don't much care for Siobhan. She's a selfish, cold and vain young woman, but I don't believe any of that family are that mercenary, except of course over buying and selling horseflesh.'

'I understand you, sir, but the sudden possibility of acquiring a great deal of money can have a remarkable effect on even the least mercenary characters. You'd be surprised what it does to the psyche—the sudden realization of the possibility of acquiring great wealth and power.'

'But the girl's going to become a nun, for heaven's sake! Great wealth and power won't do her any good at all in a nunnery.'

'There's nothing to stop her coming out of the nunnery in a year or two.'

'Can you really believe Siobhan O'Flaherty could be as calculating as that?'

'We don't believe anything yet, sir. We're just making routine inquiries—getting a general picture. Don't forget that there is another possibility—Mr Ramsay Hardcastle was in the woods that day.'

'How would Ramsay get at the flask?'

'I went to Penchester to ask him.'

'Poor old Ramsay wouldn't have dreamed of poisoning my father and he certainly wouldn't have used a rope to bring him down off his horse. With Ramsay it's all hot air. He'd never actually harm anyone.'

'He was in a very emotional state that morning after being attacked by your father.'

'I've often seen Ramsay in a very emotional state, but I've never seen him behave violently. It's not in his character.'

'Slipping something into a flask may not seem to the doer a very violent act. People can be singularly unrealistic. They make excuses for themselves.'

'I see that, but I reckon you'd agree with me if you knew him.'

'I expect I would. May I ask what was your own relationship with your father?'

Rodney looked at him. 'Ah,' he said, 'now we come to it. It
was a fair to middling-good relationship. I wasn't all that
fond of him. He wasn't that sort of father. But I'm his eldest
son. He wanted me to keep up Hangholt and the pack of
hounds and generally follow in his footsteps. He'd earned it
all and he wanted to keep it in the family, so he set up a trust
to cover all that. Not that I see any of it until after his death
—' He stopped in sudden realization, looked up at Charter,
and smiled. 'Yes. Of course. That does give me a strong motive for wanting him dead. If I needed the money now.'

'And do you?'

He thought for a moment and then said, 'Yes. In a way
I do. Of course I'm not stuck for a bob. I'm pretty well off.
There are trusts for my children too. And when my father
went to Ireland buying horses for the Hunt he'd buy them
for me and the kids too. Never for Sara. He's never much
liked Sara. She's too independent. I'm independent too but
I'm his son, so that's all right. He expected outsiders who
had been admitted to the charmed circle to toe the line and
behave with due humility and gratitude. My Sara isn't like
that, thank God. If she were I wouldn't have spent five
years in hot pursuit of her up and down the land. But that's
beside the point.

'Now let me think this thing out. I've been too busy since
it happened. What difference does it make to me?' He folded
his hands between his knees and looked at the ground. Then
he looked up.

'Yes. I have to say it *will* make a great difference to the
farm. I've never had enough capital to do what I wanted to
do here. It's part of the Hangholt estate and my father gave
it to me when he bought Hangholt. We started off by
building up the milk herd. You can picture the capital
investment involved in that. We did moderately well but
then the milk quotas took the bottom out so we switched to
mostly arable. We're extremely efficient. Too efficient. Now
I'm negotiating to set aside at least a fifth of my land but it

goes right against the grain to be paid for keeping good land idle.'

'Your father's death won't alter the Common Market Agricultural policy.'

'No, but it will allow me to do something I've been interested in for a long time.' He stood up and walked up and down thoughtfully. 'I'll get in touch with them at once and go down as soon as they can see me.'

Charter exchanged mystified glances with the rural sergeant.

'Who, sir?'

He swung on them excitedly. 'Why, the people in the Duchy of Cornwall—the Prince of Wales's people running the organic farming. That's what I'll do here now. I won't set any land aside. With the money from the trust I'll be able to carry the cost of setting the whole thing up, and the income from my father's business will cover the waiting time until we can make it profitable. Just think. We chuck nitrates on to the land at £110 a ton, three hundredweight to an acre, to increase output per acre, and keep on doing it. Then we're paid to set land aside because we're over-producing. Better to use all your acreage and produce less per acre. And you get rid of all the pollution that way. Use clover for grassland and break-crops for your arable so you put the nitrogen in naturally.'

He looked at the open-mouthed policemen, threw back his head and roared with laughter.

'That's given me a beauty of a motive, hasn't it? My father would have had no truck with organic farming. So make the most of that. Now I've got to leave you. Come back again if you've any more questions. I've got to get out to see over my spring sowing and I've not finished with my shepherd yet—and, heaven help us, here comes the gamekeeper from Hangholt.'

As they went to the door a small wizened old man, as brown as a nut, popped his head over the half-door, holding up two enormous eggs.

'Good morning, sir,' he said. 'These are the goose eggs

for Abby. She wanted to hatch 'em out for Easter so I said I'd save some for her.'

'I've two minutes for you, Harry. No more,' said Rodney, ushering them all out into the yard.

'Go on into the kitchen, Harry,' he said. 'The children are there, so you can give the eggs to Abby. Ask Jen to give you a cup of tea and she'd better pop a slug of brandy in it. You'll need it after crawling about after all those nests.'

He shook hands affably, if distractedly, and turned away.

They walked away round the house.

'What was he doing with the nests?' asked Charter, and the rural sergeant smiled.

'It's a huge flock of Canada Geese, sir, up by the lake at Hangholt Manor. They're the terror of the neighbourhood. They light down on a field—any field—for miles around and they graze it bare. Enormous, beautiful birds but dreadful thieves. Harry blows the eggs and puts the empty eggs back in the nest. Otherwise she'd lay some more.'

'Seems a bit heartless to me,' said Charter.

'You wouldn't think so if you were a farmer with grazing or corn. They say three geese will eat as much as one cow. Well, sir, it seems Mr Rodney Hardcastle is in the clear.'

'All that money. It makes a good motive.'

'Sir,' protested the sergeant, 'you could see the man was thinking it all out as he went along. He wasn't waiting for his father's death to go organic.'

'How do we know he isn't a brilliantly clever man and a consummate actor? That could all have been an act for our benefit. He could have gone to the Kennels the night before the meet, laced the flask, and hung around near his father during the hunt so he could remove it. He was one of the first on the scene. It's not impossible.'

'No, sir, I suppose we'll have to bear it in mind. I've got it all down here.' He waved his memo pad. 'But I still don't believe a word of it.'

They got into the car.

'Neither do I,' said Charter. 'Now, a sandwich in Stumpington and then for Messrs Pratt and Whatsisname on

Stumpington High Street. Two o'clock I said and he'd
better be there.'

'He was in York on Saturday,' said Cobbold. 'I don't
think he can be involved.'

'Oh yes he can,' said Charter. 'We don't know where he
was on Saturday. His wife has merely told us he was in
York. But I look forward to meeting Mr Pratt. He can fill
us in on Hunt politics too. With special reference to Mr
Hartley Godwin.'

CHAPTER 13

Roger Pratt rose from his desk and came courteously to
greet them.

'Good morning, sir,' said Charter. 'I'm Detective Chief
Superintendent John Charter from Police Headquarters
at Penchester. And I expect you already know Sergeant
Cobbold.'

'Good morning, Sergeant,' said Pratt. 'We know each
other well, Mr Charter. Our paths cross every so often,
don't they, Sergeant?'

'They do indeed, sir. I hope you're keeping well?'

'Thank you. What can I do for you, Mr Charter?'

John Charter had been allowing himself to speculate on
a feeling that he had seen Roger Pratt before and it was
with a sense of great satisfaction that he pinned the memory
down. The solicitor bore a strong resemblance in features
to the gentleman in the portrait in the study at the Old
Rectory. His bearing and manner were however more remi-
niscent of the lady on the other side of the fireplace.

'We'd like to look at the will,' he said baldly.

Roger Pratt got up without a word, went to the door and
spoke to someone outside. 'I have it waiting for you,' he
said, as he came back and sat down. 'I know the provisions,
of course. I looked them over when he told me that he was
coming to see me this week about it.'

'Did he say what he was going to do?'

'No, he didn't, but I fear he was going to change it. Mrs Hardcastle had told him she was going back to Ireland. He would have cut her out of the will but he couldn't reverse the trust for Dandy. I doubt whether he would have considered doing such a thing anyway.'

'That gives Mrs Hardcastle a strong motive.'

'I don't think it does, Mr Charter. Mrs Hardcastle is a very unusual young woman. She doesn't seem to take any interest whatever in ordinary everyday arrangements about money. She comes of a happy-go-lucky, irresponsible family of Irish horse-breeders who live in a mouldering country house in great discomfort. She's highly intelligent and when Charles brought her here she threw off the shabby country gear and became the elegant young lady he wanted her to be. But you've seen Eithne. They don't really care about clothes or comfort. They don't plan for the future. For Dandy she might, but that won't be necessary. She's very cold but I really can't see her as a murderess.'

'So the will provides no motive except for Mrs Hardcastle?'

'No. There are bequests to a few old former servants and Hunt servants. Everything else goes to Mrs Hardcastle except for one rather extraordinary bequest. Fifty thousand pounds to a Mrs Antonia Hyde.'

'Indeed! Who is Mrs Antonia Hyde?'

'She's a distant connection of the Penfoldshires. They live at No. 110 High Street, a few doors away. The husband's in the wine trade. Often away abroad.'

'What was her connection with Mr Hardcastle?'

'I know of no connection.'

'She didn't work for him?'

'No.'

'I see. Were they on dining terms?'

'I've never seen either of them at Hangholt Manor, though they were friends of the young Hardcastles at Hangholt Farm.'

'What sort of relationship did Rodney Hardcastle have with his father?'

'Perfectly friendly. They didn't live in each other's pockets but there was no ill-feeling. Charles Hardcastle wasn't generous with his money but there was this enormous trust which could of course be used as collateral. Rodney knew great wealth would be coming to him. He wasn't impatient. He and young Dandy will both be immensely rich. Hangholt Manor goes to Rodney. There was never any question of that going to Siobhan. Rodney was the heir. Charles was extremely fond of his first wife, who died soon after he bought Hangholt. But Dandy will be able to buy his own Hangholt if he wants to.'

'Who are the trustees?'

'Francis Hardcastle and myself for Rodney. Rodney and myself for Dandy. Here is the will. Do you want to look at it?'

'No, thank you, Mr Pratt. That's all I need to know for the present. Now, the inquest is to be held on Friday morning in the Town Hall at Penchester. It will almost certainly be adjourned. So, although the PM has been done, I'm afraid the body won't be released for some time yet. If there is an arrest the defence will want to have a look. The funeral arrangements will have to wait. Will you explain that to Mrs Hardcastle or shall I?'

'I believe I had better do it myself,' said Roger thoughtfully. 'I'll go over there right away.'

'And you'll explain that she will be asked to appear at the inquest?'

'Of course. Poor girl. She won't have my wife. Won't have anyone. Her sister is there, but she's only nineteen and a widow herself.'

'She has her fiancé.'

'Yes.' He sounded doubtful.

'Dr Cresswell isn't popular?'

'Oh yes, he has always been extremely popular. That wife of his gave him a hard time. Everyone was on his side. But neither he nor Eithne seem exactly happy. Of course, the wife had the money. That's why he lives in Stumpington. She took the country house.'

'Did they have any children?'

'No. She wasn't the maternal type.'

'Any girlfriends before Eithne?'

'Well, he was thought to have had a short liaison with a young pathologist at St Christopher's, a Dr Prideaux, but it came to nothing.'

'Dr Prideaux? That's extremely interesting. I wonder what the two Irish girls will do. Will they go home?'

'I expect they will and Hangholt Manor will be let.'

'Then I think I know who will rent it.'

Roger Pratt frowned.

'Hartley Godwin,' said Charter, fishing.

'He may well. Much good it will do him.'

'Do you intend taking on the Mastership yourself, sir?'

'I'm too busy, and not rich enough. But if we can set up a Joint-Mastership with two or three of us I think I could take a hand. But certainly not with Godwin.'

'People seem to think Godwin would be capable of it,' said Charter.

'He is an ambitious man,' said Roger Pratt. 'But I fail to see why the Can and Ash should help him to fulfil his ambitions. He's American. Let him hunt with the Old Chatham in New York or the Pickering at Valley Forge or perhaps even the Orange County.'

'Might be difficult, perhaps,' hinted Charter gently and Pratt swung to face him. 'What do we know about him? He's a New Yorker. Where did he get his money? How do we know he hasn't got Mafia connections? We know nothing about his background. Here in Penfoldshire we like to know people's backgrounds. Hartley Godwin was one of Charles Hardcastle's totally irrational crazes. It would have lasted another couple of years at most.'

'The hunt servants seem to respect him.'

'So they ought. He behaves impeccably and he earned his hunt button by sheer hard work. I've nothing against him as a member. But he's too clever by half and if he became Master he might be off back to the States any day. And, liberal though one may be, he'll find himself up against all sorts of diehard prejudice with the landowners and farmers in this sort of country.'

'Do you really think so, sir? Don't you think you may be under-rating the people round here?'

Roger Pratt looked at him in great surprise and seemed to be wrestling with a new idea. Then he said more calmly, 'Well, perhaps I am. You may be right.'

'I hope you noticed, Sergeant,' said Charter, 'that our obliging young pathologist may, it now appears, have reason to bear a grudge against the doctor?'

'Yes, sir. And we seem to have found the lady of the Kennels cottage.'

'We have indeed. And that's where we're going now. But she isn't going to be our murderer. If she knew Siobhan was going back to Ireland she had everything to hope for. But she may have something for us. How on earth did they keep it quiet?'

'The husband travels a lot. I suppose she'd go over whenever he was away. Leave the lights on at home. Nobody'd know where she was.'

But there was no reply at No. 110, High Street.

Roger Pratt telephoned the White Hart that evening to explain to Charter that there was to be a short memorial service at the church in Hangholt village on the Thursday of the week following the inquest.

'This week's hunting has naturally been cancelled but we intend to get out again a week on Saturday. Everyone feels we can't hunt again without paying some sort of tribute, so Mrs Hardcastle has agreed to a memorial service for the family and Hunt members. There'll be no public announcement—not that that'll keep them away. It seems to be the proper thing to do. It may be weeks before the body is released for the funeral. And it will be a chance to get the family together to read the will. We can't wait indefinitely for that.'

CHAPTER 14

The car park outside the Town Hall at Penchester was crammed with cars like a market day and the crowd gathering on both sides of the road was so large, and getting larger, that several policemen had been brought in to control it.

When Rogers brought the grey Mercedes to a halt at the bottom of the steps they surged forward to gawp at Siobhan and Eithne. Siobhan wore black. Her blonde hair was brushed smoothly under a pill-box hat borrowed from Maggie. Neither of the O'Flaherty girls had ever willingly bought a hat. She looked pale and even distinguished. Eithne was sheet-white and the purple of her tweed coat was reflected in the shadows underneath her strained eyes.

Maggie walked between them, touching them and nodding reassuringly at them like a mother-hen.

The sound the crowd made was not a murmur of sympathy but a deep soft growl. The wave of resentment was almost palpable and it startled the two girls, who had expected to be gazed at with sympathy. Siobhan's eyes widened in horrified amazement. She grabbed Eithne's hand and almost ran up the steps and through the swing doors, leaving the gathering TV reporters with their outstretched microphones foiled on the steps. Siobhan pulled Eithne round beside her against the wall and they leaned there for a moment breathing fast. Maggie came hurrying after them.

Roger Pratt came forward and took Siobhan's hand, Mabel at his shoulder.

'Are you all right?' asked Mabel. 'Shall I come and sit with you?'

Siobhan shook her head. 'We've Maggie with us,' she said.

'I'm sorry,' said Roger, 'that you have to go through this. I suppose the public interest was inevitable—MFH and

hunt saboteurs and all that. But it will be quite straightforward. It's Hawkins. A civilized chap. I reckon it'll be
adjourned. It shouldn't take long. Will you and Eithne and
Maggie come and lunch with Mabel and me afterwards?
I've booked a private room at the White Hart.'

'It's very good of you,' said Siobhan, 'but you saw those
people out there. I'll not stay in this place a minute longer
than I have to. We'll go straight back to Hangholt and the
sooner we can go away back to Ireland the better. I hate
them. Why do they do that? What do they know about it?
It's because we're Irish.'

'Siobhan, look! It's the mob instinct and it's the same the
world over. It isn't because you're Irish, it's because of the
money. So much money. And they like a bit of drama.
That's all it is.'

'I hate them,' she said again in a shaking voice and
Maggie put an anxious arm round her.

The inquest lasted longer than Roger had expected and
he wondered if the TV cameras outside had something to
do with this. The courtroom was crammed with what to
Siobhan seemed avid eyes. The Press were there in force
and there was a jury of eight people. The witnesses sitting
in the body of the court included Ramsay Hardcastle,
Harriet Lincoln, Dr Cresswell, Norman, Tony and Jill.
Ramsay looked embarrassed and seemed unwilling to meet
anybody's eyes.

Siobhan was called to give evidence of identification.
She then listened in cold resentment to the rest of the
proceedings. She gripped the hands of Eithne and Maggie
in a fury when the representative of the WEN Life Insurance
Company got up to question the witnesses. 'What's it got
to do with him?' she asked fiercely.

'Sh! Sh!' soothed Maggie, patting her shoulder. 'What
does it matter, my dear? It's only their routine. It doesn't
mean anything.'

Harriet was called to give evidence of the attack on
her and as she described falling into darkness among the
thudding sound of hooves, Eithne swayed and, to the great

excitement of all the spectators, fainted into Roger Pratt's
arms. It was very hot in the courtroom. Dr Cresswell jumped
up to go to her and together they helped her out. Siobhan
moved as though to follow but turned then to Maggie and
whispered to her. Reluctantly Maggie followed them.

The television news people got pictures of Eithne being
helped into the Mercedes by Roger and Donald. They
hopefully held out their microphones to her and called out
'Won't you speak to us, Mrs O'Dowd?' and, 'What did it
feel like when you heard your brother-in-law had fallen
under the hooves of his horse, just as your husband did at
the Curragh?' She did not even hear them, much less answer,
but on the lunch-time news there was a short account and
flashback to Patrick O'Dowd's death, with pictures of the
ambulance taking him away and a distraught Eithne running to him. Then followed shots of Charles at a lawn meet
and of Charter stonewalling as he went to the inquest, and
Siobhan running up the steps of Stumpington town hall. It
made a riveting news item and ensured that pictures of
Eithne and Siobhan were plastered over all the front pages
next day.

The rural sergeant gave evidence next, followed by Dr
Cresswell, the pathologist who had done the PM, and
Ramsay Hardcastle and his friends. Everyone got the im-
pression that the hunt saboteurs were the chief suspects.
The police asked for an adjournment, which was granted,
and it was over.

After the inquest Charter headed for the White Hart with
the sergeant, hoping to find that Mr Hartley Godwin would
be staying there, since he had attended the inquest. He was,
and he asked the police officers to join him in his suite.

'Good morning, Mr Charter, I've been expecting you.
May I ask them to send up coffee for you? A smoked salmon
sandwich? No? Then please sit down.'

Having seen Godwin across the court room, Charter
was not surprised at the sheer pleasure derived from the
contemplation of such a beautifully-put-together human

being. He was on the tall side and of slim, athletic build.
He moved like an athlete and like a Negro, softly and
smoothly as if his bones were made of oil. Every movement
seemed to flow out of the one before. His head was beauti-
fully shaped and covered with cropped curls. The bone
structure of his face was good to look at and his eyes were
calm and amused. His voice was well modulated but the
accent was mid-Atlantic, not the clipped, certain tones of
those sons of African potentates educated at English public
schools.

It was the only suite the White Hart boasted and com-
prised the oak-panelled bedroom with the four-poster bed,
where Charles II and his brother, York, were reputed to
have spent a night as children, and a small, comfortable
sitting-room with an 18th-century stencilled wallpaper,
looking out on the High Street.

Sitting upright but totally relaxed in the chintz armchair,
Godwin looked questioningly at Charter and he began.

'Can you give me any information, sir, about the set-up
of the Canfield and Old Ashley Hunt, which might have a
bearing on the death of the Master?'

'I don't really think I can. He was a choleric man. He
annoyed several people. But one can't imagine anyone
killing him because they were annoyed. By far the most
likely answer is the hunt saboteurs.'

'An accident?'

'Probably an accident. Possibly something more culpable.'

'Murder?'

'I should have thought manslaughter more likely.'

'That would of course be the most satisfactory solution
for the Canfield and Old Ashley.'

'It remains the most likely.'

'I am told, sir, that Mr Hardcastle had become obsessed
with the idea that you should be his successor.'

'Obsessed? Is that the sort of language they've been using?
It is true that he had decided that I would be the best choice
for Master.'

'Are you well qualified to be Master? I ask because foxhunting is a field in which I'm not at all knowledgeable. So I have to ask for guidance.'

'I have all the qualifications bar one.'

'And what is that?'

'A white skin.' He smiled and Charter found himself smiling back in spite of himself.

'Have you any idea who murdered Charles Hardcastle?'

'None whatever.'

'Did you murder him yourself?'

'In order to become Master of the Can and Ash? Good heavens, it's not the Quorn, Mr Charter. And I hardly think—even to be Master of the Quorn—it would be a conceivable scenario, always supposing I needed the éclat of being MFH. But I don't. All this to me is relaxation and amusement. I'm interested in the tactics, so to speak, of the foxhunt and I'm even more interested in the conservation aspect. I would have liked to learn to run a Hunt successfully and if Charles had lived I might have done it. Now I never will. I'd have enjoyed returning to the States having run the Canfield and Old Ashley for a year or two, but it's not important.'

'What is your present occupation, sir.'

'I'm marking time. A little politics, a little law, a little public speaking. In a year or two I'll decide whether to go home to run for the Senate or perhaps stop here and eat my dinners at Gray's Inn and end up wearing a curly white wig. Perhaps I'll be the first Old Bailey Judge to wear a black skin.'

'Many possibilities seem open to you, sir.'

Hartley Godwin smiled at him. 'I create possibilities for myself,' he said. 'You find it surprising to meet a black man from the United States who hunts with the Canfield and Old Ashley. You probably expected an African prince. Well, like an African prince, I read Law and Classics at Oxford and I was actually elected to the Bullingdon. It has nothing whatever to do with luck and everything to do with much determination, some native ability and a lot of very hard

work. Of course it couldn't have happened without my
father's money.'

'Have you met with any difficulties in the Hunt, sir?'

'Tactfully put. I am accepted by the mounted subscribers
and the foot-followers. Some of them ask me to dinner every
now and again and not all of them pat themselves on the
back for doing it. As for the Hunt servants, I was a bit of a
nine days' wonder to begin with. But when they saw my
horses and my gear, my clothes, my boots, my box, my rugs,
and when they saw that I know what I'm doing and the
terms I'm on with the Master, they began quite happily to
treat me like any other of the mounted followers. Now they
don't notice any difference. But if I had departed from
convention in the smallest particular, worn ill-fitting boots
or ridden an ill-conditioned horse, skylarked over fences or
thrust myself to the fore, it would be a different story.
An Anglo-Saxon Caucasian would be allowed one or two
failings of that sort. As I don't do any of those forbidden
things—as I behave correctly and tactfully, am helpful
without being officious and useful because I know what I'm
doing—they accept me as one of themselves. I have the
highest respect for the Hunt servants. They are sensible,
efficient, and kindly. They get on with their jobs and never
grumble and they put up very civilly with the rest of us and
our assumptions.'

'I believe you don't get on particularly well with the Hunt
Secretary, sir?'

'Not so far.'

'What seems to be the trouble?'

'Charles Hardcastle. I'll be able to sort it out quite easily
now.'

'Was there any truth in the suggestion that Mr Hardcastle
fired the Whipper-in to make room for you to get experience
of hunting hounds?'

'Arrant nonsense. Charles fired Peter Thorn for insubordination. Roger Pratt was irrational on that subject. Charles
liked to annoy him and Roger Pratt allowed himself to be
annoyed. I was *learning* from Peter Thorn.'

'Why did Charles Hardcastle choose you to be his successor rather than Roger Pratt?'

'Roger Pratt couldn't afford to do it on his own. Charles knew that I am interested in working with hounds. I'm interested in the breeding. I went into it a bit in the States. Many of our best hounds are French, possibly descended from the *chien de Gascoigne*. Lafayette presented us with a pack of French hounds at the end of the eighteenth century, after the War of Independence. I've been making something of a study, a comparison of the French, English and Welsh hounds. Charles was very interested. And I've also been getting up the subject of the politics of Field Sports in this country and studying the effect on ecology and conservation.'

'What is the effect?'

'Foxhunting has a good effect ecologically. I don't think anyone disputes that. And, incidentally, it's the most humane way of controlling the fox.'

'That's interesting, sir, but I wonder whether they asked the fox?'

'If you asked the fox he'd vote for no control at all and we'd soon be overrun. If he had to vote for being gassed or shot or snared, I think he'd vote for being hunted. If we catch him he's killed instantly. If we don't he gets away unscathed. All the other methods, even if they're in the hands of experts, and they very often aren't, end up with foxes dying slowly in great pain.'

'It sounds convincing.'

'It is. Read the Scott Henderson Report on the inquiry set up by the Attlee Government. That was the only independent inquiry ever and they came down heavily for control by packs of hounds. They felt it was immoral for anyone to enjoy the hunt, so they cut out the followers who help to pay for the whole thing but even so it's an interesting conclusion. Packs of foxhounds run by civil servants.'

'It does seem a little uncivilized to hunt for sport when the whole thing ends in a death.'

'That's a perfectly tenable position but surely everyone must decide for himself. And I do think there's one thing people don't understand about foxhunting. The followers on the whole have nothing whatever to do with catching the fox. To most of them it's a good gallop and some stiff jumps across country. The real hunting people despise them for it, but there it is.'

'Well, it's another sort of death I have to deal with, sir. May I ask where you were last Saturday? Were you out that day?'

'I was in London that day and the day before at an International meeting of PEN.

'Can you substantiate that, sir?'

'I think so. I was one of the speakers. Some people will probably remember me. I was there till quite late in the evening on both days.'

'You won't be leaving the country in the near future, sir?'

'No. I'll be here for the memorial service and I'll be hunting on Saturday. When I'm in Penfoldshire I stay here. If I'm not here I can be found at my London flat. Here's my card.'

Charter took the glossy embossed square on which he found the address: Hartley Godwin, Pinbolt House, Pin Lane, London EC1. 'If you are ever in the City do call and see me,' suggested Godwin. 'I'll show you the Scott Henderson Report and various other publications and books and pictures to do with foxhunting.'

'Thank you, sir. I'd enjoy that.'

'Interesting that, sir,' said Cobbold, as they left the White Hart.

'Interesting, but hardly helpful. Not the vestige of a motive there.'

CHAPTER 15

On Monday morning they arrived at Hangholt Farm before the Press arrived for their daily vigil, greeted the uniformed man on duty, drove round the rambling Elizabethan farm-

house to the stableyard, looked in at the kitchen door and
found Sara and Harriet drinking coffee at the large kitchen
table.

'I'm sorry to barge in,' said Charter. 'We're working on
the principle that, in the country, try the back first.'

'Hello, Mr Charter,' said Sara, 'come and join us. Hello,
Sergeant.'

She went to the dresser and got two more blue and white
mugs. 'How do you like it? What about you, Sergeant, milk
and sugar? Fine. Here you are.'

They sat companionably round the table, the sergeant at
the far end with his memo pad poised.

'Have you come to interview me again?' asked Harriet.
'I was frightfully rude to you last time. I do apologize but
I expect you could tell that I wasn't myself that day.'

'It's for me to apologize,' Charter said. 'It's good of you
to give us coffee, Mrs Hardcastle. I could see that I'd blotted
my copybook with you good and proper.'

This humble behaviour represented enormous guile. He
knew that this cosy approach might net him facts about
the hunting community he could never find out on his
own.

'Well, you had rather blotted it,' said Sara. 'It was rotten
of you to upset Harriet when she wasn't well but I put it
down to enthusiasm and I've forgiven you. And if we can
help we will, won't we, Harriet? I do want you to find out
if my father-in-law was murdered. It seems so unlikely and
yet he did behave impossibly to everyone, so I suppose if
there was someone about who was inclined to murder he
was a very likely murderee.'

'And would you say that there is someone about in your
hunt who is inclined to murder?'

'No, of course I wouldn't. But now that I know that one
of them probably *was*, I must confess that I have been
turning ideas over in my head. In fact, Harriet and I have
been comparing notes about it.'

'Tell me about it.'

'Well, *I* know them much better and longer, but Harriet's

highly intelligent and brings a fresher view. Together we've decided that Ramsay Hardcastle is a possibility in a way, though we don't think he would be a murderer except in very exceptional circumstances.'

'Like being beaten up in public by his brother?'

'Exactly. He was a bit beside himself that day. Roger Pratt is simply out of the question because of his character. He couldn't possibly do such a thing. And nor could Mabel, of course.'

'You'd be surprised how people can act out of character when things go wrong for them.'

'Don't quibble. Now, if Hartley Godwin wanted to murder anyone, he'd do it with effortless aplomb, but we don't think he'd want to. Everything comes to that gentleman so easily that he couldn't want *anything* enough. NB. You'd have to want to murder someone terribly badly to actually get down to doing it.

'Peter Thorn is totally incapable of a mean murder. So, of course, is dear old Jim Caudle. Tom Stringer is a very strong character. He thinks too much, perhaps, like Cassius (that's Harriet for you), but our verdict is "No". Much too sensible and level-headed.

'Dr Cresswell. We both think he's selfish and he's got a chip on his shoulder but he was very nice to his horrid wife and he's off to Ireland soon with Eithne anyway and he doesn't stand to gain anything so why should he want to murder Charles?

'We think Eithne is tragic and unlucky and a *femme fatale* without any intention of being one, but no one could acquire her by murdering Charles and she most certainly wouldn't murder anyone. She and Siobhan won't even hunt because the nuns taught them that it's wrong to hunt animals (which incidentally makes our good old ferret fancier, Tom Stringer, a monster of iniquity).

'Siobhan is a very strange mixture—total iron underneath the prettiness. She's the obvious one if she were keen on money, but I don't believe she is.'

'She's going into a convent.'

'Nonsense! Impossible! It doesn't hang together. She isn't the type.'

'How do you know?' asked Harriet. 'She's impenetrable. How do you know what's going on behind those stony eyes? She hates you all here. All she wants is to go back to Ireland. And she probably loathed making love with that cross old man. Oh, sorry, Sara! He was your father-in-law.'

'Be my guest,' smiled Sara. 'He *was* a horrid old man. I can say it to you, though of course I wouldn't to Roddy or the children. It's OK for them to be pious about him if they want to, now that he's dead.'

'Well,' Harriet went on, 'a convent might seem like perfect peace and rest to her after the shouting and hectoring.'

'Specially,' said Sara, 'if she's totally frigid, which does seem possible and would explain a lot.'

'My God, you women are deadly,' said Charter, shaken.

'No, we aren't,' said Sara. 'This would be uncalled-for as gossip but this is a murder inquiry. You've got to look at all the possibilities, however excruciating for the suspects.'

'Thank you,' he said. 'I wish all suspects would agree. It's what I'm trying to do and you are of great assistance to me.'

A shadow fell across the half-open door and Tom Stringer appeared in the opening.

'Good morning, ma'am,' he said. 'Is the shepherd about? I've come with the pick-up to collect the dead ewe and lambs. He's not in the yard.'

He noticed the policemen. 'Good morning, sir. 'Morning, Derek.'

'Oh, hello, Tom,' said Sara, jumping up. 'I'm sorry I can't offer you a cup of coffee this morning. We're being interviewed by the Superintendent. But I think Jack'll be up the thirty-acre if he's not in the covered yard.'

'Right you are, ma'am.' He went away.

'Harriet!' said Sara as she went back to her place. 'What on earth's the matter?'

'It was him!' said Harriet. 'It was him there in the woods. I know it was. I thought it was the "Antis" but now I'm sure it was him. I couldn't mistake him. It's the way he moves and his height and the gipsy hair.'

'Where was he?' asked Charter sharply, no longer relaxed and companionable.

'Oh—not near me. I'm sure not near enough. But I suppose he could have worked round and got behind me. And now I remember what frightened Atalanta. Someone behind me threw something hard. It fell ahead of me and I turned my head to look at it and Atalanta jumped and it was then that the arm came round my neck.' She shuddered a little and Sara put a comforting hand over hers.

'He's tall too,' said Charter. 'It's not impossible. I'll have to have a word with him.'

'Not here,' said Sara firmly. 'Please not here. We're on good terms with them all. I really would prefer—'

'Did he see you looking at him?' asked Charter sharply of Harriet.

'No, I'm sure he didn't,' she said. 'It was only as he turned away that I remembered. It's the way he moves, so silently.'

'I'll get him interviewed at the Kennels. Don't worry, Mrs Hardcastle. And now, having consumed your very good coffee, which has given me fresh heart, I must address a few questions to Miss Lincoln.'

'I'll go,' said Sara. 'I'll be out in the tack room if anyone wants me.'

She wandered out to the stableyard with a wave.

'Now, Miss Lincoln,' Charter began, 'I have to ask this question, purely, I assure you, as a matter of routine. Did you yourself have any reason to murder the Master? Anyone who finds the body, you see, immediately comes under suspicion unless we can, as I know we can in this case, clear them.'

'No, Mr Charter, I didn't have any motive and I didn't murder him. I first met him at that lunch at Hangholt.'

'Good. I knew all that. One more question. When you fell into the sound of the thundering hooves, do you think they were more than just Atalanta plunging about and taking off? Could someone have approached you on horse-back?'

'And let one horse he was leading go, so that I heard that one thundering past me as well as Atalanta? Well, I don't mind telling you, I've been turning that over in my mind and the last thing I would be likely to do until all this is over is to consult Donald Cresswell about my health or anything else. I wouldn't care to be alone with him, though I can't imagine why he should do such a thing.'

'People are often both clever and irrational and murderers more irrational than most. He might just be stark raving mad.'

'No. That's cheating. So could Hartley Godwin, or Roger Pratt, or any of us be stark staring mad.'

'It's not a game,' he said grimly. 'I mean it, Harriet. Watch yourself. That policeman on the door is there because one attempt has already been made on your life. I don't in fact believe that he meant to kill you, but I'm not prepared to take a chance on it. And especially now you've identified Tom Stringer as having been near you in the woods.'

'Yes,' she said. 'Yes, I will. Thank you.'

'So it was Tom Stringer who attacked the girl,' said the rural sergeant.

'I doubt it,' said Charter. 'But he almost certainly saw something. What interests me is why he won't say.'

'He's a funny chap, sir.'

'I'll have a talk with him as soon as I get back from Ireland.'

'From Ireland, sir?'

'Unless the O'Flahertys are coming over for the service I'm going over to have a word with them.'

'You still suspect Mrs Siobhan Hardcastle, sir?'

'I do, Sergeant.'

He telephoned Siobhan from the White Hart to ask whether her parents would be coming over.

'No, they're not,' she said. 'They never leave Monahoe. My father won't leave anyone in charge of the horses. And anyway, I'm sending Eithne back home to them tomorrow. Why should she go through another peepshow? It'll be just like the inquest only worse.'

'I think you are wise. You need permission from the police for anyone connected with a murder case to leave the country but I think in this case we can stretch a point. As long as she understands that she must stay at Monahoe and make herself available for questioning whenever we need her. What time is she flying?'

'The midday flight. You don't need to talk to her, do you?'

'I may talk to her in Ireland, but we'll leave her in peace for the time being.'

Hanging up, he dialled the police station and had himself booked on the same flight, feeling slightly guilty, but fairly sure that if he had confessed to Siobhan that he planned to travel with her young sister she would immediately have cancelled Eithne's flight.

At an early hour he arrived at the front door of the Manor in a police car. Maggie came to the door looking flustered.

'Good morning,' he said with a guileless smile. 'It seems that Mrs O'Dowd is booked on the same flight as I am so I thought it might help if I gave her a lift to the airport.'

'Why, how kind of you,' she said with a pleased smile. 'I'm sure she'll be very glad to be looked after on the flight.'

Siobhan came out in a filmy white dressing-gown looking astonished and affronted and even suspicious, holding Dandy by the hand.

Wrapped in her dark purple coat, with a long black scarf wrapped round her shoulders and over her head, Eithne looked the epitome of Greek tragedy as she embraced Maggie and Siobhan and Dandy and got into the car.

'If you're going to Monahoe,' said Siobhan, 'you'll be giving my parents a shock. They don't know about Charles yet. Eithne is to break it to them.'

'Perhaps it would be better if I spared her that and told them myself?' he suggested.

'No doubt you'll do as you please,' said Siobhan, and she

turned and went into the house. As the car drew away
Dandy burst into tears and Maggie picked him up and
cuddled him and stood there waving his hand to them until
they were out of sight.

CHAPTER 16

Eithne was still white as a sheet when she got on to the
plane at Heathrow with Charter. He behaved to her like a
father, protective, patient, firm. He was frankly worried
about her. Her hands were trembling, her eyes dark-ringed
and wide with strain. She was, after all, only nineteen,
widow or not, and he had seen this sort of collapse before.
Something was troubling her beyond her memories.

He bought her magazines to read but she smiled and
shook her head.

'I thought you liked them,' he said. 'I noticed a lot of
them in your sister's room.'

'Siobhan and I are different people,' said Eithne. 'You
see how I dress. I don't look at pictures of fashion plates.
I'll never wear fashionable clothes. Patrick didn't like
women like that.'

'And Charles did?'

'Charles did.'

'And you and Siobhan do whatever your husbands want?'

'Yes. Of course.'

'I suppose you learned that from the nuns too?'

'I suppose we did.'

'It does seem a little odd to me that you are coming home
to your parents.'

'Who else should I go to?'

'Well, I thought you were engaged to Dr Cresswell.'

She turned her head away.

'I'm sorry,' he said. 'I didn't mean to upset you.'

'Donald is busy closing down his practice. He'll come
over later. Besides, it wasn't me who wanted to come.

Everybody seemed to want me out of the way. It was Donald said I should go. And Siobhan. And then you came with the car. What could I do?'

'My dear girl, you fainted at the inquest. They were all worried about you. This has been a shock, worse for you than for others, because it must have reminded you. Everyone wanted to spare you.'

'I never faint. It was the heat in there. I'm not such a fool as you think. I'm really not feeble. After I've seen my mother and father I may come back.'

'You know, you do puzzle me a bit. Now that Charles Hardcastle is gone you can all do as you wish. You ought to be happy for Siobhan and Dandy and Donald Cresswell and yourself. What's the matter?'

'Nothing,' she said, turning away again.

'Well, I hope it is nothing,' he said. 'If you know anything I ought to know you really ought to tell me. Once a murder has taken place you can't safely protect people. Someone who has committed murder has gone over the edge. Murder comes much more easily once you've taken the plunge. It's frightening. I've seen it. Anyone who hides anything has to be prepared for a dreadful responsibility.'

She shook her head from side to side and he patted her hand reassuringly.

'Think about it later,' he said. 'Worry never did anyone any good. If, when you've had time to think things out, you decide that you have something to say to me, you can telephone me at the police station in Stumpington. You can leave a message for me there and if you like I can phone you at Monahoe.'

'You're very kind,' she said, and slept for the rest of the flight. He wakened her as they taxied to a halt. They took a train to Wexlow and a taxi up to Monahoe by way of Monahoe village.

'I want to see your parents alone,' said Charter. 'Is there anywhere in the village where you'd like to stop for a while?'

Eithne was sitting up eagerly and looking about her. Some colour had stolen into her cheeks and now she smiled.

'Stop at the pub over there,' she said. 'I'll go in to Mrs Flynn.'

'I'll tell her you're here.' He got out of the car and tapped at the door of the rather dingy-looking house which, surprisingly, had a shop front displaying not bottles but groceries.

A large plump woman with her plentiful silver hair in a bun came to the door, shedding a voluminous pinafore. When he told her his errand, she broke into smiles of delight.

'Of course I'll look after her, the darling,' she said. 'Where is she? Come on out of there, my poppet. You'll stop with me till your father and Mrs O'Flaherty come down after you.' She put her arms around Eithne as she got out of the car. Eithne was beaming.

'Goodbye, Mrs O'Dowd,' said Charter. 'You're in good hands now.'

She turned back to him. 'I've been in good hands all the way,' she said. 'You couldn't have been kinder. Thank you. And I might be phoning you at Stumpington.'

The taxi-driver drove on and the two women stood and waved after them until they were out of sight. Charter found this strangely touching.

The taxi-driver was garrulous.

'Going up to visit Monahoe are you, sir? Lovely place he's got up there on the mountain, looking right down over the green hills to the sea. And lovely daughters he's got. Have you seen them at all? The one's in England and—'

'Yes, I've seen them. Both beautiful girls.'

'They grew up like tinkers' children. Never played with any but the O'Briens.' He pointed ahead and to the right where, some distance away, a plume of smoke rose above trees.

'They never had their noses out of a book all the same. You'd see them walking about barefoot and they'd be reading as they walked along. Of course they went away to the nuns. It was the sisters gave them their education. If ever they were away it was either to the nuns or with their father to the bloodstock sales at Dublin. And he'd buy them each

an outfit to go to Dublin. You never saw the one of them in
a decent frock except they were going to Dublin to the sales.
The horses at Monahoe are housed like lords—nothing but
the best for the livestock—but if ever those girls ate anything
but bacon and cabbage I'd be surprised. They let the girls
sell the hens' eggs and they'd sometimes buy themselves a
few bits and pieces with the proceeds. Then the great English
man of business comes over buying horses and that lovely
bit of a girl she ups and marries him and away off with him
back to England. Sad. Sad for the other too. No sooner
married to the jockey than the lad has an unlucky fall.
Wasn't it her came with you off the train?'

'It was. You saw her go in to Mrs Flynn at the public
house. The family will send down for her later on.'

'They won't do that, sir. They'll come down in the car.'

They drove through the park gates which were standing
open looking as if they were unlikely ever to close again
since each was drunkenly off its hinges. Along a rutted drive
through roughly fenced grassland sweeping away downhill
on either side. On one side of the drive two donkeys were
standing. On the other side some brood mares were grazing
with their foals at foot.

On to a wide gravel sweep misted over with grass in front
of a crumbling flight of steps up to a vast pillared entrance.
The pale gold of the stone was stained with years of rain-
water from leaking gutters. Some of the panes in the Georgian windows were cracked.

'Please wait,' he told the driver. 'I shouldn't be more than
an hour, if that.' He walked up the steps past the cracked
stone urns and rang the bell. The door opened almost
simultaneously and a tall man with curly silver hair came
out carrying a bucket filled with grain in each hand, saw
him and said, 'Hello, there! Whoever you may be! You're
welcome. I'll be back in a minute. It's time for the hens. Go
on in.' Two labradors came bounding down the steps after
him as he got into a battered old Aston Martin sports car.
The dogs raced after him as he drove on to the grass and
away down the field to where a range of equally battered

hen houses could be seen at the bottom of the slope. Wondering how he would coax the car up the slope again, Charter turned and went into the house. There was no one about. He looked round the circular hall with its flight of stone steps that parted halfway up to the next floor to become two graceful flights curving away from each other to join the curved landing above. He looked into a large drawing-room lit by a row of tall windows through which could be seen distant blue mountains. Two buckets stood under projecting bays to catch the drops from the ceilings whose discolouration showed where the rain came in. Several rather grand portraits hung on the pale-rose-brocaded walls.

Behind the stairway was the green baize door, much the worse for wear, beyond which a stone passage led into the enormous kitchens. Warmth and good cooking-smells came out to meet him as he opened the door. A wooden chopping-block was laden with fresh vegetables. Shining pots and pans were stacked haphazard on an old-fashioned pan rack. Several decanters stood on a dresser. The scrubbed deal table was strewn with newspapers, books and knitting and two pairs of reading glasses lay side by side. The dresser shelves were filled with pots and dishes and books. A skinny dark girl in a huge white apron was sitting at the table sifting flour into a large mixing bowl. At the vast cooking range stood a small woman in a similar huge apron, stirring a thick rich stew in a cast-iron pan. Dark hair flecked with grey fell straight and lank over a high forehead, dark brows, hollow cheeks. She looked up.

'Excuse me, ma'am,' said Charter, looking into Eithne's eyes, 'I am a police officer from England. I would be glad of a few words with you and your husband. I met him at the door and he told me to go on in.'

A look of cold resentment came over her face, wiping out the dawning smile of welcome.

'We have nothing whatever to do with the Provos,' she said, 'and we have absolutely nothing to say to a British police officer.'

'It's not connected with the IRA,' said Charter.

Only then did a look of fear come over her face.

'Is it the girls?' she asked quickly. 'It's not the girls or Dandy?'

'No, it's not the girls or Dandy,' he told her quickly and reassuringly. 'I'm afraid it's your son-in-law.'

A look of great relief was followed by a sudden joyful realization, immediately quenched. She turned away and took off her apron.

'You had better come into the drawing-room and tell us about it. My husband will be here in a moment. I won't be long, Rosie dear. Just finish the pastry and then you can cut up the apples.'

She led him to the drawing-room and motioned him to sit on an ottoman. She sat down opposite him, very upright in a rosewood chair. She pushed her hair back behind her ears. Then a smile of great pleasure and affection came over her face as her husband came in. He came towards Charter with his hand held out, smiling with enormous charm which appeared to be quite spontaneous.

'Welcome to Monahoe,' he said. 'I'm sorry you got such a cavalier welcome. Livestock dictates life style, I'm afraid. I'm Brodrick O'Flaherty and this is my wife, Rose. Is it a horse you're after?'

'No, Brody,' said Rose. 'This man is come over from England. He's an English policeman and it's Charles.'

All the welcome died and Brody's eyes became stony. Charter felt some regret. He would have liked to be asked into that warm kitchen and given a glass of wine and then perhaps invited to share the delectable-smelling stew. He felt sure that Rosie would sit at table with them and that the taxi-driver would be bidden to come in and join them. It was a pity.

'What is it, then?' asked Brody.

'I have bad news for you,' he said. 'I have your daughter's permission to break it to you. Her husband fell from his horse out hunting last Saturday and he is dead.'

Rose gasped and put her hands over her mouth. Brody's eyes narrowed on Charter, who got an impression of some hurried rearrangement of ideas, some urgent calculation. From that moment he was convinced that there had been a plot and that Siobhan was implicated in it. Something had not gone according to plan, but that there was a plan he was quite sure. The news did not hurt them but it interfered with, or changed, some arrangement or expectation. Perhaps it was the timing that was not in order. Perhaps he had died too soon.

Brody said, 'Why weren't we told at once?'

'Your daughter thought it would do no good. She told me you were not fond of your son-in-law.'

'That's true,' said Brody bitterly. 'A man older than I am.'

'Eithne will be a help to her,' said Rose. 'I'm glad Eithne is with her.'

'She isn't,' said Charter. 'I brought Eithne with me.'

Rose jumped up. 'Where is she, then? Have you left her outside?'

'No,' said Charter. 'She's at Mrs Flynn's in the village. Mrs Flynn is looking after her until you go to fetch her. She was distressed by the similarity between Charles Hardcastle's death and that of her husband. Her sister thought she would be better with you and I decided to come on ahead and tell you what had happened to spare her more distress.'

'Then Siobhan will be here within the week?' asked Rose.

'I'm afraid it may not be as soon as that,' said Charter. 'You see, there is a possibility that Mr Hardcastle may not have died naturally. Until our investigation is completed no one connected with Charles Hardcastle may leave the country. Even Eithne will be expected to stop here and hold herself in readiness in case we need to talk to her again.'

'She should have brought Dandy,' said Rose. 'Eithne is much better with Dandy. Siobhan will have too much to think of. The child will be neglected.'

She stood up. 'I must go to Siobhan and Dandy.'

Brody went to her and, putting his hands on her shoulders, he made her sink back on to her chair.

'You are going nowhere,' he said. 'They have all their friends, and Rodney and Sara, and Donald Cresswell. Do you think they won't all look after Siobhan? Anyway, you know that Siobhan is quite well able to look after herself. Eithne will be needing you more.' He turned to Charter. 'Eithne is a brave girl, but this is too much. It's only a year since young Patrick was killed.' He turned back to Rose. 'Siobhan will soon be home and then we'll have the three of them, Eithne, Dandy, and Siobhan.'

They looked at each other and smiled with delight at the idea.

'Before I go, sir, there are a few questions I have to ask you.'

'As you wish,' said Brody.

'I believe your daughter intended to leave her husband and come back to Ireland before this accident?' said Charter.

'She did.'

'And was that agreeable to Mr Hardcastle?'

'Agreeable or not,' said Brody, 'she intended to come and would have come.'

'Would Mr Hardcastle have agreed to that?'

'He couldn't very well have stopped her.'

'But he was going to change his will. The trust for young Dandy was, luckily for him and for your daughter, irreversible. But there would have been no provision for his mother.'

'My daughter wanted none,' said Brody grandly.

'But now that her husband is dead she will get a very large provision.'

'It is immaterial to her.'

'Then she is a very extraordinary young woman.'

'Yes, she is that,' said Brody. 'But where she's going she'll have no use for large sums of money.'

'It is true, then, that she is going into a convent?'

'Yes, I'm sorry to say it.'

'Then perhaps she plans to give you some of the money? Perhaps that would be a consideration with her.' His eyes went to the buckets.

'I'd rather see this place in ruins around me,' said Brody magnificently, 'than patch it up with that barbarian's money.'

'It seems surprising that she should consider leaving her son. Mr Hardcastle would surely have got custody of the boy.'

'He'd never get it. A child goes with the mother.'

'Even if she goes into a convent?'

'Eithne and her doctor are to look after him. Siobhan will see him every day. They are moving to Wexlow to be near the convent. Dr Cresswell is buying a practice there. The chances are that Dandy would spend his time between the two parents.'

'But now that won't be necessary. Dandy can stay here full time.'

'My daughter would not kill for any reason. And if she were able to kill it would not be for any motive connected with Dandy. She is a good girl, a brave girl, with many splendid qualities, but she isn't a maternal girl. Would she be joining the nuns if she were? We've been worried that Dandy was left too much in the hands of the servants. Charles Hardcastle paid no attention to Dandy either. They would have sorted it out one way or another. Don't forget that Dandy is not the heir. Charles has a son by his first marriage. It's he will inherit Hangholt and the business. In any case, killing isn't in Siobhan's stars. She and Eithne are gentle girls. They won't even hunt, which is sheer sentimentalism taught them by one of the sisters.'

'They are strong-minded, though,' said Charter, 'even if gentle. To refuse to hunt in these circumstances with a father who owns hunters and deals in bloodstock needs some strength of mind.'

'I would be sorry to have a daughter devoid of strength of mind,' Brody replied. 'But strength of mind is a different thing from violence.'

'Well, I think that is all for now. Perhaps, just as a matter of routine, you would give me the address of the nuns.'

Rose went to a desk and brought out a letter which she

handed to Charter. It was addressed to Mrs Rose O'Flaherty
by the Reverend Mother of St Mary's Convent near Wexlow
and it confirmed that Mrs Siobhan Hardcastle was invited to
spend three months at the convent from the following July for
the purpose of exploring the possibility that she might have a
vocation to enter the novitiate at some later date. The writer
made it clear that there could be no promise of automatic
entry. The circumstances were sad and somewhat unusual.
It was all in the hands of God.

'Thank you,' he said. 'That does answer my question.
And now I had better be going. I have a plane to catch. My
taxi is outside.'

'What?' said Rose. 'Has he been sitting out there in the
cold all this time?'

She went out of the room and Charter heard her calling:
'Rosie dear, will you go out to the man in the taxi, I think
it must be Seamus, and take him a cup of strong tea and
the sugar bowl? Hurry on out, there's a good girl.'

She came back into the room and stood by the door.

'If you want to wash, it's on the first floor at the end of
the passage on the right.'

'Thank you.' He made to go.

Brody said, 'Pull down hard once and don't leave go. It
should work quite easily this time since no one's been up
there for a while.'

No tea was offered him when he came down and they
bade him goodbye unsmiling. Neither offered him a hand.
He ran down the steps and got into the taxi.

'The airport. As fast as you can.'

'The airport is it?' said Seamus mildly. 'That's a long
way. But don't you be minding me. I'll get you there.'

As they drove away Charter saw Brody and Rose come
out and get into the Aston Martin, no doubt on their way
to collect Eithne.

'Well,' he said to Seamus, 'you were lucky to get a cup
of tea.'

'You'd hardly expect any different, would you now?' said
Seamus comfortably. 'An English policeman and a Black

and Tan (you'll know what a Black and Tan was, from the
time of the Troubles), they'd be as like as two peas in a pod
to Brody O'Flaherty. He wouldn't forget what they did to
his father. It was the Black and Tans gave Thady O'Flaherty
his lame leg. He had to cut and run for America. Mind you,
it was there he made the grand fortune he used to buy
the house and lands at Monahoe. But a son of Thaddeus
O'Flaherty won't ever love the English.'

'Is he IRA, then?'

'He is not. Mind you, he might not be all that far from
the Provos in his way of thinking on politics but Brody
O'Flaherty wouldn't hurt a living soul.'

CHAPTER 17

Charter arrived back in England on the first plane on
Thursday morning and Sergeant Cobbold picked him up at
the airport and drove him to Hangholt Church for the
memorial service.

'Now, Sergeant,' he said, 'I want you to look out for Mrs
Hyde at the church. She'll want to be there, but if she thinks
the word has got about on who slept up at the Kennels, she
won't be. We've got to trace her. She may have something
for us about the last night before the hunt. Come to think
of it, we'd look right fools if it was her all along.'

'I've thought about that, sir, and I don't know how we
could ever be sure it isn't. With the run of the Kennels'
cottage she could have monkeyed about at will with tablets
and hunting flasks and, as nobody was aware she went
there, who would ever have known? She wasn't to know
he'd blow her cover by leaving her all that money openly
in his will.'

'We'll look silly if she's fled the country.' But Charter
didn't look at all worried.

They stood at the back of the little Norman church
which was filled to overflowing, a disillusioning spectacle

for those who knew how little Charles Hardcastle was mourned.

Antonia Hyde was not there.

In the small walled churchyard tucked into a small plateau on the slope, a cold wind whipped down from the hill as the family came out of the church. The crowds of onlookers, cameramen, reporters and acquaintances stared them out of countenance.

Towering over Siobhan protectively, Rodney took her arm and led her to the car. Maggie hurried forward to join her.

Charter happened to be looking at Donald Cresswell at that moment and, watching him then, he knew with blinding certainty that the man was dying for love of Siobhan. He couldn't keep his eyes off her and he couldn't hide the hunger in them. It was all he could do to stop himself from going to her. Charter could almost feel the antagonism in him. He couldn't endure another man's arm supporting her, another man's voice soothing her, another man standing between her and the crowds lining the path, eyeing her curiously, murmuring angrily, hating her.

Donald Cresswell turned away and, as he turned, his eyes met those of John Charter and fastened on them in palpable shock. Charter looked at him composedly and raised a hand in greeting, but there was no doubt in his mind that Cresswell had betrayed himself—and knew it. Engaged to Eithne or not, it was Siobhan he loved.

The funeral baked meats were eaten at Hangholt Farm in the absence of the widow. Afterwards the family gathered at the Manor for the reading of the will.

Roger Pratt was looking out for Charter and as soon as he walked into the room he took his arm and led him out into the hall.

'I hoped you'd come,' he said. 'That information I gave you about the will was wrong. I gave it to you in good faith but in going through the file I've found an envelope he deposited here without revealing what was in it. It turns out to be a codicil to the will I drew up for him. Properly witnessed. Perfectly legal.'

'Dated?'

'Eighteen months ago.'

'And?'

'It more or less cuts Siobhan out. She gets fifty thousand pounds. Exactly the same as Antonia Hyde.'

'My God! Then there was no motive for her!'

'I don't think she was ever told. She has certainly seemed to me to have been under the impression that she would inherit largely. I'll go ahead now. I felt I should tell you that you'd been wrongly informed.'

'Thank you.'

To Roger Pratt's great relief Siobhan flatly refused to attend the reading of the will. When the clause bequeathing to the widow no more than £50,000 was read out there was a great gasp from everybody assembled in the room. An even greater gasp came after the reading of the bequest to Antonia Hyde. Wild surmises were soon running like wild-fire from Hangholt to Stumpington, to Penchester, and even, a little later, to London.

Charter ran upstairs as soon as the will was read. Maggie followed him, protesting angrily, and rushed ahead of him to burst into Siobhan's sitting-room and warn her of his approach. Charter walked straight in after her and found Siobhan lying on her stomach in front of the fire reading a magazine with her heels waving in the air. She had changed into jeans and shirt. Charter couldn't be sure, but he got the impression that she snatched her thumb out of her mouth as he came in.

She rolled over and sat up. 'It's all right, Maggie,' she said. 'It's all right.'

Maggie had tears in her eyes. 'It's not fair,' she said. 'He's coming to tell you—he wants to see how you'll take it—it's cruel!'

'Please go at once,' said Charter and, looking at him, Maggie went, shutting the door behind her.

'Well, what is it?' asked Siobhan, sitting cross-legged on

the rug and waving him to a chair. 'Is it to do with the will?'

'Did you know the provisions of the will?'

'Not exactly, but I knew he meant to give me whatever wasn't already tied up for Rodney and Dandy.'

'Well, he hasn't. No one knew it, not even Roger Pratt, but eighteen months ago he changed his will. All you get is fifty thousand pounds.'

She looked at him and said nothing.

'Well, doesn't that surprise you?'

'No. He did what he wanted to do with his money. It was his money not mine.'

'Aren't you angry? Disappointed?'

'Why should I be? Fifty thousand pounds is a lot of money. I've never had so much money in all my life. And all for me. I can do what I like with it.' She was smiling.

He looked at her, perplexed, and remembered what Roger Pratt had said: 'She doesn't understand ordinary common arrangements about money.'

'I hope you won't do that,' he said. 'It's not all that much. You ought to invest it. But that's not my business. I'm sure there'll be plenty of people to advise you about investments. Perhaps the Reverend Mother of your convent.'

He was beginning to understand why Maggie felt she must protect Siobhan and Eithne. He himself was beginning to feel rather like an exasperated uncle. He was strangely reluctant to go on but he said, 'Did you know that your husband left a large sum of money to Mrs Antonia Hyde?'

'Did he?' This time she looked stunned.

'I'm afraid he did. Fifty thousand pounds.'

She shook her head and was silent.

'Why do you think he did that? Were they related?'

She looked up at him quite calmly. 'I suppose she must have been his mistress,' she said. 'I didn't know he had one. I thought he only cared about his business and the Hunt. I'm not going to think about it. It doesn't matter.' Then she flushed suddenly. 'It was a horrible thing to do!' she said. 'To give her the same as me! You can guess what they're all saying down there. But I knew he was cruel.'

'Well, thank you,' he said, getting up. 'I'll leave you now. Shall I call your housekeeper to you?'

'No,' she said. 'I'm perfectly all right. When can I go?'

'To Ireland?'

'To Ireland.'

'I don't know, Mrs Hardcastle,' he said. 'I don't know at all.'

He looked at her and was quite unable to judge what sort of woman she was.

Telephone calls to No. 110 High Street still went unanswered and Charter put the Stumpington police on to finding Mrs Hyde as a matter of urgency. For the last few days the Press had tended to concentrate on the local robberies simply because the man in charge was photogenic, articulate, and very ready to talk to them. As they received no encouragement from John Charter they began to run stories about hunt saboteurs annoying the hunt-followers and hunt-followers beating up hunt saboteurs. They hinted that not enough was being done to trace the saboteurs. Those who had attacked Abigail were easily found and brought in for questioning. They were released when they were able to prove that on the day in question, finding discretion the better part of valour, they had adjourned to a pub in Penchester, the Coach and Horses.

Charter decided to seek out the rest of the saboteurs on their own ground.

'I'm going hunting tomorrow, Sergeant,' he said on Friday afternoon.

'Foxhunting, sir?'

'Fox- and hunt-saboteur-hunting.'

'Do you think in the circumstances they'll be out, sir?'

'Perhaps not the ones we're after, but if there are any others about they may give us a line on last Saturday's lot. Besides, I've never hunted before. This will help me to understand what's going on between the solicitor and Hartley Godwin for one thing, and what sort of circumstances could put the Master off alone somewhere in the middle of a hunt, and what Tom Stringer gets up to.'

'Well, good luck, sir. Have you got the gear?'

'It seems that after Cheltenham it's quite acceptable, if not correct, to appear in what's called ratcatcher. I'm just going off to the saddler in the High Street to buy some breeches and a bowler. My old tweed jacket will do quite well but I suppose I must get some rubber riding boots.'

'But you'll need a horse, sir.'

'Mrs Rodney Hardcastle has promised to mount me.'

'You should see some sport, then. They're up on the Hill tomorrow. The end of season hunts tend to be high ones, above the plough. They say the foxes up there are quite a different breed from the Vale foxes. They say they never come down off the Hill. They go like blazes up there in the open and you can see them for miles. It's like a Christmas card, coursing rather than scenting. The horses get a bit lively too, particularly if there's any wind.'

'My mount is said to be a patent safety hunter, large but docile.'

'Well, the best of British luck, sir! I hope it won't be blowing a gale.'

It wasn't, but there was a lively breeze blowing.

A middle-aged woman drove up the narrow lane ahead of him to the farmyard on the hill, where the meet was. She backed her Land-Rover into a barn, got out, and began to set up a table on which she put out glasses and several Thermoses of mulled wine, helped by various foot-followers.

Charter caught sight of Mabel Pratt riding side-saddle on a cobby grey mare and it occurred to him that, if you want to learn something, the best thing to do is to ask someone who is likely to know the answer.

He walked his big chestnut gelding over to her and tipped his bowler.

'Good morning, ma'am.'

'Good morning, Mr Charter.'

'Can you please explain to me, Mrs Pratt, why your husband feels so strongly about Mr Hartley Godwin, and whether this could have given rise to problems within the

Hunt which might have a bearing on the Master's death?'

'Come with me,' she said, and they walked their horses away along a path at the edge of a ploughed field. To the right was an old stone rectory, it's sheltered garden full of narcissus tossing their heads in the long grass, glossy dark green leaves and deep pink flowers of japonica against a wall, and a tiny pure white magnolia stellata on a bank. Birds were singing, the sun poured light.

'It was all Charles, making mischief,' she explained. 'Roger has always been very liberal and not in the least prejudiced. Charles was a right old diehard. For some reason Hartley Godwin completely won him over. Roger was very suspicious of Hartley. He was convinced that he must have Mafia connections. Charles enjoyed manœuvring Roger into the position of being the fuddy-duddy diehard and that made Roger even more determined not to be won over for the wrong sort of reason. But when you meet Hartley you'll find he is very level-headed, knows exactly what he wants and will effortlessly achieve it. If you watch them both today I think you'll find that the whole situation between them has changed. Watch them together. No, I won't say any more. Just watch.'

As they walked back to the meet they found a small field gathering round the Huntsman and the pack. Roger was Acting Master. Hartley Godwin, looking magnificent in his scarlet coat, mounted on a chestnut hunter that, without being in the least showy, would undoubtedly have been placed in any county show, was Field Master for the day. Among the onlookers were several cameramen and reporters.

Foot-followers and mounted followers were waving to each other, kissing, swooping on children and giving them great bear hugs. A beaming Peter Thorn was holding someone's two-year-old child on the saddle in front of him and she was gurgling with delight. Charter thought of Charles Hardcastle with some sympathy. If the poor chap could have seen what was going on he might have felt it rather a poor show just a fortnight after his death.

Having taken their pictures and got their copy, the Press began to leave. Slogging on foot after the field was an experience they would forgo. Charter was wearing his bowler tipped well forward and not a single pressman recognized him.

Jim Caudle blew his horn and the pack streamed off out of the farmyard. Their way took them uphill until the lane they were following opened up on to the wide sloping upland covered with ancient turf. They trotted several hundred yards and put hounds into a spinney between two slopes, sheltered from the wind. Mabel had disappeared so he must wait for a suitable moment to ask her what had, within the space of a few days, brought about the change in Roger Pratt and Hartley Godwin. As they trotted slowly up the lane together they were deep in conversation and apparently on terms of almost brotherly affection. Several times they broke into laughter at each other's remarks and when Roger finally left Hartley to control the field while he cantered on with hounds and Huntsman, he raised a hand in farewell and went on, smiling broadly, apparently very well pleased with himself.

Charter concentrated on getting on good terms with his chestnut and found himself perfectly capable of handling him in the headlong canters and sudden turns and pauses that ensued. He was even able to keep his eyes open for any saboteurs which might be dotted about the landscape. None turned up on this day except one, and he made himself known by shouting at the Huntsman as he approached a formidable-looking oxer. In a dark green peaked cap, a somewhat tattered blue anorak, and jeans which looked as if they had grown on him, he stood beside the jump brandishing a stick and calling out, 'I hope you fall and break your bloody neck!'

The Huntsman sailed over the jump, quite unaware of this charitable injunction. But John Charter, following him, riding an unfamiliar horse, concentrating partly on the jump ahead and partly on the pugnacious young man, made a mess of the jump. They cleared it with difficulty, the chestnut pecked on landing and Charter went over his head.

As he was gathering himself together, Charter was surprised and affronted at receiving a great blow from the stick wielded by the young man in the peaked cap. The blow fell across his shoulders and hurt him very much. So did a second on his upper arm. Then he was up and moving and in two seconds flat the young man, open-mouthed, was on his back and winded, and the stick broken in two by the judicious application of force from Charter's hunting boot.

Harriet came cantering back, leading Charter's horse. He hesitated, wanting to haul in the boy, but Harriet handed him the reins firmly, impatient to catch up with the hunt. Charter remounted and cantered on beside her as the boy ran away and disappeared into a copse beyond the jump.

'Are you all right?' asked Harriet anxiously, and he smiled at her.

'Absolutely,' he answered, 'I'd better be. Young idiot. He'll learn not to vent his wrath against the foxhunting community on the body of a policeman. Don't be surprised if I hand you the reins and leap off in pursuit of that young man when we next catch sight of him. I want him for questioning.'

They were galloping neck and neck together along the ridge of the hill, the wind making fleeting silver shadows on the grass, the sun warm on their hands and faces. A skylark hung in the high clear air pouring out its song. Far away in the Vale they could see the towers and curtain-walls and battlements of Penfold Castle, white in the blue distance at the edge of its reedy lake. Then they were in the midst of the mounted field. A few minutes later Charter spurred his horse after Mabel Pratt's springy-actioned cob.

'Found you.' he said. 'Nice animal.'

'Surprising, isn't it?' she said, smiling. 'She's of unknown breeding and not a great looker. That's why everyone's startled at seeing what a lovely performer she is.'

'Now,' he said imploringly, 'dear, delightful Mrs Pratt, we are no longer policeman and murder suspect. I do beg of you, as one inquisitive hunting person to what I take to be another: what has brought about this sudden extraordinary *rapprochement* between your husband and Hartley Godwin?'

She threw back her head and laughed and Charter was wholly charmed.

'It was the most exquisite piece of tact on the part of Hartley Godwin,' she explained. 'Would you believe it? He managed it with one long-drawn-out lunch at the Connaught. Roger had to go up to London on Wednesday and Hartley said he wanted to discuss some lobbying he's doing for the Field Sports Society and invited him to lunch. Roger went rather reluctantly but they sorted everything out. Hartley told him he's perfectly happy to go on under Rodney and Roger. The farthest thing from his mind was the ambition to make it a triumvirate. He totally reassured Roger about his background which, it seems, was showbiz two generations ago. (Have you ever heard of Harry Godwin? I can't say that I had.) This provided the wherewithal for publishing ventures by Hartley's father, who made millions and then diversified into liquor and other things and made billions. He paid for Hartley to read law at Oxford and eat his dinners and all the rest of it. Hartley knows everyone and we're dining with him in London with the American Ambassador (who is a friend of his father's) and one or two legal people Roger is charmed to meet. It was a *tour de force*. Hartley defers to Roger in the most tactful way. Now, watch out! We're going down to the river and I reckon we might be fording it down there if it isn't in flood.'

The fox they were after seemed unaware of the widespread belief that the Hill foxes stay on the Hill and never descend into the Vale. It led them inexorably downwards to the brooks where the River Pen was foaming and frothing over rocks.

'It may be too deep already,' said Mabel. 'But if we do wade across, don't forget to kick your animal on hard. Some of them sometimes take it into their heads to lie down in the water, which is humiliating for the rider.'

'And wet.'

'Exactly.'

They slithered down a steepish, muddy path and joined the riders and the pack waiting beside the river. The Huntsman was conferring with Roger and Hartley, then he turned and trotted away with hounds, and Roger waved the field on after him.

'It's too deep,' said Mabel. 'They'll go on, to the bridge. We'll lose the fox but it can't be helped. Come on.'

A strange, wailing shout startled those left within earshot and was succeeded by a splash from somewhere upstream.

'What's that?' said Mabel, halting and turning her head.

'Someone in the river,' said Charter, and urged his horse on down to the water's edge, followed by Mabel. Some of the foot-followers had gathered on the opposite bank near Tom Stringer's Land-Rover. Having handed his terriers to one of the group he was getting a rope out of the Land-Rover. One old countryman was already wellington-deep in the water, stretching out a long stick vainly for the victim to catch on to. A green peaked cap came floating down the stream.

'It's that boy who shouted at Jim!' said Mabel, taking the reins as Charter flung himself off his horse. 'To me!' he shouted to Tom.

The rope came hurtling over, attached to a piece of wood. Charter caught it and several of the field came to his help as the weakly-splashing, gasping youth came floating fast down the river, spinning round in circles.

'His boots'll have filled,' said one of the foot-followers with a mixture of anxiety lest the boy should drown and satisfaction at his having got himself into difficulties.

The boy managed to grab the rope with one hand and, with a struggle, got his other hand up to join it. Hanging on, knuckles white, he started pulling himself hand over hand towards the bank. Charter noticed that he looked first towards the foot-followers' side, which was nearer, and chose to deliver himself into the hands of the mounted followers, an unfortunate decision as the Land-Rover was on the other side. They all started shouting, 'The other way! The other way!' and pointing to the other bank. He stopped and hung there, gasping, in the middle.

With great aplomb, Tom Stringer handed the end of the rope to his friends and, grasping the taut rope with both hands, lowered himself into the water. He pulled himself out to the boy, grabbed him by the jersey and dragged him slowly to the shore, hand over hand, with great effort. Everybody cheered as they stumbled out and up the opposite bank, their arms round each other.

From there on the foot-followers took over, putting them both into the Land-Rover and driving them off to where they could be dried and warmed and given hot drinks laced with brandy.

Before they got into the Land-Rover Charter put his hands up to his mouth, trumpetwise, and shouted, 'Tom Stringer! Get that man's name and address and tell Derek Cobbold to hold him!' The dripping Tom turned to look back, puzzled, then caught on and waved reassuringly. 'I'll do that, sir!' he called.

The mounted followers got on their horses again and moved off. Charter tipped his bowler to Mabel. 'That's my quarry,' he said. 'I'm afraid I've got to go.'

'I'll come with you,' she said. 'We'll go back to the farmyard where the meet was and I'll see to loading.'

'You'll miss the hunt.'

'Who cares for that? I'm assisting the police. We do want to get this over and done with.'

'We're doing our best,' he said.

'How soon?'

'Can't tell. I think I've picked him out on the horizon, but I've got to wait until I see the whites of his eyes.'

CHAPTER 18

When Charter got to the police station at Stumpington he found Cobbold, who had just arrived in search of him, but no prisoner waiting to be interrogated. The rural sergeant had heard nothing from Stringer and no message had been telephoned in.

'I'll get over to the Kennels,' said Charter, furious with himself and Tom Stringer and annoyed at having to postpone the long bath and rub-down and the hot toddy he had hoped would not be long delayed.

On the way he recounted his adventures to the sergeant and told him, 'I want this young man in for questioning right away. What do you think Tom Stringer is playing at?'

'Probably interrogating him himself,' said Cobbold comfortably. 'Perhaps he saw him hit the girl. Or perhaps he knows he *didn't* hit the girl because he saw someone else hit her. If that's it, he might let the young man go with a ticking-off. He likes to play God. He'd be fair, too.'

'If that's so, why doesn't he tell us what he saw?'

'Playing God again. Might think he'd tell the chap. Hold it over him.'

'Blackmail?'

'I don't think so. It wouldn't be straightforward blackmail. Not with Tom. He'd like to feel he had a hold over the chap. Especially if it's the doctor—one of the nobs. Highly educated.'

As they drove into the yard by the flesh house Tom Stringer was parking his Land-Rover and unloading spades, swophooks and terriers.

'Oh hello, sir,' he said innocently, but refusing to meet Charter's eye. 'That was a pretty smart bit of work we did over there. I'll just put my Jack Russells away and then I'll be with you.'

'The name and address, Mr Stringer,' said Charter firmly.

'What name and address, sir?'

'The name and address of the hunt saboteur who fell in the river. I asked you to get his name and address and hand him over to Sergeant Cobbold.'

'I'm sorry, sir. We were freezing cold and wet. Mr Hardy took us back to his place and gave us hot baths and hot drinks and Mrs Hardy popped our things in the drier. I telephoned the station but Derek wasn't there.'

'Someone was on duty.'

'You said Derek, sir.'

'Look, Mr Stringer, you're not stupid. Don't pretend that you are. Have you let him go?'

'Couldn't stop him, sir. Once his things were dry he just went. I was in the other room watching the television and waiting for me trousers.'

'And you let him go without taking his name and address.'

'Well, I thought Derek would do that when he got back. I know his first name's Paul.'

'Mr Stringer, I repeat, you are not stupid. I can think of only one reason for your letting that boy go. You don't want us to find out who the Antis were who were in the woods that day. That means you are afraid they might be able to tell us where *you* were when the Master fell and Miss Lincoln was struck down.'

'I've nothing to hide.'

'Supposing I told you that we know you were on the scene shortly after the Master fell?'

'What if I was?'

'Then you are being remarkably and foolishly secretive about it. Did you see anything at all that might be of help to us?'

'I wasn't near enough to see anything.'

'I'm wondering if you weren't near enough to have *done* something.'

Tom shut the door of the Land-Rover and walked past the Superintendent towards the terrier pens, the Jack Russells yapping and jumping up round his legs.

'I've got to put my terriers in their pens,' he said un-graciously.

'I advise you to think very carefully what you are doing, Mr Stringer. It's your duty to cooperate with the police. If you have some ploy of your own, give it up. Hiding infor-mation about a murder case can be dangerous.'

A crackling sound from the car sent the sergeant to talk

to the station. He called Charter on a high, urgent note and Charter sprinted after him, leaving Tom Stringer open-mouthed looking after them, still playing the dim-witted yokel.

'It's Mrs Hardcastle, sir. She's called the station to speak to you. She won't give any message. She says it's very urgent, a matter of life and death, and they say she was crying and shaking so she could hardly speak.'

'Good God. Is this going to be a confession?'

'No, sir, I don't think so. It sounds—well, you can hardly credit it, but the thing that comes to mind is kidnapping. She wants you there at once but not in a police car. She says you're to go in a delivery van so no one will know who you are.'

'Come on! Get there!'

'They're laying on a van for us to pick up outside the Cattleman Pub. Shall we go straight there?'

'Right! Get there fast!'

'This is ridiculous,' he said, after a moment, as the sergeant negotiated the narrow lane at speed. 'You can't have a kidnapping by coincidence slap in the middle of a murder inquiry.'

'Not unless it's a part of the murder inquiry, sir.'

'Why? He couldn't think we'd let it distract us from him, could he? Perhaps they think we're on to them. They know they won't get any of Charles Hardcastle's money. This would be a way of getting the cash out of probate. So much for the non-mercenary lady heading for a nunnery. I always knew it wasn't true.'

But when they drew up in the stableyard beside the Manor and walked to a side door where Siobhan was waiting for them with Maggie at her side he began to wonder. This was a different Siobhan altogether. For the first time he believed she was showing genuine feeling. She looked almost old, her hair unkempt, her face white, with black shadows under the eyes, and a film of moisture over all. She was sweating with fear. It crossed Charter's mind that Dr Cresswell might have doped her into the right frame of mind but the pupils were quite normal and after all one did quite naturally sweat with fear.

She put out a shaking hand and pulled the Superintendent into the house.

'It's Dandy,' she said. 'Someone's got Dandy. They want money. A lot of money. I don't know how to get it. There's something called probate. You must get Roger Pratt. They want it now. You must help me. They said they'd throw him to hounds if I don't pay up.'

Charter took both her hands in his. 'Well, I can tell you now,' he said, 'they won't do that. For one thing, we'll put a guard on at the Kennels at once. Sergeant, find a telephone and arrange that right away! And for another, they don't mean it. Kidnappers always tell the mother that sort of thing to make the parents pay up.'

He gazed into Siobhan's eyes compellingly. 'Now, quietly, quietly, Mrs Hardcastle. Let's go upstairs and sit down. Just tell us what happened and I assure you we'll find him for you.'

She took them up to her sitting-room, running and stumbling. The room was untidy, cold, dismal, last night's ashes still in the grate. She walked towards the window-seat, then swung round. 'No,' she said, 'not near the window. They might see you. They said no police.'

They sat facing each other by the cold hearth.

The sergeant came into the room. 'All arranged, sir,' he said. 'And the chap at the Kennels will be wearing a brown overall. He'll look like one of the Kennels' staff. No one will take him for a policeman.'

'Now,' said Charter. 'Tell me everything from the beginning.'

She ran her hands through her hair, pushing it back behind her ears in a way that reminded him of Rose O'Flaherty in the drawing-room at Monahoe. She clasped her hands together and talked in a trembling voice.

'When I went to his room early this morning everything was all over the place and he was gone. Then I got this phone call saying, "We've got him. You're rich. You'll pay up. We'll let you know." I begged them to let me speak to him but they wouldn't. They said he was all right. So far. But if I didn't get the money he'd be dead. They were considering ways of doing it but the probability was they'd feed him to hounds.' She covered her face with her hands. 'Dandy,' she said, and rocked to and fro.

'Where was his nanny?'

'She left before Charles died. They had a row and she stormed out. Eithne looked after him while she was here. I wish she hadn't gone. I can't manage on my own. I need her.' She was shaking like a leaf.

'Sergeant,' said Charter, 'go and find someone. There's a housekeeper called Maggie. Ask her for some brandy and a glass. Now, Mrs Hardcastle. This is very distressing for you, no question about that. But you don't help Dandy by giving in like this. I'm going to give you some brandy and then I think we must call your doctor.'

'No.'

'Why not? He'll be able to prescribe a sedative.'

'I don't want a sedative. I've got to find Dandy. I must be awake. I don't want Donald Cresswell. I want Eithne. Anyway, Donald's away.'

'Away? Since when?'

'He's gone to some medical meeting.'

'Where?'

'I don't know. Do you think I could care?'

'Shall I telephone your parents in Ireland and ask for Eithne to come back? Though I must tell you that it's better to change nothing in the household until we've got Dandy back. Any change might alarm the kidnappers. We want as little coming and going as possible.'

'Then don't think of telephoning. I'll go to my parents as soon as we find Dandy. We'll get out of this horrible place.'

'They won't hurt him,' said Charter. 'The threats are to frighten you. Why would they hurt a small boy? He's no threat to them. They are probably opportunists who reckon they can get some of your husband's money out of you.'

'I must get it for them. How do I get it?'

'We'll talk to your lawyer and get him to organize it. Now, Mrs Hardcastle, I'm going to get in touch with Scotland Yard and arrange for some officers from our Regional Crime Squad to come and move in to the house to help me to organize the search for Dandy. They'll bring all sorts of sophisticated equipment with them. They'll tap your phone and record all messages. They are very experienced and with their help we'll get Dandy back.'

'But you'll stay?'

'I'll certainly stay until they get here. But after that I may have to leave. You can trust them and if you don't understand what they're up to and want to talk to me, just tell them.'

'I must get the money. They said I'm to bring it to them. They'll let me know when.'

'Then we must wait until they do. But I promise you Dandy's safety will be the only criterion.'

The door opened and Maggie came in and put her arms round Siobhan, rocking her to and fro. She looked angrily at the Superintendent.

'Do as she wants,' she said. 'He's her *child*!'

The sergeant came in with the brandy and Charter said, 'Pour some brandy for Mrs Hardcastle, Sergeant, and get her to sip it slowly. I want a word with Mrs Philpot.'

She followed him out of the room and he said to her, 'You must try to keep her calm. Get rugs, hot-water bottles. Let her lie down. Light the fire. Brandy. Hot broth. Glucose drinks.'

'Right,' she said. 'You can rely on me to see to her. What are you going to do?'

'I'll be here until the Regional Crime Squad officers get here. Don't worry. And don't be alarmed if they come in over the fields. They won't look like police officers and they won't be in a police vehicle.'

She turned away, then swung back to say, 'You may think I treat them both like children but that girl here has had enough. Five years with that dreadful man. And the other poor kid! Losing the husband within a month! Within a month! Life is very unfair to some people!' and she opened the door and went in, closing it behind her very softly as if it was an invalid's room.

Charter went downstairs wondering whether the human warmth and kindness and physical comfort supplied by Maggie could possibly outweigh the cloying encouragement to self-pity which might do more harm than almost any fresh blow fate might deal.

He was busy setting up the organization of the police operation on the kidnapping until late that night. No trace could be found of any engagement at a medical conference for Donald Cresswell. His receptionists said they had no idea where he was. He had done his evening surgery as usual on Friday night and had none on this particular Saturday. Charter considered putting out a general call for him but he had no evidence and he could see no possibility of convincing the Assistant Chief Constable that any such move could be justified.

The search for Antonia Hyde had come up with a telephone number near Bath and it was established that she had left the Hunt early on the previous Saturday and was heading for Bath with her sister by the time the Master fell from his horse. They knew nothing of his death until the next day. Antonia agreed at once to travel home and would be available for questioning next morning.

Charter got to bed at one.

CHAPTER 19

Charter lay in bed considering Donald Cresswell. After a while he got up and turned the light on, walked up and down, put his head out of the window to feel a cool breath on his cheek, hear a dog barking far away, and see dark shadows along the High Street thrown by a bright moon whose cold light almost quenched the reddish glow edging

the silhouettes of the Stumpington night skyline. A church
bell struck two.

He sat down at the desk by the window and concentrated
hard. After a time he took a piece of paper and began to
write.

Four different plots involved in the murder of Charles
Hardcastle and its aftermath.

Two puzzling facts:

1. Siobhan was leaving her husband to go to Ireland
not to a lover, but to a convent. Everyone agreed that she
was not the type to become a nun.

2. Eithne was engaged to Donald Cresswell and
planned to live with him in Ireland next door to the
convent with Siobhan's child, but was surely not in love
with him.

But—third fact: Donald Cresswell was painfully in love
with Siobhan.

Try this: It isn't Eithne who is marrying Donald Cresswell but Siobhan. It isn't Siobhan who is going into the
convent but Eithne. Eithne, who has lost her young husband, who hasn't got over it, and perhaps never will.

This was the first plot, a plot to get Siobhan away from
Charles Hardcastle *with Dandy*. This was the plot in which
Rose and Brody O'Flaherty were involved.

Suppose Eithne tells her parents she is going to the
nuns. They are horrified and send her over to Siobhan,
hoping that Dandy and Siobhan may help to change
her mind. Instead, the two girls invent this plan to get
Siobhan away from her husband.

It is a mad scheme, but it had a chance of success.
Charles would be unlikely to visit the convent and they
could hope that he would not visit Ireland at all without
warning. In any case, he'd had one heart attack already.
By the time Dandy was old enough to interest him,
Charles might well be dead. Dandy would presumably
go to prep school and Eton when the time came, but that
was all far ahead. The chances were that there might be

no trouble at all about custody of Dandy for the next few years. Charles had no time for small children. So the game was worth the candle.

Now if this plot was entirely innocent how would they all react to the news of Charles Hardcastle's death? They ought all to be relieved and delighted, but they quite clearly weren't. Perhaps Rose and Brody were, but they had had no time when I was there to contemplate the possibilities, and the possibility that Charles might have been murdered had not had time to sink in. Eithne was distraught. Why? Charles's death relieved her from the responsibility of lying about who was engaged to be married and who was entering the novitiate. She should have been happy. The same held for Siobhan. Once Charles was dead, the original innocent plot to get Dandy away from him, could be abandoned. But she didn't abandon it. When I interviewed her, less than 24 hours after Charles's death, when it was still generally believed that his death was accidental or caused by the hunt saboteurs, she kept up the pretence that she was going into the convent. Was this to show she could have no mercenary motive for wanting him dead? How did she know that she needed such an 'alibi'? Either she knew he had been murdered or someone else told her he had been murdered. That someone must be Donald Cresswell. True, we did mention the possibility ourselves but I don't think Siobhan is the quick-witted sort of murderess who could work that out and act on it in the middle of an interrogation. She had already decided to stick to the original plot before we ever got there. Could that conceivably be done by an innocent woman? Yes, it could. Donald could have told her it would look funny to the police and be embarrassing in front of their friends. He could have suggested gradually revealing the truth later on. So it's not conclusive that Siobhan was in on that.

Now for the second plot. This was the original slow murder plot, the motive for which was almost certainly money.

Everyone connected with Charles Hardcastle, including Siobhan and his lawyer, believed that she was residual legatee after Rodney and Dandy had received their trust funds. No one could therefore expect to benefit except Siobhan and anyone whom Siobhan intended to marry. If I'm right, then that means Donald Cresswell. Cresswell knew that as soon as Siobhan told Charles she was leaving him Charles would go to see Roger Pratt and change his will, cutting her out. Cresswell had got rather used to thinking of himself and Siobhan as guardians of a child with a huge trust fund to make life easy for him and when Charles had the heart attack he must have realized that there was a good chance for Siobhan to inherit a huge amount if Charles died before he was told that she meant to go. The slight heart attack must have given Cresswell the idea of nudging Charles on a bit by removing the potassium from the mix of heart and blood pressure pills, thus making the new prescription for digitalis a slow killer rather than a life-saver. He hoped Charles would die of apparently natural causes before Siobhan told him anything. In the meantime, Cresswell sold his practice and that in itself would make him feel insecure.

It's unlikely, though not impossible, in view of Siobhan's unsophisticated approach to money matters, that she was in on this original plan. If she *were* in on it she would *not* have told Charles she was going to leave him. It was that premature revelation that forced Donald Cresswell to abandon a slow, subtle murder method for a hasty and ill-judged fast one. This surely indicates that he didn't involve her in the slow one. Did he involve her in the fast one? It's impossible to tell.

So the third plot was the plot to get rid of Charles fast, so that he wouldn't be able to keep the appointment with Roger Pratt to change his will.

Donald Cresswell decided to put an extra dose of digitalis in the hunting flask to speed up the murder plan. He intended to stick close to the MFH throughout the Hunt in case anything happened. Then he would be present and able to remove the flask during his examination of the victim. This was a ridiculous assumption. The murder in mid-hunt, shadowing the MFH in case he fell, was all very risky, and as it happened, when the Master fell, he *had* eluded Cresswell, quite by chance, by suddenly dashing off after the straying hounds. Cresswell suddenly discovered that he had lost his prey.

He must have panicked and dashed off in search of Charles, only to meet Rodney Hardcastle and Hugo and learn that the MFH had fallen from his horse and was very likely dead. So he arrived at the scene with Rodney, already flustered and having to ad-lib where he had expected everything to go like clockwork. At any moment horsemen, hounds, police, foot-followers, might arrive on the scene and there would be no chance of collaring the flask unobserved.

Luckily for him, Rodney sent Hugo away and went himself in search of the police. The only problem now was Harriet Lincoln. He tried to entice her away and failed. By then he must have been gibbering. Most opportunist murderers probably are. He hit Harriet over the head and got the flask, but even as he did it, he must have known that he was completely destroying his chance of writing a death certificate and having the whole thing seen as an accident. Now his only possible chance of getting away with it was if people believed that the saboteurs had done it.

I don't see how we'd ever have proved anything if he hadn't gone off half-cock and attacked the girl. NB. We haven't found the flask.

Now, was Siobhan in on this third plot for disposing of Charles Hardcastle at great speed before he could change the will? She has been in a distraught state since hearing that Charles was murdered. That could be because she suddenly realized that if anyone had a motive for murdering him it was Donald Cresswell. But she *could* be distraught because Donald had bungled it. If they were in it together they would have been certain the death would be regarded as natural causes. The panic attack on Miss

Lincoln ruled that out. If Siobhan thought she could rely on Donald up till then, she must now have realized that she couldn't. He'd done one thoroughly stupid thing. He might at any moment do another. She must be watching her step all the time and can't hope for a happy outcome.

Her behaviour since the crime is perfectly consistent with either theory—that she was in it with Cresswell, or that she was not.

So now we go on to the fourth plot: the kidnapping of Dandy.

For a day or two Cresswell thought the saboteurs were the chief suspects. But the attitude of the crowd to Siobhan at the inquest and the service must have made him fear that the police, too, were suspicious of her. He may have had two motives for the kidnapping. First, to take our minds off Siobhan. Second, to get some of the money. He knows now that he isn't going to see any of it unless Siobhan can get it quickly out of probate. In order to help her to pay a kidnapping ransom, the police might just assist her to do that. Then he arranges for her to deliver it somewhere which can be a jumping-off ground for them to escape, probably overseas. He's absolutely raving if he thinks he can get away with it but what else can he do? He's going for the jackpot and, if he loses, he won't be any worse off.

I don't think for a minute that Siobhan was in on the kidnapping plan. He decided that she must believe in the kidnapping if she's to convince the police. Cresswell must have telephoned Siobhan and bullied her in his disguised, kidnapper's voice, because he knows that she's as tough as old boots in spite of the fragile appearance, and he has to break her so she'll convince us. All this may be right but there is almost no evidence at all. It may equally be all wrong and a complete farrago on my part. We'll have to find out where he went today and if he could have taken Dandy with him. Try the airlines and ferry companies for Ireland and see if we can put him near Monahoe today. I wouldn't be surprised if he spun Eithne a yarn and has her looking after Dandy.

How do you smuggle a small boy who doesn't belong

to you out of the country? You've got no passport. First
you make sure he wants to go. You tell him he's going to
Eithne. You probably give him a mild sedative as well.
You take him to Northern Ireland, hire a car and drive
down to Monahoe, then straight back to the airport. He'd
want to be back almost before he left. Check the times.
He may have taken Dandy quite early in the night. He
could be in Ireland within hours.

He'd tell Brody not to get in touch with Siobhan. Tell
him the phone is tapped. Siobhan sent the boy away
against the wishes of the trustees. It's true she ought not
to remove him without permission from the trustees. The
O'Flahertys would swallow some such story.

He jerked himself awake. It was nearly two o'clock. Something was nagging at the back of his mind and he knew he
couldn't go to sleep until he'd dealt with it. And then he
had it. Tom Stringer! He had been so busy all evening
with, first, Siobhan and then the arrangements at Police
Headquarters at Penchester, that he had completely forgotten the theory that Tom Stringer might be holding his
knowledge of what took place in the woods on the day the
MFH was killed over a murderer who, Charter felt sure,
was by now a madman. Although he had no concrete
evidence of anything, he was so sure that he was right that
he quickly put on dark trousers, dark pullover and trainers,
and went downstairs carrying a torch.

A sleepy night porter let him out and he headed for the
hotel car park.

CHAPTER 20

Charter left the car outside the Kennels guest cottage and
walked in via the grassyards. The landscape was bathed in
moonlight. Not a good night for creeping around the Kennels undisturbed, but Charter was good at this sort of

thing. To his surprise, he disturbed a badger padding along purposefully in the moonlight. When it saw him it changed direction and moved fast out of sight. He moved in his trainers, almost as silently as the badger and, as he reached the stableyard he saw the police guard patrolling the entrance gates, which were shut. He ducked out of sight and made for Tom Stringer's house. During all this time, concentrating as he was on moving without a sound, it never entered his head to look behind him.

He arrived at the gate and was cautiously stretching out a hand to open it when he heard a sharp noise coming from the direction of the flesh house.

He froze and listened. The noise came again and was cut off, as if urgently suppressed. Then silence. Charter went cautiously towards the flesh house and collided with one of the offal bins, which gave out a hollow booming sound. He sprinted silently the rest of the way. Resounding through his mind was the threat to throw Dandy to hounds. Somehow that made him picture the huge deep freeze in which Tom Stringer had said you could lose a few horses . . . He opened the double doors and switched on the lights, expecting to hear a scuffle. There was no scuffle, no sound at all. He walked round the main skinning room. No one there and nowhere to hide. He moved on into the room with the freezer at the back, walked round, and examined the freezer. It was padlocked shut. There was no one in that room either, but he came across a second door which led out of the side of the building, either back to the flesh house yard, or behind it, into the grassyards.

If anyone had been hiding in the flesh house they could easily have stolen out through this door as he was going in by the other. On the other hand, who would be hiding in the flesh house? It was probably rats. All the same, he sprinted out into the moonlight again and made for the cottage. An owl hooted softly. He vaulted over the gate. If he lurked in the garden, patrolling back and front, he would be there if anyone came.

It was as he turned to hide in the deeper shadows under

the apple trees that the watcher pounced, hitting him scientifically over the head with a cosh.

He was lying on a cold, hard surface. His throat felt choked with a strong smell of disinfectant and a stronger animal smell. His head was throbbing and he felt slightly sick. He was aware of purposeful movement all around him and of light touches all over his body and breathing on his cheek and neck. It was as if he was lying in the cold embrace of some monstrous, moving, live, massive, creature. And there was a far-off sound that was loud and urgent and terrifying in its associations, though he couldn't quite tell why. Then as if something had switched on suddenly in his head, he knew. Hounds were baying, padding all around him, sniffing at him, touching him with their paws. If the blood could freeze in one's veins Charter's blood froze in his veins. Foxhunting friends had told him long ago the story of the Huntsman who was reputed to have gone unexpectedly into the hound lodges in the middle of the night and been eaten up all except the palms of his hands. At the time everyone had laughed at the story and reminded each other that the same thing had happened to Jezebel. When they went to bury her they found nothing but the skull and the feet and the extremities of the hands.

Charter began to sweat and his breath came fast and shallow. He forced himself to survey the situation sensibly and remembered that it was Saturday, that these same hounds had been hunting and that he had seen them, had been hunting with them. Hadn't Jim Caudle said that hounds are fed the minute they return from hunting? Then these hounds were replete. His flesh still cringed away from their touch and from the strong smell that surrounded him and filled his nostrils and his throat until he wanted to retch and cough.

It must be highly unlikely that hounds would eat a fully clothed man. But still they circled round and still they raised their heads and bayed. Then he understood that hounds would catch the scent of terror and be excited by it. He must scotch it at once. He went limp and forced himself to breathe slowly and deeply from his abdomen, willing himself to concentrate on his own body and not on the hounds; on the sensations he could feel in his muscles, and on the breath he took in and its passage through his whole body infusing his limbs with lightness and strength and then letting the breath flow out of him as he breathed out, leaving his body limp and relaxed, his weight seeming to go down through the cold tiles into the ground and into the depths of the earth. His body seemed part of the earth. He cleaned his mind of all images and looked quietly into darkness.

Suddenly he realized that hounds were no longer baying but had padded back to their bench and were settling down again into their straw bedding. He could smell the fresh, tobaccoey goodness of it. He lifted his head and began to consider trying to raise himself up, and the two questions of whether he should dare to try and whether indeed he was physically capable of the exertion. He had reached an affirmative answer to both questions by the time the door opened, the lights went on, and Nancy Thorn was leaning over him while Peter talked to hounds.

'Get up,' said Nancy, 'and come out after me. Can you walk?'

He got up slowly and she took his hand and led him out. Then the lights went off, the door shut, and Peter Thorn was at his side with a strong arm round his shoulders.

'My man on the gate,' he said, and it came out in a sort of croak. 'Must search. Man who hit me may be still about.'

'You go and tell him, Nance,' said Peter, and she sprang away into the darkness in her nightgown. Peter helped Charter into the sitting-room of his house and into a chair.

'How did you know I was there?' asked Charter.

'Hounds were baying,' explained Peter. 'When they make a noise like that and don't stop, there must be something up.'

'But isn't the hound place locked at night?'

'It's locked all right, sir, but the key hangs on the wall

outside. Not everybody'd know it but plenty would. I'll go and help your chap search. We'll comb the place. Will you be all right? Nancy'll be back soon but I want to send her to old Jim. Can't have anything going on in Kennels without the old boy knows it. He's in charge.'

'I'm fine,' said Charter and lay back wearily.

Half an hour later Nancy and Peter came in looking flushed and excited, but no one had been found. Charter had put his head under the tap in the kitchen and washed his hands and face and was feeling much more lively.

'Well,' he said, 'now we know this chap's a nutter. If your deep freeze hadn't been locked, who knows, he might have shoved me in there. I'd have been cold meat by now. I'm going after him. He must have dragged me into the hound lodges and I'm no light weight. He must be a big strong chap.'

'Unless there was a gang of them, sir.'

He raised his eyebrows. 'You're right. That is a possibility. That bump on the head has made me stupid. I'd better get back to bed.'

Nancy came in with a cup of coffee and Peter seized a bottle. 'I'll lace it with rum, sir. That's a good pick-me-up.'

'Thank you.' He sipped the mellow, powerful mixture and warmth and wellbeing stole through him. 'Thank you both,' he said. 'I feel a little more like myself after that.'

'What's this chap after, sir? Is he the one that murdered the Master?'

'We haven't proved yet that he was murdered. But I think that's the chap. And he's up to worse mischief than that. So let me know if you hear anything out of the ordinary. Don't be surprised if a few more chaps in blue turn up here tomorrow. I'm sorry you've had a broken night.'

'That's all right, sir. No meet tomorrow. It's Sunday.'

He shook hands with them both. Wonderful people. Salt of the earth. The bump on his head seemed to make him think in clichés. But he felt he was recovered enough to drive back to the White Hart. There, the night porter made him sandwiches and more coffee and he slept until 9.0 the next morning and woke without much of a headache.

CHAPTER 21

The rural sergeant, full of amazement at last night's happenings and reproaches for having been left out of them, joined him for breakfast.

'You're absolutely right, Sergeant,' said Charter. 'I ought to have taken you with me. Yes, do help yourself to rolls. There's a cup. Have some coffee. It would never have happened if you had been there.'

'You could have been torn in pieces by hounds, sir. It's no joke. There's a story about one Huntsman who's supposed to have gone out to his hounds unexpectedly at night—'

'I know, Sergeant, I know. They ate him up, all but the palms of his hands. I was contemplating that story all the time I was lying there. But I'm puzzled. Why should the chap want to get me eaten by hounds? It would do him no good at all. *You* know all I know. Besides, he couldn't even be sure they *would* eat me. They undoubtedly gave the matter some consideration, but suddenly they all made up their minds to return to their bench and go to sleep. I've no idea why. I only thank God I wasn't bleeding freely from the bang on the head.'

'Like sharks,' said the rural sergeant.

'Yes,' said Charter. 'Just like sharks. Only no water. I've got a thick skull, I'm glad to say.'

'You have indeed, sir,' agreed the sergeant, so heartily that Charter gave him a sideways look. He was quite serious.

'The thing is, sir,' he said, picking his words carefully, 'it seems to me that that bump on the head may have taken some of your faculties.'

'Indeed?'

'Only temporarily, of course.'

'Thank you for small mercies. What have I missed?'

'The fact, sir, that last night's affair very likely has nothing to do with the case.'

'Indeed?'

'You've been carried away, sir, by the message about the little boy being thrown to hounds. And that made you concentrate on the Kennels. But the kidnapper only invented that as the most horrific threat he could think of to make Mrs Hardcastle give him the money. You told her that yourself. He had no real plan to throw a three-year-old boy to foxhounds. And that being so, sir, the last place he'd take the boy or go near himself, is the Kennels. Seeing he'd warned everybody to look there.'

'Sergeant, you are quite right. But then who hit me over the head?'

'Well, sir, when it grew light this morning the Hunt servants found the carcase of a deer lying in the drive near the flesh house. At first they just thought someone had dumped it there for them, but its throat was cut and that means a nasty racket. Did you get the feeling, sir, that there was someone in the flesh house when you went in there?'

'Yes. I heard a scuffle. I thought it was rats, but I got a feeling first that someone was there.'

'I reckon there was, sir, and more than one. They were deer-poachers. Lot of money in it. You go out in a gang into the woods at night, you shine your headlights to dazzle the deer. They freeze with fright. Then some of you creep up on them and slit their throats. You can shoot them but that advertises your presence. Anyone sees car lights and hears shots at night in the woods might guess what you're about. People get very angry. Sometimes you find deer bleeding to death in the woods. It's all absolutely against the law. You can't kill deer without a game licence. You load them in your van, skin them, carve them up in neat pieces, and store them in a ruddy great deep freeze until you can do the rounds of the local restaurants and hotels. You sell them at the back door. Or perhaps you take them up to London. All you need is a van and some ice.

'I reckon this lot were pretty small fry. Probably out of work. No premises. No refrigerated van. So they used the flesh house to store the carcases. No one goes there at night. It's a way away from the houses and stables and lodges. There's a quiet cul-de-sac lane where they could park. From there they could get to the grassyards and come quietly up to the flesh house. If they were careful not to put the lights on until they had shut the doors no one would see them. There aren't any windows. I checked with Peter Thorn and he says there would be plenty of room in the deep freeze and they could store the stuff at the back. No one would be any the wiser. They're checking the freezer now.

'When you came into the flesh house they hid and then they scarpered, dropping the carcase. But one of them hit you first. They probably thought you were on to them.'

'So they threw me to hounds.'

'I reckon, sir, they just shoved you into the nearest available place away from the flesh house where you wouldn't be seen too quickly. I don't expect they meant more than that. Mind you, it's a lucrative business. They would stand to lose a very convenient free storage space if you reported them. And they wouldn't know who you were. Criminal thing to do. They couldn't know you wouldn't be —injured.'

'So I might have been. Your theory makes sense, Sergeant, and you've caught some deer-poachers, but I'm not sure I believe in deer-poachers finding the key of the hound lodges and wasting time throwing me in. Surely they'd have just hit me and left me lying there. I'm not entirely sure that it wasn't Peter Thorn who put me in with hounds.'

'Why him, sir?'

'Because he's still the likeliest, after the doctor, to have put the digitalis in the flask. The vet's prescribing it for his wife's mare could have put the idea into his head. He had access to the flask. And then he could easily have followed the Master into the woods. Who more likely than the

Whipper-in to be worried about hounds straying on to the line? He could have gone after the flask and struck the girl on the head and been seen doing it by Tom Stringer. Then, seeing me on guard outside Stringer's door last night, may have frightened him to death.'

'But he rescued you.'

'Yes, he did, didn't he? But he may have waited till he thought I was a goner. He only came in after hounds had stopped baying. Then, when he found me unhurt, he could have played the American cavalry coming to the rescue. Whoever put me in there knew his way about the Kennels and was familiar with hounds. Who else would dare to open the door of the hound lodges in the middle of the night?'

'The doctor might have visited Kennels as a Hunt member and noticed where the keys were kept.'

'So might many others.'

'If he was desperate I suppose a murderer might do it regardless'.

'Yes he might, but unfortunately we still have no hard evidence of anything.'

'Peter Thorn would have no reason to kidnap the boy.'

'No. But Nancy could look after the boy if he did.'

'A nice girl like that, sir?'

'We've only the evidence of her own words that she's a nice girl. And now we're going to call on Mrs Antonia Hyde.'

'Are you sure you're up to it, sir? You look very white, if you don't mind my saying so.'

'No. 110, High Street, Sergeant. Come on. And if I talk nonsense we'll know I'm not fit, and you can call in the men in the white coats.'

This time Antonia answered the door. She was fortyish, good-looking, with blonde, straight, smooth hair, good bones, a hard expression. She wore gold earrings and bangles and chains, a designer woollen dress, and ballet shoes. An Irish wolfhound came to the door with her.

'Hello,' she said. 'I'm Antonia de Roffeyss. I drove back

from my sister overnight to be here. I'm sorry you'd been searching for me. I didn't think you'd need to interview everyone in the Hunt.'

'Detective Chief Superintendent John Charter,' he replied, as she led them to her drawing-room. 'And Sergeant Cobbold.'

'Hello, Sergeant. I know you, don't I?'

She led them into a bright room, as perfect in its way but quite different from, the Kennels Cottage.

Antonia caught Charter glancing round with approval and smiled. 'You like it, Mr Charter? I don't, as you see, go in for the wholesale designer look.'

He smiled. 'It's much prettier like this.'

'Do sit down.' She sank gracefully into a chair and waited. The wolfhound lay at her feet and gazed fixedly into her eyes.

Charter paused for a moment, searching for a tactful way of approaching the embarrassing question.

'Don't worry,' she said. 'I know what you want to ask me. That fifty thousand pounds. It's typical of Charles. He wouldn't give a thought to how it would look to people here —that it would destroy my reputation and make everything clear to Tony. Not that I care about anyone but Tony.'

'I don't imagine Mr Hardcastle expected to die.'

'It's all much too important to leave such things to chance. Were you surprised?'

'No, Mrs Hyde. I had expected something of the sort.'

'You're brighter than any of this lot round here then. No one ever suspected. How they could believe a man like that with a woman like Siobhan for a wife would live chaste. She's been treated all her life as if she'd break in half if you so much as looked at her too hard. Selfish, cold, discontented. Incapable of ever being contented. I've known from the beginning she never could be, with Charles.'

'Did you know that she planned to leave him?'

She looked up sharply. 'I don't believe it,' she said. 'He would have told me.'

'She's going to go back to Ireland and become a nun.'

'What! You can't be serious! She's not the type. Now the widowed young sister, she might do it. Poor girl. I'd understand it if she went off her head and decided to take the veil. They hadn't been married a month when the husband was killed. But this one's shallow. No Reverend Mother would ever believe she had a vocation. I know what I'm talking about. I was brought up by the Canonesses of St Augustine at Bruges. I know nuns.'

'They have accepted her.'

'Are you certain of that?'

'We've checked.'

'Then I would check again if I were you. That girl is perfectly capable of killing Charles herself. It wouldn't surprise me if she did. She'd make up some fantasy about it. Pretend to herself she had no alternative. Underbred little egoist.'

'That seems a little sweeping,' said Charter.

'Irish horse-copers', she said contemptuously. 'Well, that doesn't rate with us.'

'You mean with the de Roffeyss?'

She looked at him narrowly. 'Why shouldn't I use my maiden name?'

'It has a ring to it,' said Charter cautiously. 'But why should you?'

She burst out laughing. 'Come off it, Mr Charter, you know quite well Antonia de Roffeyss has a cachet plain Antonia Hyde couldn't possibly match.'

'Hardly plain Antonia Hyde.'

'Thank you. Well, I sometimes use that name to show that I'm something more than the ageing mistress of a man who, a year after taking up with me, got married to an Irish horse-coper's daughter.'

'Not a good description of Brody O'Flaherty,' he said, oddly stung.

Her lip trembled. She stood up and walked about the room, then swung round to laugh at him. 'But how clever of you, Superintendent! And how insidious! You've made me talk myself into the position of chief suspect.'

'No,' he said. 'If you were tempted to kill it would hardly be Charles Hardcastle. Now, your husband, that's a different matter. When will he be home?'

'This evening.'

'We'll want to see him.'

'Come when you wish. He'll be here for a week if nothing comes up. But Tony would never have killed Charles even if he knew about Charles and me.'

'And did he know?'

'Do you know I truthfully don't know whether he did or not. Tony's very restrained. I only went to Charles when Tony was away so I don't think he could have known. But he's the sort of man who wouldn't ever say. I can imagine him coming home unexpectedly one night and finding me gone. He'd never ask. He wouldn't want to embarrass me.'

'He might still be very angry both with you and with Charles Hardcastle.'

'I must have been mad. I can't think how I could have done it.'

She looked quite calm but she was almost wringing her hands.

'How on earth did you manage to keep it secret? Isn't there a cleaning woman at the cottage?'

'Yes, of course there is. But she comes regularly and only on Wednesdays. Charles's chauffeur brings her and lets her in. She hasn't got a key. And I always bring an overnight bag. I never leave anything there for her to find. We couldn't spend much time together there. We used to meet sometimes at his London flat. We never went out to restaurants or theatres together. I sometimes said I was with my sister near Bath and she would always cover for me. She knew.'

'It doesn't sound as if it was much fun for you.'

She laughed wryly. 'No. Not much fun at all. Charles was simply obsessive about keeping it a secret. He was determined not to give Siobhan the chance to sue him for divorce. He was afraid she'd take him for everything he had. And all that—the success, the vast amounts of money—

that was terribly important to him. He couldn't bear the thought of anyone making demands on it. Not even his wife. Oh no, Mr Charter, he wasn't a man to marry. I suppose I was simply bored to death, with Tony away so often. And Charles had a certain aura about him.

'I gave him up, of course, when he told me he was going to get married. And then, when things went wrong between them, he was lost. He used to tell me what a terrible mistake he'd made. Between them over there in Ireland they'd bewitched him. He knew she was far too young but he was head over heels. He'd been the same about me. Over sixty and still given to utterly wayward enthusiasms.'

'Did your husband get on with him?'

'Tony didn't like him but he took up hunting for my sake. He thinks it's part of my background and he didn't want me to have to give anything up if he could help it so he gave up his flying instead and bought a horse. We still go up together occasionally and he sometimes flies himself to his sommelier get-to-gethers, which I can't stand, but he's a real hunting man now. Comes to all the functions and even does some fund raising. He's not in the least a negligible person but he's not quite one of us if you understand me.'

'I wish I didn't. As a de Roffeyss—you hardly need to pay homage to the petty snobberies of the British middle classes. Were you at the Kennels cottage the night before the meet last week when Charles Hardcastle was killed?'

'No, I wasn't. Tony was away but I had my sister stopping with me for the lawn meet.'

'So you can't tell me anything about his hunting flask and where he filled it?'

'No, I'm sorry. Perhaps Donald Cresswell can help you.'

'Donald Cresswell?'

'Charles phoned me that evening and mentioned that Donald had popped in out of the blue. He was rather surprised and a little put out. I might easily have been there that night.' Carefully repressing any display of interest in this piece of news Charter asked, 'Did the MFH ever offer you a swig from his flask?'

'No, never. Charles was much too busy ever to offer his flask. He was like a general running a battle. He never stopped to do the polite.'

'Thank you very much, Mrs Hyde. I don't think we'll need you again.'

She showed them out and stood looking after them as they walked away.

Charter exchanged jubilant glances with the rural sergeant.

'You never know your luck, do you?' he said. 'Still circumstantial, but it does give him the opportunity and why else would he have gone there that night? A thing he'd never done before.'

'But what motive has he, sir?'

'The good old human motives, Sergeant, love and greed. He is totally besotted with Siobhan Hardcastle and he's kidnapped her child to get her husband's money so he can run off with her to South America or the Antipodes. He's mad to think that he can get away with it but he may work some pretty nasty mayhem if we don't stop him soon. I'll explain as we go along.'

'But, sir,' panted the bewildered sergeant as he followed him to the car, 'she isn't in love with him. He's engaged to her sister.'

'That was a put-up job from the beginning, Sergeant. Eithne is quite clearly not the sort of girl to forget that young husband of hers so soon.

'It's she who wanted to take the veil. They pretended it was Siobhan because they thought in their innocence that Charles Hardcastle would let her go to the nuns whereas he'd never let her go to another man. And, hard as nails though she seems, she didn't want to go without Dandy.'

'But they'd never get the nuns to lie for them.'

'They weren't asked to lie for them. They entered Eithne in Siobhan's name. When they enter they take a saint's name so why should the nuns ever find out it was the other sister? So, when we asked, we got the right answer. Yes, Mrs Siobhan Hardcastle was seeking to enter the novitiate.'

'Then *she* was planning to marry Cresswell.'

'He's the only available man and he wants her and he'll look after her and Dandy and he knows how to make himself charming to women.'

'But, sir, all very well. He went to the cottage that night. But how could he have got the stuff into the flask with the Master there watching him? And why the flask? He could have gone to the bathroom and put it in something there or in the chap's drink.'

'I don't suppose for a moment that the Master offered drinks. He probably threw him out almost at once. And that explains why he put it in the flask. It must have been lying there. Hardcastle must have looked the other way and given him the chance to tip the brandy out and put his own mixture in. We may find the brandy in a flowerpot.'

As they got into the car the Sergeant said thoughtfully, 'Odd name, de Ruffs, sir. Do you think it's foreign?'

'Oh, English, Sergeant, as English as they come.'

When they got to the White Hart an urgent message was waiting for them which took them straight to the Kennels.

Peter Thorn went into Tom Stringer's cottage at ten o'clock that morning to tell him the news of the deer poachers. Tom was often away for hours at a time earth-stopping or collecting carcases but he wasn't doing either on a Sunday. Peter went through the empty kitchen into the empty garden. There was no one in the terrier pens. Then he saw the door of the ferret house was open. Tom only left that door open when he was inside. Relieved, Peter walked over and looked in. He recoiled with a strangled sound half-moan half-scream, and ran for his own house white as a sheet.

An hour later Charter and the rural sergeant arrived on the scene. By then they had got the ferrets off the corpse and put them back in their pens. The Scene of Crime men were still busy. The photographers had finished. The lab men shook their heads. They had never before had to gather clues where six ferrets had been let loose to destroy the evidence.

Tom Stringer was lying on his side, his face a dreadful yellow colour, bruises darkening on forehead and chin. His own gun lay on the ground beside him. The throat was completely eaten away. The smell of blood mingled with the stronger smell of ferret in the small space, which was crowded with policemen carefully stepping over the corpse and brushing past each other and walking outside to leave room for others and to take in great gulps of fresh air. No one actually threw up.

'I believe in your deer poachers all right,' Charter said later, 'but I reckon it was Cresswell had a go at me. Then he went on after Stringer. Whatever Stringer said to him, he must have known he'd never be safe while Stringer was alive'.

'I suppose Tom might have decided to bleed him for money, sir, but most of all he'd have wanted to feel he was in charge. I told you he was big-headed. Dr Cresswell was squirming and Tom quite liked that.'

'I would have saved him if I'd got there earlier. I wouldn't be surprised if pushing me in with hounds didn't give Cresswell the idea of using the ferrets to disguise the wound and mess up the forensic evidence in Tom Stringer's outhouse. Perhaps he hoped we'd think it was accidental death. Chap tripped over his own gun. He's raving, Sergeant. I'm worried about what he'll do to that child if he decides to cut his losses.'

Charter telephoned the ACC to report progress. The ACC agreed to the putting out of a general call for Dr Cresswell if he failed to turn up for morning surgery on Monday but flatly refused to authorize any earlier action. 'No hard evidence at all,' he said firmly. 'A respected country practitioner. We'd end up with egg on our faces. You keep after him, John, and get the evidence.'

Charter rang off, exasperated. Calls to Monahoe got nothing but the engaged signal. He considered alerting the Garda but rejected the idea. A kidnap situation was too delicate to be handled by police briefed from another country. Better to get himself flown there at once. Probably quicker too.

'You know, Sergeant,' said Charter, 'he could have told them their phone would be tapped. Spun a yarn. Told them to hide Dandy. He only needed a few days and he wouldn't want a child on his hands. But now Dandy's his hostage. Maybe his only chance. I've got to get over to Ireland again.'

'Sir, I've been wondering about Mrs Hyde.'

'You're right, Sergeant. We put a man on 110 High Street right away. He may have heard the Master telling her he had the doctor with him. I reckon he hasn't time to do anything about it, but better safe than sorry. I'm going to Monahoe now. Then you check the surgery tomorrow and we put out the call. In the meantime, if Dandy is with Eithne I want to get to him before Donald Cresswell does.'

CHAPTER 22

This time he thundered on the knocker at Monahoe and got no answer. The double doors were fastened. The windows at the front were all shut fast. He walked round the house. The stableyard was deserted. The back door of the house was locked and even one or two shutters up. Neither of the kitchen windows were locked and it took him only a little exertion to lift one of the sashes and clamber in.

He looked round in astonishment. It was like the *Marie Celeste*. A half-eaten meal was still on the table, going mouldy by degrees. A few flies disturbed by his entrance were settling on the food again. No dogs. No human beings. He went to the front part of the house and did a quick tour of all the ground-floor rooms, then upstairs into all the bedrooms. The house was deserted. And the telephone was off the hook. He put it back again and returned to the kitchen. He stood there and remembered what had been there last time he visited Monahoe. The spectacles and the knitting were gone. And he knew there was something else missing if he could only think what. Then he remembered.

All the decanters were gone from the dresser. He climbed
out of the window again and went back to the stableyard.
The boxes were filled with clean straw, the racks heaped
with sweet-smelling hay. Water was laid on from the mains
in every box. Buckets of feed were standing prepared in the
feed room. Beyond it was a long low stone building. He
looked in through the door and found a large untidy room
with a big communal table, television, comfortable chairs
and sofas. Up a steep flight of stairs was a dormitory with
six beds, three of which were made up. Obviously the
quarters of the stable lads, but they too were deserted.

He went back to the taxi. The mares and foals were
grazing near the house. 'Right,' he said. 'Down the field,
Seamus. Take me to the O'Briens.'

This was bluff but he remembered the smoke he had seen
rising up beyond the hen houses in the valley beyond the
woods.

Seamus said quite without surprise, 'Down the field it is,
sir.'

'Good man,' said Charter. 'I knew you'd be able to help
me. I need to speak to the O'Flahertys, not for my good
but for their own. How long since they went to join the
O'Briens?'

'It was Saturday as ever was, sir. Midday. I heard it all
from Mrs Flynn. They'd all disappeared before tea-time.
Left the telephone off the hook, she said, and sent the stable
lads home. It was something to do with the boy Dandy and
the English lawyers. They had to hide him away. She
made me swear I wouldn't tell, but seeing as you know it
already . . .'

'Wait for me here,' said Charter as they reached the
bottom of the field.

'You'll be needing me to show you the way,' said Seamus,
and took him to a stile which led into the wood.

They came out into open country and there in the valley
beyond the wood, sheltered by the sloping meadow above,
was the O'Brien encampment. The centre of it was a long
low farm building opening straight into the field. There

were only two caravans, though rectangular patches of bleached grass showed that several more had lately been standing there. And to Charter's surprise there were no cars, no horses and, as he looked about him, no men. A washing-line was strung between two trees and a girl was hanging out washing.

'Where are the men?' he asked and Seamus explained, 'It's the horse fair at Ballyfinnane in the morning. All the lads and the men are up there with the horseflesh. It's the last fair of the winter. They'll up sticks soon and off to England for the summer.'

'And the Derby,' said Charter. 'So this is where they spend their winters.'

'It's nice and snug,' said Seamus with a wink. 'They don't get chivvied from pillar to post. The children can go to school every now and then in the village when they feel the whim come upon them. And no one tries to put them in a council house.'

Several children and six or more lurcher-type dogs became aware of their approach and came running to meet them.

'Get off with you!' said Seamus. 'They'll likely be in the house over there. Let us be, you young rips! Imps of Satan all of you!'

The children stood aside and followed them in procession to the house. There they were met by a large woman of about sixty, of imposing bearing, and robed head to foot in what looked like brown rags. All the other women Charter saw were wearing summer dresses and shrunken cardigans, their legs bare, down-at-heel sandals on their feet. This lady wore laced-up boots.

'Here's a gentleman from England, Bevinda O'Brien,' said Seamus. 'He's after the O'Flahertys. It's important he should see them.'

Bevinda turned on her heel without a word and went into the house. Seconds later Rose O'Flaherty, followed by Brody, came running out to them.

'It's you,' said Rose, stopping and faltering, her eyes

going to where the children were playing. 'Is it Dandy
you're after?'

'Yes,' Charter replied. 'And I'm looking for him for Mrs
Hardcastle. She doesn't know where he is.'

Brody stood at her shoulder, both of them shocked into
silence.

'Who brought him here?' asked Charter.

'Mother of God!' said Rose. 'What have we done?'

'What is it?' asked Brody. 'I knew there was something
queer about it. Is Donald Cresswell a villain?'

'I've no proof,' said Charter, 'but I believe he is. I think
he killed your son-in-law and kidnapped Dandy to get a
large ransom. And I'm afraid I can't give you any assurance
about your daughter. She may have been involved in all of
it except this last bad business of using Dandy. Where is
he?'

They looked at each other and Brody nodded. Rose turned
back to Charter. 'You're quite right,' she said, 'we've got
him here with us. Donald brought him yesterday. He said
Siobhan had sent him to be away from the crowds and the
Press. He said she would be coming over after him as soon
as she could. Siobhan has done nothing wrong. She never
has, has she, Brody? Eithne was the naughty one.'

'Hush, Rose,' said Brody. 'We know she's done nothing.
The police will find the proof of it. Don't worry yourself.'

'Did Cresswell tell you not to phone Siobhan?' asked
Charter.

'Yes. He said the phones at Hangholt would be tapped
and that Siobhan could be in trouble for sending the boy
out of the country without permission from the trustees. So
he told us to hide him away and to tell anyone who came
after him from England that we never saw him.'

A flock of ragged, bright-cheeked, dark-eyed children
came racing across the grass, shrieking with laughter. Two
little girls were rolling over and over down the slope and a
filthy little boy with curly blond hair was trotting after them.
Unable to catch them up, he threw himself on to the grass

and began solemnly to roll after them. A bigger boy bent and gave him a gentle push and he landed at their feet beaming all over his face, jumped up and flung himself at Rose's legs. Brody bent to pick him up.

'He's very well here,' he said. 'You won't need to take him back, will you?'

'Let's sit down and have a talk about it,' said Charter, and they all sat down on the grass.

'Thank you, Seamus,' said Brody. 'You can wait with your car now.'

Disappointed, Seamus removed himself.

Rose waved to the girl with the washing in her arms and she dropped it all on the ground and came running barelegged across the grass.

'It's you!' she said. 'As soon as my mother waved I knew it was you! Is it Dandy?'

She stood smiling at him anxiously.

'Sit down, Eithne,' said Brody. 'Sit down and hear what the man has to say.'

She sat cross-legged on the grass, folded her hands and gazed at Charter with a sort of hero-worship he had met before.

Bevinda O'Brien came out of the house followed by young Rosie, her great-niece, who had been spending the summer working for the O'Flahertys. Rosie was carrying a tray laid with cups and saucers, milk jug, and silver sugar bowl. Bevinda was carrying the teapot and a younger girl held up a large blue dish on which reposed a rich brown ginger cake. All this was set down on the ground and, as Bevinda turned majestically away, beckoning the girls to accompany her, Brody O'Flaherty said, 'This is Mr John Charter. Mrs Bevinda O'Brien.'

A pitying smile came over the thin, commanding, face. 'Oh, it's plain Mr Charter, is it? Then it wouldn't be the gentleman from the English police?'

'Well, yes, Bevinda, that's who it is,' said Rose pleadingly.

Bevinda looked down at her and lifted a hand in what looked almost like a benediction. 'Never you worry yourself,

Mrs O'Flaherty,' she said. 'It's all round the village by now. You know the tongue the Flynn woman has on her. It's nothing to us. You arrange everything to suit yourselves. You'll be telling me when you've made up your minds,' and she made her stately way back to the house with her attendants.

'That's a splendid lady,' said Charter. 'Now what I want you to do is to move Dandy away from here. I can see he won't want to go, but Donald Cresswell may come back for him. He may want to use him as hostage. I want you all to go, if you will. Go somewhere Donald Cresswell won't know about. Take Dandy to the seaside if you like. It will only be for a day or two longer. Go in your own car. Don't use Seamus. And don't tell anyone here where you plan to go. I would like to know and to have a phone number so I can let Siobhan talk to you if necessary.'

'Will Siobhan be all right?' asked Rose.

'I can't tell you that yet,' he said. 'I wish I could.'

'Siobhan wouldn't do anything wrong,' said Eithne, pleading with him.

'We can't tell that yet,' he told her. 'But if I were you I wouldn't go into the convent just yet. Dandy may need you.'

'The convent?' She looked as if she had never heard of it. 'No,' she said, 'I'll let that wait.'

Charter smiled at her, reasonably sure that the convent would wait in vain.

'Tell me,' said Rose. 'Why did Donald Cresswell do it?'

'I don't know yet,' he said. 'Now, you've got your things here with you. Where's your car? At the top of that meadow? Right. Then please go to it now and choose where you'll go.'

Rose and Brody looked at each other and nodded.

'Good,' said Charter. 'Write it down for me.'

They did so.

'I'm staying with you,' said Eithne. 'I want to be with Siobhan.'

'Impossible,' he told her. 'I want you all out of the way

in case Cresswell tries to take more hostages. I do seriously believe the man is mad.'

'And what will happen to Siobhan?' asked Rose.

'I can't tell,' he said. 'But I promise you I'll do my best for her. Now go.'

'Don't you claim to know anything about my girl,' Rose said, eyeing him fiercely. 'That girl you met in England isn't my girl. He made a zombie out of her. She wasn't thinking straight.' Her eyes filled with tears.

'Don't upset yourself, Rosie,' said Brody, putting his arms round her.

Rose turned away from him to cry out to Charter, 'Have you ever given a thought to that housekeeper of theirs? Morbidly interested in both my girls and more in their sex life than anything else. Unhealthy. Siobhan's my daughter but I can see her faults. Listen to that woman and you'd think she had none.'

It was only much later that Charter realized what Rose had said. He was hardly listening to her and later he was too busy organizing a reception for Donald Cresswell at Ballyfinnane to turn it over in his mind as he would otherwise have done.

'Come along, woman,' said Brody. 'The man here has work to do and we must get this boy away.'

Charter took a respectful leave of Bevinda O'Brien, who would see to the Monahoe livestock, and walked back with Seamus. Two of the girls followed them up through the woods each with an armful of halters for bringing in the mares and foals.

Before heading for the airport Charter telephoned Penchester and learned that nothing had been seen or heard of Donald Cresswell, that he might well have returned to Ireland, and that a ransom demand had been telephoned to Siobhan. The taped voice had asked for £500,000 and Siobhan was told to bring it to Ireland to Ballyfinnane.

'There's a horse fair there tomorrow,' he said.

'Well, they won't let her go,' he was told.' They've got

the money together. The solicitor got the whole family to contribute and the bank agreed and sent it round in a briefcase but they've advised her to tell him when he calls that it will take a little longer. She was hysterical about it but they say she settled down in the end. They don't want her out of our jurisdiction. We might run into all sorts of difficulties in Ireland.'

'Well,' he said, 'you can tell her that Dandy is safe. I've found him with the sister. She knew nothing of the kidnapping. Thought Siobhan Hardcastle had sent him over to get him away from the press furore.'

'That's wonderful news. We'll tell her first thing in the morning. They have her heavily sedated after the scenes we had this morning.'

'I think you ought to tell her now.'

'I'll pass on that message.'

'And in view of the mention of Ballyfinnane I reckon I stop here. I'm liaising with the Garda. We'll have Ballyfinnane horse fair pretty well surrounded.'

CHAPTER 23

It was at 7.0 a.m. next morning that Charter was interrupted in the middle of a hearty breakfast of bacon, kidneys and sausages at the country hotel near Ballyfinnane where the Irish police had put him up for the night. It was a very embarrassed senior officer of the Regional Serious Crime squad calling from Hangholt Manor.

'Sir,' he said, 'you're not going to believe this. I don't really believe it myself. Your young woman in the kidnap case, the mother of the boy. She's disappeared.'

'Disappeared?'

'In the middle of the night. Vanished together with the housekeeper.'

'What were you doing to let them go?'

'We didn't let them go. They crept out by a back window,

that fat middle-aged lady and all. Climbed over a fence and scarpered off over the fields.'

'When did this happen?'

'We don't know. The nasty truth is they drugged us. Chloral hydrate in the coffee. And we thought we'd put her out at least until morning. That's why we thought it was no use trying to wake her to tell her the good news. The housekeeper took the pills for her. They must have chucked them away.'

'You great chaps let yourselves be drugged by two particularly unworldly women? No, I'm sorry. No recriminations. Not the time for it. Any idea where they've gone?'

'They took the briefcase with the ransom.'

'Oh my God! They're heading for Ballyfinnane!'

'We've been on to the airports and the ferries. They haven't been seen on any regular flights or boats.'

'Any private planes nearby? Had they any pilot friends? Good God, what about Tony Hyde? Would she go to Antonia Hyde's husband? Yes, she would, for Dandy. And Antonia would be all for it in those circumstances. Get someone along fast to No. 110 High Street, Stumpington. Ask if the husband has flown to Ireland. That's the only way I can think of that they'd get there in time for the horse fair. I'll have to leave all that to you. Keep in touch through the station at Ballyfinnane.

'Right. I needn't say how sorry I am.'

'Let me know if you get Tony Hyde and, if he did fly them over, where and when he landed them.'

'Right.'

Charter arrived at the horse fair at about eight o'clock. The sun was shining, dispelling the chill of an early spring morning. The fair took place in a broad flat field rimmed by drystone walls. At one end was a winding stream, at the other a clump of stunted trees still bare of shoots. The salt wind came straight in from the sea. A slight tang in the air and a gull or two soaring against a pale sky showed that the shore was not far away. The surrounding fields sloped down from the middle and looked like a display of plump

green cushions frilled with grey stone. The country roads
that led to Ballyfinnane were hidden by green banks shored
up with stones.

There were few women about but everywhere the men
were lounging, each with a pony or a mare or a horse
or a string of them, tended by the tail of youngsters each
seemed to hold in fee for running errands. An aproned
blacksmith plying his trade in a corner was surrounded
by spectators, encouraging, criticizing, and telling stories.
Some were singing sad songs. Some were laughing
riotously. It was all very good-humoured but none of
them failed to scrutinize appraisingly every animal that
came in sight.

Charter was kitted out as unobtrusively as possible in the
flat cap, grey flannels with a darn in one knee, scuffed
leather shoes and open-necked shirt which appeared to be
uniform wear at an Irish horse fair. He was a dark horse
and attracted some attention as a possible buyer. He drank
a bottle of beer purchased from a plain clothes man from
Dublin, and reports reached him at regular intervals from
various parts of the fair.

Quite early in the day he learned that a stranger had
parked his shabby horse-box at the far end of the line of
boxes, carts and trailers, that edged the field. The driver
was unknown to any of the police. He was described as
fair-haired wearing a beard. False beard? Dyed hair? Charter sauntered as near as he dared, but the driver was sitting
morosely in the cab of the box and it would be risky to go
too close. Charter began to patrol, never too near, but never
completely out of sight.

The tinkers came past him at about half past ten, thread-
ing their way among the horse-pens and the parked cars
and jeeps and the stalls where you could get a cup of tea or
a glass of beer. The boy wore the flat cap, a crumpled shirt
and tie and an anorak at least two sizes too big for him,
flannels, and trainers. He was leading a shaggy pony with
a haynet attached to the Ds on the saddle, and was shuffling
along, his hands in his pockets, looking down at the ground

and whistling nervously through his teeth. The woman wore a black shawl wrapped round her shoulders and over her head, and a nondescript long skirt with a drooping, uneven hem. She walked mincingly in large flat laced-up shoes.

They walked unhurriedly the length of the horse fair and over towards the line of boxes and trailers. And yes, it was at the very farthest of them that they stopped, appeared to confer with each other, then went up to the driver's cab and tapped on the window. The fair-haired man got down and went round to lower the ramp. He wore a trim, fair beard and looked nothing like Donald Cresswell.

The boy unknotted the haynet and got into the trailer and began to tie it to a hook. The woman stood holding the halter, looking self-conscious and stiff. That woman had never held a pony on a halter in her life before. Charter began to run and as he ran he thought: The haynet! Of course, the haynet! The money's in a plastic bag inside! And as he ran, the fair bearded man slammed the ramp shut, fastened it on both sides and went quickly back to his cab, leaving Maggie holding the pony and screaming at the top of her voice.

Charter grabbed her and dragged her with him. 'Leave the pony,' he said. 'This is John Charter. You've got to come with me and help me stop that man. I'm going to need help with Siobhan. This place is slewing with Irish policemen but I'm not sure what their drill is. He's got a gun, you can be sure of it.'

He pushed her into the car he'd hired the day before, got into the driver's seat and they were speeding after the horse-box. It was only a few hundred yards ahead of them but it suddenly appeared, coming back towards them round a bend in the road. Charter thanked God for the Irish police. They must have set up some sort of road block. He backed into a farm track and turned round.

Cresswell made straight for Monahoe and Charter followed. They arrived at the gravel sweep in time to see Cresswell dragging the 'boy' up the steps, trying the door, then pulling her after him around the house to the back. Siobhan was fighting him and he appeared to be remonstrating with her, imploring her, and all the time he held a pistol in one hand. When he saw it, Charter knew it was destined for a double death pact and he resolved with absolute determination that whatever now happened it would not be that. Let Donald Cresswell shoot himself. Come hell or high water, he was not going to shoot Siobhan. As they disappeared round the side of the house, the haynet bumping on Cresswell's hip, Charter and Maggie were out of the car and running after them.

By the time they got to the kitchen window they could hear voices inside. Charter lifted the sash and Maggie hitched up her skirts and followed him in, panting. As they went through the kitchen she picked up a heavy cast-iron frying-pan from the pan rack.

'That's lethal,' said Charter. 'I've got a gun,' and he showed it to her as they ran up the stairs.

Upstairs, Cresswell's voice could be heard talking and talking, begging, imploring. No word could be heard from Siobhan. Charter took Maggie by the hand and led her into a bedroom to confer.

'Mrs Philpot,' he said. 'Maggie! Look, the Irish police will soon be here. But when they come he'll shoot her. The man's insane. If I go straight in with my gun she'll be the first to go. I daren't risk it. He may shoot himself but it may be her. I'm going up on the roof. I found out the layout when I came here yesterday. The trouble is they're dormer windows. He'll see my shadow and God knows what he'll do. I need a diversion. Will you wait seven minutes and then start making the most unholy row on the landing below him? Don't, whatever you do, go up to the room. He'll shoot you as sure as I'm standing here if you do. Just a noise from the landing below.'

'Of course.' She looked at her watch and his. 'From now,' she said.

'Wonderful woman! Now!'

He went up the stairs like a shadow and on up to the top

floor where Cresswell could be heard almost weeping as he harangued the girl. He got to the attic where he had seen the skylight. Quietly lifting a table underneath this, he climbed up, opened it and scrambled through on to the roof. There he found a narrow walkway between the balustrade and the dormer windows. As he approached the fourth window he heard them. He pressed his ear to the window-frame. She was very quietly pleading for Dandy.

'Just tell me where he is, Donald. I'll help you all I can. We'll go away. But just tell me where I can find Dandy.'

'It's no use,' he kept saying. 'It's no use! It was all for you! It's no use!' Then his voice changed. 'You don't have any idea, do you, what I've done for you? You don't give a damn.'

The seven minutes were just about up, but in any case this was the moment. Any minute now he would shoot her. Or perhaps, please God, himself.

Charter jumped into view at the window, shouting, and smashing the pane with an almighty kick. Donald's gun veered towards him and Charter felt his hand explode as the gun was shot out of it. Everything then happened at once. Donald turned the gun towards Siobhan. Charter went in through the window, broken glass and all, the door of the room opened to reveal Maggie brandishing her pan, Charter hurled himself at Cresswell's gun hand, deflecting it upwards, and Maggie charged across the room and brought the heavy iron pan down on the back of Cresswell's head. The gun fell to the ground. Donald Cresswell folded into himself and crumpled on to the floor. Maggie's eyes met Charter's and then she collapsed, shuddering and moaning.

For a moment, Siobhan and Charter stood frozen, looking down at the still body. That it was now a body seemed unquestionable. The skull was crushed. Charter bent over him to look at the damage, then straightened up at last and said to Siobhan, 'I'm afraid he's dead.'

A look of stark horror came over Siobhan's face and she

launched herself at him, screaming and beating at him with her fists.

'He didn't tell me! He didn't tell me! We'll never find Dandy now! He didn't tell me where he is! Why did you do it?'

He grabbed her into his arms. 'Hush,' he said. 'Stop it! We've found Dandy. Dandy is with Eithne. He took Dandy to Eithne and told her you had sent him. They're with your parents now. Be still.'

She stopped shaking and he released her at once.

'It's really all right,' he told her.

She lifted a grimy tear-stained face to him.

'Where?' she asked.

'With Eithne and your parents by the sea. You can go there right away. But I think I hear the cavalry approaching. You and Maggie need a little care. Look after Maggie. She saved your life.'

The last he saw of them they were both on the floor in each other's arms sobbing and laughing at the same time.

By the time he got down to the hall it was full of police officers, nurses, and ambulance men. Someone who looked like a pathologist walked towards him. He had had enough of pathologists. This was a matter for the Irish police. And anyway it was time he got back to Penchester. There was no evidence that Siobhan was Cresswell's accomplice, no proof that he ever had an accomplice. Who was going to try to extradite her to England? Let the question marks remain.

'May I bandage your wrist?' asked a pretty nurse.

'No,' he said gruffly and walked out of the house. More police cars were arriving. An ambulance stood by the steps. He went down the steps and walked away. The victim, Charles Hardcastle, the horror that was Tom Stringer's death, the guilt or innocence of the boy-girl in the room upstairs would be discussed at length by TV presenters, psychologists, policemen. For the moment he had had enough.

And then he stopped dead in his tracks. For suddenly, thanks to Rose, he knew that Siobhan had never been Donald Cresswell's accomplice. Siobhan had done nothing more reprehensible than to dream up, together with her sister, a hare-brained plan to bamboozle Charles Hardcastle into letting her and Dandy go. That foolish scheme had not, after all, been a wild attempt at an alibi to show that she didn't want her husband's money. No alibi was needed because it was true that all she had wanted was to be free of the man and to go back to Ireland. Everyone agreed, (and he hadn't taken nearly enough notice of this) that Siobhan O'Flaherty wasn't mercenary. If she had been, surely she would have tried to please her wealthy husband, surely she would have hunted, forgetting Sister Imelda's compassion for the fox. He turned and walked swiftly back to the house.

Who had, over the past few years, developed a morbid sympathy for Siobhan and Eithne? Who had hated Charles Hardcastle so much that she went bright red with anger every time his name was mentioned? Who had access to medicine cupboards at Hangholt Manor? Who had gone with Siobhan and Eithne to visit Nancy Thorn's sick mare and had the chance to steal the digitalis and throw suspicion on the Hunt servants? Who would have hoped to live with Siobhan and Donald and enjoy the amenities of Monahoe, finding a niche for herself as housekeeper-nanny to the grateful couple?

And now that everything had gone wrong and Donald Cresswell was revealed as a murderer, in whose interest was it that he should die before he could reveal her part in what he had done? Who had gone in bravely to rescue Siobhan, yet struck down Donald Cresswell seconds after Charter had deflected the bullet meant for Siobhan?

And then he thought of the look in Maggie's eyes as she raised them from her dreadful handiwork? Shocked, yes, shocked and horrified. But, as they met his, hadn't there been something else as well? Something that could only be described as triumph?

He went slowly up the stairs. As he went into the crowded room the sight of Siobhan's hands tightly clasped in Maggie's made him feel sick. He walked over to them and, leaning down, gently separated the hands and lifted Siobhan to her feet. Maggie's breath went in with a hiss as she looked up into his face. He led Siobhan away to be looked after and taken to Dandy. And Maggie went on crying and crying, the veiled triumph in her eyes slowly turning to desolation.